Three Two Compare

Three Two Compare

ESTHER RILEY

Copyright © 2016 by Esther Riley.

Library of Congress Control Number:		2016916660
ISBN:	Hardcover	978-1-5245-4958-9
	Softcover	978-1-5245-4957-2
	eBook	978-1-5245-4956-5

All rights reserved. No part of this book may be reproduced or transmitted in any form or by any means, electronic or mechanical, including photocopying, recording, or by any information storage and retrieval system, without permission in writing from the copyright owner.

This is a work of fiction. Names, characters, places and incidents either are the product of the author's imagination or are used fictitiously, and any resemblance to any actual persons, living or dead, events, or locales is entirely coincidental.

Any people depicted in stock imagery provided by Thinkstock are models, and such images are being used for illustrative purposes only. Certain stock imagery © Thinkstock.

Print information available on the last page.

Rev. date: 10/06/2016

To order additional copies of this book, contact:
Xlibris
1-888-795-4274
www.Xlibris.com
Orders@Xlibris.com
750823

This book is in memory of my parents Harry and Martha Jackson. "Only if you could see me now…I believe you can in the spiritual realm."
Thank You to:

Family:

My husband and best friend David, Thank you for the love, support and giving me the courage to push forth. I love you.

My grandmother Mrs. Georgia H you've inspired me to live my dreams.

The rest of my entire family, you always knew I loved to write; be creative, and love to be humorous. Dreams do come true.

Mentors:

Lynda D, Francis-Ray, George R, Judith P, Robert R, Carolyn H and Valerie R

Technical and Marketing:

Charles B, Eddie E, and Kellie A.

Special Thanks:

Thank you to all of the readers who waited patiently to read this book. Be on the lookout for more of writings coming soon.

INTRODUCTION

You are about to journey into the lives of Roselita Macalaonez, Brandon Bright and Gordon Gem.

Three people, who challenge, tangled love, which causes each of them to get lost by their own lustful thoughts.

As each one is about to experience the corruptive nature of being just friends,

These urbanites couldn't have imagined the connective tissue called desire that could lead to such destructive ends.

Witness the difficult circumstances as each person's life unfold before your eyes.

You'll feel the electrifying wave of what it means to be in love verses loved.

CHAPTER ONE

It was five o'clock p.m. when Roselita Macalaonez got stuck in the evening commute. While she waited for traffic to move, Roselita turned the air conditioner on full blast. Roselita sat upright, relaxed her head on the headrest, and glanced at the tawny car on the left side of her onyx car. Roselita noticed an elegant gentleman giving her a captivating smile that made her body feel moist inside. Roselita kept her composure as she returned his greeting with an approving smile. Roselita diverted her eyes back to the traffic in front of her as she reached forward, turning on the radio to her favorite station, KLSX 107.8 FM, to ease her troubled mind. The meteorologist announced the weather. It is eighty-nine degrees outside with the humidity feeling as though it is one hundred degrees. After the weather report, it is time for smooth jazz in the evening. Roselita said, "Now this is what I call winding down after a day of working hard." The radio personality announced the next song, "This is 'Got to be love,' by Monte. You are listening to smooth jazz with Richard Crest on KLSX 107.8 FM." Roselita allowed the soothing sound of the music to flow through her ears as the traffic crept forward. Roselita reminded herself, "This isn't the time to be letting myself get mushy and sentimental; I'm not in any mood to be searching for Mr. Marriage material." Roselita continued to muse, "I have been single for the last two years. I'm a News reporter writing for social media about why some men can't keep one woman." Roselita added, "Yes, eventually I'll settle down to get married, but right now I'm not in any mood to be setting my heart on romance." Roselita said aloud, "Could this really be happening to me or could this be another test of infatuation for me?" Roselita shifted her thoughts as the traffic started to pick up and move swiftly. Roselita exited off Highway three eighty-five by making a right turn onto Jordon Road. Roselita stopped at the grocery store before going home. Roselita and another driver raced to park in a spot that is closest to the store entrance. As Roselita turned the wheel of her car to pull into the empty spot, an elderly couple drove into the spot, leaving Roselita and the other driver to find a different parking spot. Roselita felt startled as she said, "I know that elderly couple didn't just pull in front of me, they saw that I was trying to maneuver my car into place." Roselita took a deep breath then exhaled as she prepared to go into the grocery store. Roselita realized that she needed to respect people who were much older than herself. Roselita drove around for a while until she saw another available spot. Finally parking her car, Roselita entered the store. Roselita proceeded to grab an empty shopping cart. At the same time, the elderly couple that stole her parking spot also grasped the same shopping cart. The elderly woman said to Roselita, "Excuse you. I saw this cart first." Roselita mumbled to herself, "I know she didn't just say, 'Excuse you,' as if it is my fault for taking the cart that I touched first." Roselita wanted to say, "The nerve of that elderly couple! First they took my parking spot and now they claim they had the shopping cart before me." Instead, Roselita kept all negative thoughts to herself as she greeted the elderly woman with a soothing smile and said, "Oh, I'm sorry ma'am. Go ahead--it's yours. I'll get another one." The elderly woman returned Roselita's smile with a canny smile of her own. "That's nice of you to allow me to have this cart dear." Roselita was astounded by the elderly woman's trenchant attitude towards her as Roselita pulled out another cart and let the whole situation pass over. Roselita took the empty shopping cart and proceeded towards the produce section. Roselita contemplated buying some pink grapefruit or oranges. As Roselita stood there, a man came up behind her. Before she could turn around, he said, "You know, it's much healthier to eat pink grapefruit." Roselita is so amazed by his striking voice that Roselita remained frozen as she quickly closed her eyes and said, "Lord, please let this be a ravishing man, someone who is available." Roselita opened her eyes, and then turned around only to find out that standing behind her is the same man she saw driving the tawny car, while they had been stuck in rush hour traffic. Roselita gazed into his almond shaped eyes. Roselita studied his well-proportioned body, marveling at his very appealing navy suit. The man wore matching navy nine and a half inch shoes. His obsidian hair tapered into a perfectly shaped style. What captured her attention is the thickness of his blackened goatee, which caused her heart to beat rapidly. Roselita continued to get a good view of his charming smile showing off a set of white-jade teeth. The handsome man caught her off guard as he said, "Excuse me ma'am. I didn't mean to interrupt your thinking." Roselita pretended to be startled and flirted in return, "Oh, it's okay; I enjoy it when someone offers his or her opinion about choosing produce." Roselita quickly glanced at the man's left finger to see if there was a wedding band on it. To Roselita's surprise, his left finger was bare. Roselita thought just because there isn't anything on his left finger didn't mean he was unmarried. Roselita erased that negative thought as she stood there showing her diffident side, hoping it would make a lasting impression. "I'm sorry. Please forgive me again. Let me introduce myself. My name is Gordon Gem." He extended his hand to greet Roselita's as she said, "Nice to meet you Mr. Gem. My name is Roselita Macalaonez." She tried to be sophisticated but her crafted style isn't getting her anywhere. Roselita couldn't hold her bodacious behavior any longer. That's when she said, "Mr. Gem do you always follow women whom you find to be attractive? "Gordon laughed richly, which made Roselita feel annoyed that she wanted to know what he found to be hilarious. "Miss Macalaonez, that's not the case. I was coming to the grocery store to get some ingredients for tonight's dinner." In awe, Roselita said, "I'm sorry if I came at you with such a harsh question before I even had the chance to know you." Gordon smiled and began to feel a warm sensation come over him, "No harsh feelings here. So are you married? Do you have any children? Are you in a serious relationship?" Roselita thought Gordon is being too persistent about her love status before they had fully known each other. Gordon, on the other hand, didn't find anything wrong by asking her these common questions. Gordon wanted to make sure that Roselita didn't have a special someone in her life before he made his move on her. Gordon's eyes lit up as he watched the movement of her full lips open and then close as Roselita responded back to him. Gordon tuned out

Roselita's tempered attitude as he focused on her breasts, reviewing how beautifully her five foot five inch body is curved. Gordon noticed Roselita's fully oval lips that were lightly accented with earth-tone lipstick covered with a touch of lip-gloss for shine. Roselita wore a white V-shaped blouse, which made her breasts look larger. Roselita's long navy skirt had a split, as if her body appeared slimmer and taller than her normal height. Roselita's slanted eyes sparkled. The crescent shaped pinned-up curls cascading from her hair made Roselita appear as if she were a twenty-six year old. Gordon deflected her response by being interested in getting to know her better. Gordon was trying to find a way to make Roselita become his true love. Roselita informed him that she isn't married and did not have children. Roselita went on to say that as far as being in a serious relationship, "I'm single. What about you Mr. Gem? "Gordon turned up both corners of his lips, forming a pleasant smile. "Roselita, I'm not married either and I don't have children." Roselita was flabbergasted to have learned that she might have found herself the man she'd been praying for—someone loving and caring who knows where he is going in life. Gordon said, "Please forgive my irrational behavior. It's just that I'm tired of women approaching me by playing games," Gordon continued speaking in a moderate tone so mellow that it could put a baby to sleep, but instead drew Roselita's attention. Roselita felt a calm sensation come over her as she stopped talking for a minute, wanting to hear what Gordon Gem had to say to her. "Roselita you don't have to explain, I have seen the women in my family whom had withdrawals when it comes to finding the right man for them." Gordon continued, "I'm not trying to make you feel uncomfortable, but I would like to get an opportunity to know more about you, if you will allow me to do that." Roselita knew that out of all the men she had ever encountered, none ever approached her the way that Gordon Gem did. Roselita respected the fact that Gordon is a gentleman. After hearing Gordon ask her to give him some time, Roselita softened her pruned face by breaking into a blossoming smile. At that moment, Roselita wanted to lean forward and allow her lips to lock into Gordon's, but being the sharp woman that she is, Roselita flared back up, giving Gordon stern answers. Roselita said, "Looks are charming but the mind can sometimes be deceiving." Gordon pondered Roselita's reaction as he said, "I see. Do you always go around piercing men with sarcastic remarks? It seems to me you've been hurt too many times by men who crossed your path before." Roselita was appalled because Gordon was the first man who noticed her reaction towards men. It is as if the outer shell of her walls was collapsing and Gordon could have made a breakthrough to her tough but tender heart." Roselita said, "Gordon, please accept my apology for my shrewdness. Yes you're right I have been hurt by too many men before." Being an understanding man, Gordon felt the depth of her soul. Gordon could sense that Roselita is lacking attention and comfort. "Roselita, do not let every bad experience ruin the chance for real love that could last a life time." Gordon handed Roselita his business card and said, "Miss. Macalaonez you have an edge about yourself, but I'm up for the challenge." Roselita felt nervous after realizing that Gordon seemed to be an okay man to get to know well. Roselita tried not to give Gordon any more time for their conversation. Roselita glanced down at her watch, not realizing how much time they had spent chatting. Roselita forgot she needed to be going home; Roselita took Gordon's business card and slid it into her business card case. Thanking Gordon for the conversation and for his cell phone number. Roselita turned around and walked away with a dainty swerve, making sure Gordon is still there noticing her seductive walk. Gordon stood there smiling, viewing every inch of her five foot five inch body as Roselita swayed her hips back and forth. Gordon continued to stare at her backside until he couldn't see Roselita anymore. Roselita turned right, heading into the frozen food aisle, smiling as she stopped to pull out Gordon's business card to read what is printed on it. Roselita is overwhelmed to see that Gordon is the owner of two companies, the first being Gordon's Global Network Systems and the other being E- Biz Web Design and Hosting Programming. Roselita placed the card back into the case and put it into her purse and finished grocery shopping. At the checkout lanes, Roselita looked out of the corner of her eyes and noticed Gordon a few lanes over getting ready to walk out of the store. The cashier interrupted Roselita's gaze, "Um excuse me Miss. Your total is forty-eight dollars and thirty-five cents." Roselita turned and faced the cashier as she apologized for not paying attention. Roselita replied, "Oh, I'm sorry. Here you go," as she gave the cashier her debit card. The cashier said, "Miss, I don't mean to intrude, but I once felt the same way you're feeling right now. Well now he is my husband. We also met in a grocery store. Once we were outside, we exchanged cell phone numbers and here we are today married to each other with four children." Roselita smiled at the cashier saying, "Hum, sounds interesting. Do you think the same thing could happen to me?" The cashier laughed as she said, "I don't see why not. Anything is possible. You know, sometimes you have to take a risk--but make sure he's what you've been praying for, God to bless you with someone who is compatible with you." Roselita thanked the cashier for her helpful advice and grabbed her groceries. The cashier wished Roselita all the best and said that she hoped everything would turn out perfectly. Roselita said, "Thank you for your concern. Have a good evening." It is six-thirty p.m. as Roselita made it home. Roselita pulled into her driveway, took the groceries out of the car, and entered her house. Roselita turned on the lights in her foyer and laid the mail on her maroon and cream marble table. Roselita walked into the kitchen, as she voice activated the light switch, placing her keys on the counter top. Roselita turned on her laptop to check her voice mail. The last person who called her was her mother, informing Roselita that she is going to be having a social gathering on this upcoming Friday. After listening to her mother's message, Roselita began to prepare her dinner. Roselita turned on some soothing music. While cooking, the laptop rang. Roselita glanced at her caller ID on the laptop to see who is calling. It is her friend, Brandon Bright. Roselita answered from her laptop, "This is Roselita?" Brandon seemed to be in his usual playful mood said, "Good evening my chocolate love, how are you doing?" Roselita laughed, "Good evening to you Mr. Bright, I'm doing well. How are you doing?" Brandon responded, "I'm good now that I'm talking to my chocolate love. You know I couldn't resist calling my favorite lady to see how she's doing." Roselita answered, "Okay, Brandon what is the four-one-one?" Brandon said, "What do you mean?" Roselita then replied, "Brandon stop joshing around with me. I know you have some Brandon news flash waiting to come out. Tell me what's going on with your match-making schemes." Brandon laughed, knowing that Roselita is right. Brandon had some exciting news to share with her. Brandon said, "Alright Miss Macalaonez. I couldn't fool you--but I tried." Roselita laughed harder, "Yes, Brandon you've tried. But didn't you realize that I have known you long enough to know when you're going to make your love connection moves?" Roselita and Brandon had been friends for Fourteen years. They met at Constitutes Law Firm where Brandon works as an attorney. Roselita's current company, Welcome News Express, was going through a lawsuit about an article that they published. The story had gone from good to bad. From that day forward, Brandon and Roselita developed a close-knit friendship. Brandon is more like a brother to Roselita, even though she already had a brother named Troy. Brandon had grown attached to Roselita's family, just as she had grown attached to his. They always felt so comfortable being around each other that many people thought they were a couple. Brandon continued to say, "Roselita the reason I'm calling is because yes, I do have some love connection news that I thought you might be interested to hear." Since Brandon knew a lot of high-powered attorneys, he is always inviting Roselita to different events, hoping Roselita would meet someone she would enjoy. Brandon said, "Roselita you don't sound enthused." Roselita didn't mind going to some of the events with Brandon. It's only when Brandon tried to play matchmaker that he ended up making the event dull. Brandon chuckled with a happy memory saying, "Roselita I thought I was doing such an excellent job of keeping you abreast." Roselita felt that Brandon didn't quite understand," Brandon thank you for looking out for me, but do you remember what happened last time?" Brandon said, "You mean at the Entrepreneur's Ball?" Roselita answered, "Yes, you introduced me to one of your friends named Royston Friends." Brandon said, "Ah yes. That's when I left you two alone, hoping things would have worked out." The day was Friday April eighth, the night of the Entrepreneur's Ball. Royston stood there with a smirk on his face, staring into Roselita's eyes and letting her know that Brandon had told him so much about her. Brandon told Royston that Roselita is a wonderful, radiant woman who had her head on her shoulders so tight that it would be hard to make her tilt it. As Roselita and Royston talked, she tried to ask him questions, but only ended up with blunt answers. The entire time that they spent getting to know each other was spent with Royston doing most of the talking about how conceited he is and how women who date him worshipped the ground he walked on. Roselita felt she had heard enough of Royston bragging about himself. Roselita excused herself to go look for Brandon as she was looking around for him. Roselita spotted another distinguished gentleman, but she kept her focus by trying to find her friend Brandon. Roselita finally located Brandon and flagged him down while he was on the dance floor getting his groove on. Brandon looked up and noticed Roselita waving at him. At first he thought she was signaling him to say she was having a good time, so he kept dancing. Then Brandon saw Roselita waving again, so he excused himself from the woman he was dancing with to see what Roselita's emergency was all about. Roselita told Brandon the Entrepreneur's ball was lovely, but his friend Royston had to go. Roselita told Brandon what happened between Royston Friends and her. Brandon tried to have sympathy, but it wasn't working. Brandon found it to be funny that all Roselita received was an earful of information about Royston this, Royston that and how Royston is a ladies' man. Brandon already knew Royston is obsessed with himself. Brandon also knew that it would be difficult to have a conversation without Royston talking highly of himself. Brandon told Roselita that he was sorry for trying to match her with Royston but he needed to get back to his date for the evening before she found someone else. Before Brandon returned back to the woman that he was trying to pick up, Roselita said, "Well, if I don't succeed at landing a man tonight, at least I know you were able to find someone for yourself." Brandon looked at Roselita as he smiled saying, "What do you mean I'll succeed. Do I look like some who will play on women's feelings?" Roselita smiled as she stood there looking at him, "No but you do have a smooth-way of getting ladies interested in you." Brandon said, "Roselita I'm really sorry that things didn't work out but I promise the next time they will. This time you'll be thanking me for the matchmaker help." Roselita smiled one last time as she said, "Now disappear. Your 'Miss I Need a Man tonight' is waiting for you." Brandon kissed Roselita on her cheek, followed by telling her that he loved her. Then Brandon walked in the direction of the woman who was waiting for him to return. The night ended. Brandon left the Entrepreneur's ball with the woman while Roselita went home alone. Roselita felt this would be the last time she would take Brandon's advice. Roselita assumed the only reason Brandon did this to her was so he could make fun of her inability to get a date before the night was over. Brandon thought he was trying to prove that only he could talk to women and end up dating them. While Roselita hoped she could get at least one man to date her, Brandon replied, "Well that's all behind us. Let's start over fresh. This is what I have: There is a conference that is going to take place on June twenty-third at Jack Plaza Hotel with Gordon's Global Network Systems in Ballroom A and B of the hotel. This wonderful event is being hosted by the one and only Mr. Gordon Gem." There is silence through the Internet connect for a moment. Brandon wondered if Roselita was okay because she didn't say anything for a while. Brandon thought Roselita had disconnected from him. To his surprise, he realized it was something that he said that was making Roselita quiet. Suddenly Roselita said, "Brandon I don't know about attending this event with you this time. Those last events didn't turn out right." Brandon spoke in a tranquil tone, "I understand you're upset with me but will you please attend this one and make it your final one? I promise that I won't ask you anymore." Roselita is hesitant. Roselita knew Brandon always made promises that he couldn't keep, even when he was reminded of them. Roselita decided she would give Brandon the benefit of the doubt and trust his instincts. Brandon went on to say that Gordon is a multi-millionaire who owned two businesses. Gordon earned a B.S in Bachelor of Science. Gordon owns several private Jets and a Jet Hanger. Gordon is not married, had no children, and is not in a serious relationship. Gordon is looking for a woman who could fit his description of what it meant to be a wife and mother. Brandon added, "That is the type of woman Gordon is looking for. Brandon informed Roselita this was the conversation that Gordon and he shared once before. Roselita became curious. What would a woman have to bring to the relationship in order for Gordon Gem to be satisfied? Brandon replied, "A woman would need to bring herself if she is willing to compromise certain things in a marriage." Brandon went onto say that he had an opportunity to hang out and play a game of tennis with Gordon Gem. Roselita felt that Brandon was up to his angel in disguise games again. Roselita said, "Okay Brandon, what did you tell him?" Brandon said, "Hum, let's see. I believe I told Gordon that I had a female friend who is very special to me and Gordon might find my female friend to be interesting. Gordon said, "He would love to meet my female friend." Roselita eyes widened as a moon shaped smile covered her face from cheek to cheek, showing her pearly teeth. Roselita pretended as if she hadn't met Gordon Gem before. Roselita wanted to see how Brandon would react to having her meet Gordon. So Roselita played with Brandon saying, "Wait a minute Brandon. So you told this Gordon Gem guy that you had a female friend you would like to introduce to him?" Brandon said, "Yes that's correct. I had you in mind. I know you need some time to think this over so I'll let you think it over. Please do not take long at thinking this matter over." Roselita said, "Brandon I don't know about this. Let me think about it and get back with you." Brandon assured Roselita that anything is possible if only she believed things like this could happen to her. Roselita wanted to believe it could happen to her but she started having doubts that once she had found Mr. True Love, she wouldn't know how to keep him. Just then Brandon said, "Oh Roselita stop being so predictable. Listen. Once you meet Gordon Gem, you will be able to understand why it is important that he gets married." Roselita added a faint laugh as she said, "Brandon, can you give me a day or two to think this over? Then I'll get back with you." Brandon answered, "All is good. Well my love, may you have a restful night. I'll be talking with you later." Roselita responded, "Yes and you do the same, good-night." Roselita disconnect from her laptop in talking with Brandon as she rested on her pillow. Roselita knew her answer would be "yes" about attending Gordon's conference. Roselita's heart moved with delight knowing that she would get another opportunity to meet Gordon Gem. Roselita closed her eyes imaging Gordon wrapping his firm hands around her soft waist and holding her tight. It felt as if she was a clam stuck to its shell. Roselita wondered about how good it would feel to wake up every day seeing Gordon's golden-brown body lying next to hers. Roselita imagined making breakfast for him and their children. Roselita smiled as she saw their children scrambling around the house anticipating getting ready for school. All of a sudden Roselita felt a cool sensation come across her limp body as the wind from the window gently kissed her face. Roselita smiled, realizing that she is a month away from seeing the man who could very well be the one who would change her life forever. Roselita lay there staring at the ceiling, listening to the quietness of the night as Roselita allowed her mind to take her beyond her wildest dreams. Roselita pictured Gordon's face as his eyes glistened into hers--except what appeared to be Gordon's face wasn't his. Instead Roselita saw Brandon's face flash before her eyes. Roselita wondered how this could be sense she is having a pleasant dream thinking about Gordon when Brandon's face appeared out of nowhere. Roselita rolled over on her side thinking she could shake Brandon's appearance from her sweet dreams. But his face was zoomed in so much that she couldn't sleep any more, especially after tossing and turning. Roselita arose and went downstairs to the kitchen to get a glass of water. After getting the water, she turned off the kitchen light and went back upstairs. In her bedroom she fluffed the pillows as she opened the window a little wider, allowing the night breeze to flow into the bedroom. Roselita walked over to her CD collection, pulling out Robert Bjorn's CD, gently placing it into the player. Roselita began to walk over to her bed after she selected track eight with the song entitled, "Could You Love Somebody Else?" Roselita heard the first lines in the song: "The one who's been there for you is the one you need, the one who treated you so kindly, the one who doesn't put much thought into you isn't the right one for you. Then the chorus came, "Could you love somebody else? Just when you thought you've found the right person. Do you really feel that you could have loved somebody else?" Roselita ran quickly over to the Home Coise Theater System pulling out the CD. Then Roselita turned on satellite radio to her favorite station, KLSX 107.8 FM smooth Jazz. They were playing another one of her favorite songs called, "I'm so into you," by Shyanna Rowell. Roselita finally let out a sigh of relief, hoping she found some soothing music to put her back asleep. Well, until Shyanna sang, "I'm so into you. Everything you do makes me want to spend my whole life with you." It's the simple things that you do that make me so into you. The way you love to be that gentleman paying for things makes you feel proud to be a man to stand up. Take my hand and together we shall be husband and wife, we'll share eternity." Roselita turned the satellite radio off. Roselita walked into the bathroom ran her hands under the mechanism faucet splashing cold water on her face. Roselita hoped that the coldness would ease her thoughts, but that didn't work. Roselita opened her laptop getting ready to dial, placing it back down quickly. Roselita stretched across her bed, lying on her stomach with her face into the pillow as she took a deep breath. Then Roselita exhaled, allowing her body to relax. Roselita rolled over on her side and looked at the clock. Roselita watched the numbers on the clock change as she fell asleep. Roselita went into another comfortable sleep. This time Roselita saw Brandon standing before her bent on one knee as he placed her left hand into his palm. Roselita could hear Brandon say, "Roselita Macalaonez, after knowing you for so long, I know it seems as if I took too long for this, but will you marry me?" Roselita heard herself respond to Brandon's proposal by saying, "Yes I felt you'd never ask me to marry you?" Brandon placed a diamond white gold engagement ring onto Roselita's trembling finger as he arose to kiss her. Roselita reveled briefly in the shared moment, thinking how happy Brandon made her feel. Roselita danced around, wrapping both of her arms around his neck. Roselita took in the moment of Brandon pulling her closer to him as their bodies clenched together, bringing a harmonious wave between them. Brandon gracefully kissed her forehead and then her ear lobe as he ran his hands through her flowing hair that draped her shoulders. Roselita squeezed Brandon tighter as she inhaled and then slowly released the air, feeling gladness while the inside of her body danced to the rhythm. Brandon gazed at how radiant Roselita's beauty shined. Brandon loved every inch of her five foot five inch body. Brandon looked down on Roselita's glowing brown eyes, noticing she was finally happy. Brandon kissed her neck as she held him tighter. Roselita smiled back, knowing this could really happen. They stood there so caught up into the moment that neither one wanted to let each other go, so they continued to embrace for a while longer. Roselita became comfortable with the dream that she had slept peacefully throughout the night. The next evening, her brother Troy called to see how she is doing, since he hadn't talked with her in a while.

"Hi sister, how are you doing?"

"I'm doing well, what about you?"

"I'm doing well also. I'm sorry, were you busy Roselita?"

"Oh know. I'm getting ready to exercise before I eat dinner. Why? What's happening?"

"Not much. I just called to see what my sister has been up to these days?" Roselita filled her brother in on all of the juicy details of her life, leaving nothing out. Roselita knew Troy would be ecstatic to know how things had been turning out in her life lately. Mentioning that Brandon is up to his love match making ideas again, Roselita explained that this time Brandon believed he had found the one man that could set off fireworks in Roselita's heart. Roselita had felt that Brandon is good at manipulating her brother and her mother, Mrs. Macalaonez. To always agreeing with Brandon that Roselita's love life isn't going anywhere fast enough for them all. Troy found his sister to be humorous as he agreed that Brandon could be crafty. Troy changed the subject by letting Roselita know that he and his wife Kanita were expecting their fifth child. Roselita said with consternation, "Troy you know I'm not married yet and I don't have children and here you're making and raising your own community." Troy let out a giddy chuckle saying, "Roselita its okay. It'll soon be your turn to have a family of your own. But first mother has to make a match for you." Roselita was furious with Troy. She aimed back at him, "Troy, I didn't find what you just said to be humorous." Troy then stopped laughing. He had forgotten that Roselita was extremely sensitive to all remarks made towards her. Troy apologized but told his sister she needed to ease up on the seriousness and have fun sometimes. Roselita realized that she does get defensive easily and Roselita knew she needed to relax more. Troy said, "Roselita will you be going over to mother's on this Friday night? You know mother looks forward to seeing you at her social gatherings." Roselita reminded herself how excited their mother gets, when she sees her daughter show up at her parties. Roselita sometimes wanted to tell her mother that her gatherings were getting boring, but Roselita knew if she told her mother she would break her mother's heart. Roselita's mother loved to see Roselita at her parties just so she could introduce Roselita to some of her male friends. Troy and his sister Roselita shared a laugh. They knew that their mother kept having these gatherings just for that one reason--so Roselita could date and eventually marry a man. Troy wanted to continue the conversation with Roselita but he needed to go to the grocery store before it got too late. Since his wife Kanita was on bed rest while expecting their fifth child, Troy ran errands. Kanita's parents were keeping their other four children until Sunday evening. Roselita loved knowing that her brother Troy had become successful. Troy graduated with a Master of Marketing (M.M.R) degree; majoring in Market Research. Troy met Kanita at Lynders University where they were college sweethearts. Kanita became pregnant during their sophomore year while attending Lynders University. Kanita didn't finish school, as she was pregnant with their first child. Troy married Kanita after their child turned two years old. Kanita received her Certificate in Book Keeping. Troy opened up his own Business Marketing Company while Kanita stayed home to manage the bookkeeping. Roselita knew her parents taught Troy and her well, their expectations for success runs high in their family. Roselita's parents felt that working extra can reward you with the finer things in life. Even though Roselita's father cheated on her mother throughout their lives, Roselita still looked up to her father. Roselita finished placing her dishes into the dishwasher as she straightened out the house before she went to visit her mother. Roselita drove down Interstate eighty-one with the sunroof of her car opened. Allowing the night breeze to blow on her hair, she pressed the accelerator picking up more speed. While listening to her favorite satellite radio station, smooth Jazz KLSX 107.8 FM, Roselita heard the song; "My Love Is All You Need" by Gerald Salt's come on. Roselita turned onto Orchard Lane then made another right on Dove Court. Roselita pulled up into her mother's driveway. Roselita closed the sunroof, locking the doors. As she walked up to the front door, Roselita rang the doorbell. Her mother came to the door and asked Roselita why she didn't use her spare key. Roselita told her mother that one time when she did use the spare key she walked in on her mother and her mother's fiancé Hayman. Roselita's mother and Hayman were messing around with each other, so ever since that time she has stopped using her spare key. Roselita then started ringing the doorbell, Mrs. Macalaonez said, "Baby, you don't have to feel uncomfortable being around Hayman and me. We are two consenting adults and it wasn't as if when you saw us and we were nude. Roselita didn't like when her mother would discuss her personal business with her. Realizing that they were adults, Roselita changed the subject that she and her mother were having about using the house spare key. Mrs. Macalaonez wanted to know if her daughter would be attending her social gathering on this Friday night. When Roselita was about to give her answer, her mother interrupted saying, "Baby, look at what I'm wearing on my left finger?" Roselita stood there watching the tears of joy fill her mother's face as her mother showed off her dazzling three-carat nougat engagement ring. Roselita was thrilled about her mother getting married. Roselita went in to a daze thinking about how good things were going to be just as soon as her mother is married. Roselita felt her mother should stop meddling in Roselita's love life by playing love matchmaker. Roselita thought the only reason her mother is rushing for Roselita to get married is so that Roselita could become a breeding machine, which meant more grandchildren. Mrs. Macalaonez felt that Roselita would soon be too old to have children. Then Roselita would be living in a senior high rise somewhere. Even though Mrs. Macalaonez knew that more and more women were having children in their forties, fifties and even sixties Roselita was getting older. Roselita is thirty-four years old-- practically an old woman. Roselita felt her mother didn't care that she might be enjoying her single life at the moment. Mrs. Macalaonez loved both Troy and Roselita, although Roselita envied Troy because she felt he was their mother's favorite. Troy is already married and expecting his fifth child. Roselita diverted her attention back to her mother. Roselita watched her mother's zealous oval brown eyes widen with splendor. Mrs. Macalaonez couldn't help but gaze at her cluster ring over and over again. Each time Mrs. Macalaonez smile got bigger as Roselita glanced outside of the kitchen window. Roselita saw her mother's fiancé, Hayman, pulling into the driveway and park. Hayman got out carrying a bag of clothes from the cleaners and another bag full of groceries. Roselita couldn't imagine her mother being with anyone else other than her mother's fiancé. Hayman is a stockbroker, an excellent cook, and a nurturer. Hayman isn't boring and enjoyed fixing things around her mother's home. Hayman didn't complain and loved to shower his woman Mrs. Macalaonez with surprising gifts. Roselita reminisced about the first time her mother started dating Hayman. Roselita remembered Hayman's continuous generosity, not just toward her mother, but also towards Troy and herself. Roselita hoped that when it's her turn to get married someday, she'd have as much enthusiasm as her mother. Hayman entered the kitchen, placed the groceries on the kitchen counter, and laid the clean clothes on the back of a chair. Hayman kissed his fiancée-Roselita's mother and said to her and Roselita, "Good evening. "Hayman washed his hands, took the groceries out of the bags, and began preparing dinner, asking Roselita if she is staying for dinner.

Roselita said, "As long as you're cooking I'll always stay for dinner." Mrs. Macalaonez isn't offended by her daughter's remarks. Mrs. Macalaonez knew Roselita enjoyed eating whenever Hayman cooked dinner. Hayman asked Roselita how come she never enjoys eating her mother's cooking. Roselita said, "When Troy and I were little children, her father went to college for Culinary Arts to get his Associate of Applied Science degree." Roselita continued, "Ever since our father learned how to cook, our mother would leave the cooking up to him while she kept the home clean. Our father taught Troy and I how to cook as well. I remembered one day when he said in a firm voice, 'Now children, you will learn the three levels of cooking.' Our Father continued, 'The first step is basic cooking, making microwave food. The second step is throw down, which means adding spices, and the last level is burning--not literally blackening the cook ware, but creating your own style from scratch' Hayman laughed saying, "I understand. Thank you for the information and the quick lessons in the different levels of cooking. Listen Roselita, I want you to know that I love your mother whether she can cook or not. We have a trust and a loving bond. It started out as a friendship and now it's ending in marriage to each other." Mrs. Macalaonez looked at her daughter as she embraced her saying, "Baby, I'm glad you're my daughter and I love you with all of my heart, it does my heart good to know that you're proud of me for finding someone

Whom I'm deeply in love with." Roselita said to her mother, "Don't you think it's time to tell Hayman about how father used to treat you?" Mrs. Macalaonez agreed with her daughter. Mrs. Macalaonez said, "Hayman honey, it's time you knew something about my past--that way it won't reflect upon our marriage later." Mrs. Macalaonez went onto say that it all started years ago when Troy and Roselita were little children with Troy being sixteen years old and Roselita twelve years old. Roselita saw her mother inhale heavily and slowly exhale, taking her time to speak softly. Roselita, not realizing that this could be painful for her mother to talk about, quickly interrupted her, "Mother if this is going to be too painful, you don't have to carry on with your past." Mrs. Macalaonez looked into her daughter's weary brown eyes and said, "Listen baby, don't you think that if this is too painful I wouldn't be addressing my past? It's quite all right. Your mother is okay with telling this story."

Roselita didn't say another word. Instead Roselita pulled up a chair from the kitchen table as she sat to hear the story that was never told by her mother all these years until now. Mrs. Macalaonez concluded by saying, "It was supposed to be a blissful marriage but the devastating news that my late ex-husband shared left me questioning why this had to happen to me and my family. I found out that Mr. Rio Macalaonez was having a secret affair on me. Day in and day out I thought I was doing the right things as a wife and mother of his lovely children. I tried to keep my appearance up, hoping it could keep him interested in me. I made sure everything was perfect, from cleaning, to dusting to what I had called keeping him satisfied physically, emotionally, mentally, socially, and spiritually, but none of those things seemed to spark his interest anymore. "One day his guilty conscience caught up with him. We were on our way to eat dinner with some friends of ours. I had just finished getting dressed and he was already dressed, looking distinguished, when the telephone rang. Mr. Rio Macalaonez, Troy and Roselita's late father answered it in the home office with the door slightly opened. That's when I overheard his conversation. It was one of his Auto Racing buddies, Opaque Roggins calling to speak with him. It seemed important because my late ex-husband Rio was whispering, making sure I couldn't hear what they were discussing. I overheard him working on a way to tell me something important. Mr. Rio Macalaonez said to his Auto Racing buddy, Opaque Roggins that he needed more time to make sure the children and I would be okay and safe. Just before Rio Macalaonez hung up the telephone from chatting with Opaque, Rio said, 'Yes, I'll tell her soon, but tonight isn't the night.' At that moment he told Opaque good-bye and said he'd talk with him later. The interesting part came the following week. I couldn't believe he waited a whole week just to tell me that he'd been having an affair throughout our entire marriage. After his brutal announcement, I had a hard time dealing with our marriage--especially the trusting part. I managed to forgive him. I then went into a deep depression wondering what went wrong and why he brought not only me but also our children through this. I felt if Rio didn't want to be with me or if Rio was confused, why bother getting married? Rio Macalaonez could have saved his life--let alone my life--from despair, but then I wouldn't have had my children either.

"We ended up divorcing because of Rio's infidelity. Rio Macalaonez chose to live his life without our children and me. Rio Macalaonez moved out of the house and moved in with his mistress. As time moved on, the next thing I knew I had gotten a telephone call from the morgue asking me to identify his body. I had thought Rio was in a serious car accident but later found out his mistress had given him AIDS and he died. By the end of the week here, I was having a funeral for my ex-husband." Mrs. Macalaonez fiancé, Hayman, is so caught up in the story from her past that he wanted to know what happened to her ex-husband's mistress during and after the funeral. Mrs. Macalaonez continued, "During the funeral ceremony, his mistress had the audacity to approach me, saying how sorry she was for taking Rio from my children and me. "I was stunned! I told her that because my heart was filled with compassion, I couldn't hold resentment forever. But the only question that I had been waiting to ask was, 'Why?' I told her, 'I don't mean to be harsh but, what if it was the other way around? How would you have felt towards me?' "As Rio's mistress stood there, all she could say was, 'I'm sorry and I hope that you and your children can finish making it throughout life.' I was dismayed because I couldn't believe what I was hearing. That was all she had to say after stealing my ex-husband of twenty years and then ripping our family apart. I wanted to slap her! But after seeing my children's faces, I couldn't. I knew I had to show an example of what a real woman does in a crisis, especially when the other woman is standing in her presence. After the funeral my children and I went back home. A few months later, we sold the house and moved to start our lives all over again." As Mrs. Macalaonez continued telling her story to her fiancé Hayman, Roselita had gotten up from the chair she was sitting in to put the dishes in the dishwasher and finish cleaning up the kitchen. While Mrs. Macalaonez and her Fiancé Hayman walked into the living room. When Mrs. Macalaonez finally finished her story, Hayman picked up the remote, aiming it at the plasma screen television as he sat next to his fiancée. Mrs. Macalaonez sat comfortably near her man-Hayman as Roselita finished up in the kitchen. Roselita walked into the living room. Her mother asked if she wanted to stay and watch a movie with them but Roselita felt it was getting late and she needed to be going home. Roselita made it home. Once comfortably at home, Roselita checked her voice mail for messages and sure enough, Brandon called to speak with her. Before returning his call, Roselita went into the bathroom and filled the tub with warm water. Roselita put on her white and pink robe with her name engraved on the upper right side. As Roselita went downstairs to the kitchen, Roselita poured herself a smoothie drink that she made earlier that morning. Roselita walked back upstairs to her bathroom, walked over to the built in Home Coise Theater System on the wall, and placed her favorite variety Jazz collection in the CD player. Roselita dropped her signature robe to the floor and placed her glass near the bathtub as she entered the tub to begin her night relaxation. Roselita leaned back, closing her eyes and allowing the aroma of Orange Spice and Cream to fill the room. The computer laptop rang and Roselita spoke aloud, "Music down," as she answered the laptop. The system in the bathroom ran by voice command. Roselita is able to control the Home Coise Theater System, laptop telephone, plasma television, heating and air conditioner, which were also located in the bathroom. Roselita said, "Good evening. This is Macalaonez and Macalaonez Express News. How may I help you?" Mrs. Macalaonez said, "Roselita baby, are you pretending to have your own business again?" Roselita replied, "Mother you know that I always answer the phone like this at night just in case some stranger is acting crazy on the phone." Her mother laughed saying, "I see I've taught you well." Roselita said, "Mother sorry. I do not mean to interrupt you, but aren't you and Hayman spending a lovely evening together right now?" Mrs. Macalaonez responded with, "Yes, but I wanted to make sure you had made it home safely because there was an accident on Interstate forty-five going eastbound." Roselita took the time to thank her mother for the concern. Roselita said, "Thank you mother. Yes, I'm home safely." Mrs. Macalaonez continued, "I'm glad you are home safely... I'll let you finish relaxing." Roselita activated her voice command. Roselita said, "Laptop disconnect, Home Coise Theater System sound back up." Roselita finished bathing, cleaned the tub, placed creamy cocoa butter over her body, and rubbed coconut body oil on her French pedicure toes. Roselita misted perfume on her soft bronze glowing body as she put on her silk navy chemise. Roselita walked over to the window and opened it to the quiet night as she gazed out into the darkness. Roselita opened her laptop phone as she dialed Brandon.

He answered in a firm tone, "Hello?" Roselita's voice became shaky as she said, "Brandon, good evening. It's me, Roselita."

Brandon said, "How's my sweet love doing on this brisk evening?"

Roselita relaxed her voice as it became normal, "I'm doing well. I received your message from the voice mail." Brandon answered, "I see, so what are you doing right now Miss Sweet love. Roselita giggled, knowing that she always enjoyed his playful talk even though she wished Brandon could come out and be serious by being honest with his emotions towards her. Roselita returned Brandon's question with a smart answer, "None of your business." Brandon's heavy laughter filled her heart with gladness as he said, "Mm, I like a feisty woman, especially when she's showing off how furious she can be. Can you say, 'None of your business!' but with more oomph?" Brandon asked. Roselita savored the moment as she laughed, returning the playfulness while speaking in a soothing tone, "Oh Brandon honey, would you like to be the business?" Brandon's tone of voice became rich and hearty as he said, "With pleasure. Is the meeting taking place at your house?" Both of them went back and forth, telling each other something sweet. Roselita began to picture Brandon and her embracing while watching a romantic movie together. Roselita always had a deep feeling towards Brandon but she was too reticent to let it show. Roselita fell so head-over-heels for this five foot ten inch suave man that every time they had gotten together to hang out, he made her feel nervous. Roselita knew Brandon is just too good looking with his mocha au latté self, his chest protruded, and his broad and masculine shoulders. Brandon's oval eyes were dark brown and seductive. Brandon kept his opal and curly hair short while he shaved his facial hair. When touched, it felt smooth like silk crème pie, which gave him the stud appearance of a twenty-eight year old. Brandon's hands were firm, but they could easily become soft once held. Roselita loved every inch of his body, from head to toe. Roselita loved his manly voice to his debonair charm. Roselita knew Brandon had his act together, not just professionally but also when it came to treating a woman with respect. The only thing that suppressed her feelings was Brandon's instability when it came to dating women. Roselita wanted to settle down with Brandon but realized it'd be difficult. Roselita knew it could be done, but it would take time. Roselita snapped out of her wishful thinking as she focused on the conversation she is having with Brandon. They laughed about how people do the weirdest things when driving on the highway and about how the day at work went for them. Roselita and Brandon talked a little more about the conference and how Brandon is looking forward to matching up Gordon and Roselita. Brandon mentioned that they would make a perfect match. Roselita laughed saying Brandon you are getting too carried away. Roselita knew how impassioned Brandon is, but Roselita also wanted to take her time by making sure that Gordon and she clicked before they started getting serious. Although Roselita felt deep in her heart that she and Brandon would make a better couple, Roselita thought it wouldn't hurt to give Gordon a chance. Roselita realized the decision is going to be complicated because both men were handsome and seemed to have the good qualities that she's looking for in a mate. Roselita hopes she'd choose the right man, Brandon or Gordon. Roselita saw Brandon as a potential candidate but he is too flirtatious and she hadn't the opportunity to know Gordon yet. Roselita felt she should keep her options open. Roselita wanted to do the right thing but her heart is leaning more towards her close friend Brandon Bright. As they talked, Brandon began to sing in a low key. As Roselita listened, she closed her eyes, thinking how wonderful it would be with just Brandon and her together. Roselita thought of Brandon and her having a family, suddenly she opened her eyes. As Brandon said, "You know what Roselita, I'm not good at having conversations, but there's something different about ours. What it is, I'm not sure. I can't quite understand." Roselita responded saying, "You know, maybe it is because we have grown on each other, so whether we say a lot or a little. We always seem to enjoy each other's company." Brandon replied back, "I guess you're right on that. I believe we've gotten too comfortable. There are times when you and I talk and other times when there's silence--like now when I end up singing to you." Roselita said, "Funny, because if we don't say anything we end up singing to each other instead of getting off our laptop phones and doing something productive." Brandon responded, "Now that's the truth. But it is so comfortable knowing that I'm able to do this. You know Roselita; I wouldn't waste this much time talking to another woman like I'm talking to you. Roselita felt as if it is a privilege to be talking to him on the telephone. Roselita knew how handsome

Brandon is but also felt that sometimes Brandon liked boosting his ego. Finally they let each other go as they said, "Good-Night." Roselita slept peacefully throughout the night. Roselita arrived at work and walked past her co-workers saying, "Good Morning to them." Roselita entered her office and pushed the button on the laptop checking her voice mail. Norlina Parsons left a message asking Roselita if she could cover for her because she wouldn't be in the office today. After listening to Norlina's message, Roselita deleted it, moving to the next message. It is Brandon calling to let her know that he would like to take her out to lunch. Roselita walked to the door as she turned the light off, locking the door behind her. Roselita stood in front of the elevator as she continued to say good morning to her co-workers as they passed by her. The elevator door opened and her eyes filled with curiosity when she saw a handsome man. Roselita smiled as her heart raced with satisfaction. Roselita felt a warm glow flow through her as he looked at her and said, "Good morning and how are you?" Roselita was caught up with how good the man looked that she didn't hear him say good morning to her until he laughed, "Um, I don't mean to catch you off guard, but how are you this morning?" Roselita stood frozen as she blinked her eyes several times before finally responding back, "Oh, I'm sorry. Please forgive me for staring. Where are my manners?" Roselita added, "Good Morning my name is Roselita Macalaonez." The handsome gentleman standing next to her in the elevator smiled with a beautiful candid gesture that left her mesmerized as he extended his hand to meet hers. "Hello my name is Nigel Stock nice to meet you Mrs. Macalaonez." Roselita put on her flirtatious and timid side, letting Nigel know that she isn't a Mrs. Macalaonez but instead she is Miss Macalaonez. Nigel eyebrows rose as he said, "So you're not married? Roselita smiled answering, "No but I would love to be someday." The elevator door opened as they both stepped off before they went their separate ways. Nigel said, "I hope to see more of you around here, Miss Macalaonez." Nigel winked his right eye as he walked away. Roselita's heart jolted with excitement. Roselita couldn't believe what she just saw! Roselita wanted to ask Nigel Stock to marry her, right then and there but Roselita knew that would sound crazy to even ask. Roselita walked towards the Human Resource office, unlocking the door and turning on the lights. Roselita opened her laptop and dialed

Brandon to let him know she would love to join him for lunch today. Roselita also mentioned the best time for her to go eat. Just as she hung up from her laptop telephone a man entered the office. "Good Morning ma'am, I'm here to see Norlina Parsons?"

Roselita said, "Ah, yes, Good Morning to you. Your name is?

The man answered, "My name is Jamos West."

Roselita answered him, "Well Mr. West, I'm sorry to inform you but Miss Parsons will not be in today, I'm filling in for her."

Jamos West said, "Thank you. I didn't quite catch your name?"

"Please forgive me, my name is Roselita Macalaonez." Roselita gave him a pleasant smile as Mr. Jamos West checked out her by looking up and down, sizing Roselita up to see how she would look walking next to him. Roselita walked over to the electric file cabinet, pulling out a file of vanilla folders and she carried each one back to the desk. The names of the new hires were written them. Jamos's eyes lit up as he watched her every move. Mr. Jamos West smiled childishly; liking what he was seeing when Roselita walked passed him. Mr. Jamos West took a seat and smirked while his brown eyes gazed on her behind and her legs. She sensed he was watching her every move, but when she went to sit back down at the desk, he stood up. Roselita said, "Mr. West is there something that you have forgotten or saw?" Mr. Jamos West knew he didn't forget anything and the only thing he saw was how beautiful she looked dressed in her burgundy skirt suit. Jamos West said, "No, Miss Macalaonez. It's when I'm in the presence of a beautiful woman and she's about to take her seat that I like to show courtesy."

"Well thank you Mr. West. I appreciate your manners."

"Oh you don't have to call me Mr. West. Instead you can call me Jamos."

"If you don't mind, I would prefer to call you Mr. West. After all, I'm a woman who enjoys using courtesy also."

"Miss Macalaonez, even though we've just met I can say I like your generosity."

"In that case Mr. West, shall we take your photo for the company ID?" As Roselita set up the Thirty-five millimeter digital camera, the camera became dysfunctional. During the process of Roselita repairing the Thirty-five millimeter digital camera, Mr. Jamos West tried to smooth talk Roselita. Mr. Jamos West felt he could succeed at winning Roselita's heart. "Miss Macalaonez, if you don't mind me asking, do you have a love interest? "Mr. West, once again I appreciate your consideration, but I don't mix my personal affairs with my work." Mr. Jamos West said, "I understand, but how is a man supposed to get to know a beautiful woman like you if he doesn't ask questions?" Roselita gave Jamos a grin, "Clever Mr. West. You are very clever with your choice of words." Mr. Jamos West replied, "Well Miss Macalaonez you can't knock out a man for inquiring about a lovely looking woman now, can you?" Roselita answered, "Mr. West thanks for the offer, but I'm not interested in dating you." "Miss Macalaonez, I respect your wishes. Good luck and I hope you find the man of your dreams and the two of you get married." Roselita felt Jamos wasn't her type. Roselita longed for a man with a passionate loving heart, someone--besides God--she could fall deeply in love, a man who knows where his life is going and is God-fearing. Roselita treasured the love that her parents once showed during happier times in their marriage. Roselita saw the anxiety on her mother's face as she prepared for her second marriage. Roselita realized that at this moment in her life, dating would be a hindrance to her career. The door to the office opened. Jamos forgot about talking with Roselita as he directed his attention to the woman entering the room. The woman said, "Good morning ma'am. I'm here to see Norlina Parsons? Roselita extended her hand to greet the woman, "I'm sorry but Norlina won't be in today. My name is Roselita Macalaonez and I'm filling in for her on today." She continued, "Is there something that I could help you with? "The woman replied, "Yes, I'm here to get some paper work done and take my photo ID. Roselita told the woman to have a seat...she will be right with her in a moment. Just as Roselita had finished speaking with the woman, Roselita looked over at Mr. Jamos West, noticing how attentive he now was--especially as he saw another beautiful woman walk in the room. Mr. Jamos West sat straight up in his chair and pretended to be flipping through a magazine using it as a shield. Mr. Jamos West glanced at the woman from head to toe. Mr. Jamos West could smell the scents of jasmine and lilac with a touch of cashmere. The woman wore a designer blouse with matching shoes and handbag. Her nails were French manicured as she wore a flipped up hairstyle. The woman took a seat next to Jamos while she waited on Roselita to get her information. When she sat down, she looked at Jamos giving him a sweet smile. Jamos looked over at the woman saying, "Good morning," as he looked at Roselita with a plastered grin on his face. Roselita smiled back, thinking to herself, "This is wonderful. Mr. Jamos West has found someone else to occupy his time while he's waiting." The laptop rang. It is Brandon returning Roselita's call. Brandon will be picking Roselita up for lunch at noon. The afternoon arrived. When Roselita had just finished with the last hire, Brandon pulled up in his midnight Lincoln car. Brandon just had it detailed with an extra coat of wax for the shine. The music from NIXS 102.7 FM, the hot goodies station, played as he drove into the ramp of the Welcome News Express building where Roselita was busy working. Brandon parked the car, turned off the radio, closed the sunroof and locked the doors with his key alarm system. Brandon brushed the lint from his pants, pulling out a small square box that read, "Time for Freshness," allowing the white and blue peppermints to fall gently into the palm of his hand. Brandon placed them in his mouth then pushed the button of the elevator to the lobby area of the building. The doors opened. As Brandon stepped in he began to hum the tune from "I've found my love" by Lola Fossil Brook. Just before he reached the lobby, a woman stepped in. Brandon tried to focus his attention elsewhere. Brandon marveled at how breathtaking she looked. The woman's eyes glowed as she stared at him, making her pulse race swiftly. Brandon felt if he had more time he could work his charm by having her want to be all over him. Brandon said, "Good Afternoon?" The woman on the elevator with him remained motionless for a moment as she openly studied him, looking at his muscular physique. The woman allowed her round dark brown eyes to travel to his eyes in hopes that he was single. The woman greeted Brandon in return, "Good Afternoon to you too." Brandon knew he was good at running games with women, so he used some of his pickup lines to see how she would re-act to his flirtation moves. "Excuse me, I don't mean to be of any harm but you look lovely. I'm sure your husband or man already told you that before you left the house this morning?" The woman's face became flushed, not realizing that she was being tricked into falling for the smooth Romeo pickup lines that he gives to all the women he meets. The woman laughed, "No, there wasn't any man who complimented me on how I looked this morning until now. It would have been nice to have left my home hearing those exact words. Brandon continued to ask her the questions he was hoping to get answers for, "So are you single?" "Yes, but I have four children with their ages being two, five, nine, and fifteen," the woman answered him. Brandon noticed how the woman is slowly letting her guard down and starting to open up like a flower blossoming. Brandon continued, "What's a single mother such as you doing without a man on her arm?" The woman smiled with satisfaction knowing that Brandon was making her feel important. Brandon withheld trying to pursue her any further. Brandon felt dating a woman with four children would be out of his league because he didn't have any children and he didn't want to be an already made father. Brandon didn't want to come on too strong so he kept the conversation to a minimum, "Well I hope you finish having a good afternoon." The woman replied, "Thank you and you too." The elevator door closed with the woman in it. Brandon stepped off the elevator, walked down the hallway midway, and opened the door to the human resource department of Welcome News Express. He saw Roselita seated at her desk typing away. Brandon said, "Good afternoon my Mahogany Queen?" Roselita looked up; smiling to see Brandon had made it to the office to take her out to lunch. Roselita said, "Brandon I couldn't help but notice how you seem to always put a smile on my face every time I see you." Brandon added some humor, "I know. See, only a man like me can make you melt. Now shall we go out to lunch?" Brandon took Roselita by the hand as he placed it underneath his arm as if they were a couple. Roselita felt suspicious of Brandon, knowing that he loved to be playful with her. Roselita could sense his true feelings.

"Brandon, are you getting fresh with me?"

Brandon answered comically, "Who me, Mr. 'At Your Service' Bright?" Roselita wasn't in a playful mood. As she became serious, he continued to be humorous. Roselita said, "Come on now, who else would I be talking with besides you Brandon?" Finally Roselita relaxed her face and managed to turn the corners of her mouth into a beautiful smile as the two of them shared a laugh while they walked to the elevator door. Brandon showed off his gentlemanly side as he opened the car door, seating Roselita then closing the door as he whistled a tune called, "Your love is mine" by Na'Sha Gillman.

Brandon walked over to the driver's side. As soon as he sat down he opened the sunroof and put the car into reverse as the two of them drove out of the parking lot. He made a right onto Blaine Boulevard as he picked up speed, driving forty miles per hour when the speed limit was twenty- five miles per hour through the downtown. Roselita told Brandon to slow down before he hits another vehicle. Brandon looked over at her saying, "Whose driving this car, me or you?" Roselita rolled her eyes and turned the corners of her mouth into an awkward motion as she said, "Well who wants to live--me or you?" Brandon didn't say another word as he smiled, reached for the volume button, and blasted the music louder. Brandon turned the wheel and merged into the left lane exiting Blaine Boulevard and entering Interstate four ninety- eight going southbound. Brandon turned off the radio and excused himself as he aimed for the glove compartment, pulling out a CD holder. His eyes beheld how beautiful Roselita looked; the scent of her designer perfume mesmerized him and left him and wanting to embrace her. Instead he redirected his attention back to driving, asking her about her day. Roselita said, "It started wrong. First Norlina called in, saying she wouldn't be at work. Norlina Parson gave a late notice but I filled in for her anyway. Then a new hire named Jamos West became lustful towards me until another hired a woman took his attention away. Thank goodness, the second person that showed up was a woman." Before Roselita could finish, Brandon let out a faint laugh then said, "Roselita are you in hope that some man would really make a pass at you?" Roselita became irritated by his rude remarks. Roselita felt he didn't understand that she didn't want the new hire to come onto her. Roselita snapped, "Funny Brandon, but I'm serious. Do you like it when Jilla Handsberg from your work tells everyone that you two are dating?" After her brutal attempt to get even with him, Brandon became quiet and allowed her to finish talking about how her morning had turned out crazy. Roselita said, "As I was saying, every time I walked away from the desk I could see that Mr. Jamos West, the new hired man, was checking me out." Brandon said, "Okay just because a man looks at a beautiful woman doesn't mean he's making a pass at her." Brandon tried to refrain from loud outbursts of laughter as he said, "Who picked up whose telephone number first, you or this man named Mr. West?" Roselita became so defensive by Brandon's humorous remarks that she said, "It is okay, I'll remember to be humorous the next time you try to say something serious to me." Roselita added, "Besides I thought you would be sensitive to my emotions. Now I see the real you coming out." Brandon placed his hand on Roselita's hand and quickly glanced at her. Roselita felt calm, noticing Brandon's beaming smile. Roselita wanted to kiss him, knowing how deep her love for him ran. But she returned his gesture by asking him if he was trying to reason with her so she could feel better. Brandon told Roselita that no matter what they experience together, he would always be supportive of her. Brandon pulled out a CD that read, "Lover's Soul," and selected number eight for the song entitled, "At the Beginning." Roselita pushed the control button on the side of her seat and reclined comfortably. Roselita closed her eyes and tilted her head towards Brandon, taking a deep breath and releasing it with a smile. Brandon began to sing the words to the song: "Whenever you smile, whenever I look into your eyes, I knew it was love at the beginning. Whenever I'm in your presence you make me feel complete and wonderful, your love, and your touch. You are my life and it's filled with joy, I knew it was love at the beginning. It's the little things that you do that have me loving you more and more each day. It's the way you make me feel happy. That's why we'll always be at the beginning." Roselita wasn't asleep when she heard Brandon singing. Roselita felt as if she was floating on a cloud. The song ended and Brandon stopped singing. Brandon turned right onto Willard's road, passing a car dealership on the left side when he finally approached Marlitio's Restaurant. Brandon pulled up into the overflow parking lot as he lightly tapped Roselita, informing her that they had arrived at the restaurant. Roselita sat forward, reclining her seat and fixing up her outfit. Looking into her purse, she pulled out a comb. Allowing the teeth of the comb to press against her softened relaxed hair, she then pulled out her makeup compact as she blotted her face with the powder brush, shaking off the excess powder. Stroking the bristles up and down, Roselita closed the compact, putting it gently back into her purse as she pulled out her toffee lipstick and brown lip glossy. Roselita carefully outlined her lips and then smoothed them with the toffee lipstick, rubbing both top and bottom lips together. Roselita took one last glance at her appearance before getting out of the car and entering the restaurant. "I'll drop you off at the entrance while I find a parking spot."

"Okay. I'll see you shortly." Brandon pulled up to the front door of Marlitio's Restaurant, letting Roselita out first. Roselita saw a man and woman exiting the restaurant as the man held the door to the restaurant open for Roselita to enter. Roselita greeted the unknown man with a smile and thanked him for holding the door while she went inside where she stood waiting for Brandon to park the car. Out in the parking lot, Brandon saw the unknown man and woman who was exiting the building the same time as Roselita was entering. Brandon had gotten out of the car, locking the doors with his remote alarm key. He exchanged words with the man by thanking him for holding the door of the restaurant as his woman Roselita entered. The unknown man returned the kindness by telling Brandon to enjoy the rest of the day. Brandon entered Marlitio's Restaurant and met up with Roselita. The waiter came and seated the two of them as they ordered something to drink. They looked over the menu before ordering. The waiter returned as they were both ready to place an order. Being a gentleman, Brandon allowed Roselita to place her order first. Roselita ordered the green salad, grilled salmon on a bed of Cajun rice, steamed carrots, and mashed potatoes in a light brown gravy sauce. While Brandon ordered the filet mignon, corn on the cob, sweet honey buttered dinner roll, and a loaded stuffed baked potato. After eating lunch they followed up with dessert. Roselita ordered a cup of Café Mocha Chocó-latte' while Brandon ordered a slice of cheesecake topped with strawberries and whipped cream. They talked and shared laughs until they were interrupted by an important cell phone call. Brandon looked at his caller ID, noticing it was someone from work trying to reach him. Brandon excused himself and took the call. "Hello this is Brandon?" A woman spoke, "Good afternoon Mr. Bright. This is Sally from the office. Sorry to interrupt your lunch." Brandon didn't mind being interrupted, especially if it was important. Brandon continued to talk to Sally the secretary. "Brandon, Mr. Carr would like to meet with you at two o'clock in the conference room." Brandon thanked Sally for the message and let her know he'd be back to the office shortly. Brandon returned back to the table as he focused on Roselita. Brandon surveyed Roselita from her round brown eyes to her spunky smile. As she laughed gracefully, Brandon realized that he could be making a mistake by not asking her to be his woman. Roselita noticed Brandon staring at her and said, "Is something wrong with me? Because you're staring at me like there is." Awestruck by her beauty, Brandon crossed his hands under his chin and answered, "No, I'm marveling at your radiant glow." Roselita blushed as she looked down at the table. Roselita then slowly glanced up and said, "Brandon you're such a sweet man. Thank you for the compliment." Brandon threw back his head and let out a great peal of laughter, "Ah, well it's nothing. I just felt you should know that I admire you. However, I need to get back to work. That was Sally the secretary letting me know that Mr. Carr would like to meet with me." Roselita thanked him for the lunch date as he paid the bill and left a tip for the waiter. Silence filled the car as Brandon drove Roselita back to work. Roselita rolled down the car window but quickly rolled it back up and exclaimed, "Whew, the meteorologists hit the spot. It's hot out there." Roselita unzipped her purse pulled out an electric mini fan and turned it on. Brandon looked over at her and asked, "Why would you pull out a fan when you know this car is air conditioned?"

"Well I thought you might want to save on your gas?"

Brandon said, "Yes that's correct, but I make that decision."

Roselita replied, "Excuse me for being concerned."

Brandon winked his right eye as he stroked her lips with his index finger. Roselita exhaled a long contented sigh. Brandon smiled, "Just don't let it happen again, Miss Quick I need some Air!" Roselita said, "Yes, Mr. Bright I hear you loud and clear." Brandon replied, "Okay, now let me get you some cool air and get you safely back to work." Roselita said, "Hey, you are in control Mr. Drill Sergeant." Brandon pulled up in front of Welcome News Express and got out, quickly running around to Roselita's side as he opened the car door for her. Brandon knew that he was pressed for time, needing to get back across town before two o'clock in order to meet with Mr. Carr. Standing outside the car, Roselita hoped Brandon would hug or kiss her good-bye. Instead he ran back to his side, got in, and speedily drove off. When Roselita walked into the building, she saw Pomedra Hernandez walking towards her. Roselita hoped that Pomedra would pass her by without stopping to chat with her. Pomedra said, "Roselita, how are you doing?" Roselita pretended as if she didn't see Pomedra walking in her direction. Roselita quickly answered, "Oh hey, Pomedra I'm well--and you?" Pomedra began her gossipy report on the work place. Roselita felt they should rename the company. Instead of calling it Welcome News Express, it should be named Pomedra's Gossip Express. Pomedra always has the four-one-one on everyone from every floor in the office building, as if it is part of her job description to keep employees informed of the latest office gossip. It was as if her forehead read, "Hot off the press from me, Pomedra Hernandez, the gossip queen. I have all of the latest and greatest company news." Pomedra is the secretary to the CEO of the company, Mr. Perez. Pomedra is also his mistress, which he tries to keep under cover. But he already made a couple of leaks bragging to Roselita and another close employee named Gerald that Pomedra is the best woman that a man could have. Roselita felt that Mr. Perez was in the wrong because he's married with a beautiful wife and four children ranging from one to twenty-five years old. Pomedra has a sister named Bali Hernandez who works in Welcome News Express warehouse. Out of the two of them, Bali is the settled one while Pomedra is the busy one, keeping up with the in crowd people. Pomedra continued to talk with Roselita saying, "So Miss Macalaonez, when are you going to invite your handsome male friend up to see everyone. I mean after all, he always comes to take you out for lunch but you never introduce him to us?" Roselita said, "How interesting that you should be asking that question Pomedra, because you are the only one asking to see him."

Pomedra said, "Now Roselita, you know that I'm not or am' I ... really the only one asking to meet your male friend?"

Roselita answered, "Yes, Pomedra nobody really seems to care who picks me up for my lunch dates except you."

Pomedra answered, "Okay so I'm asking. But what's the secret? Why are you hiding him from us?" Roselita responded, "Listen, Pomedra, I need to be getting back to doing some work, but I will leave you with this message: I will be keeping my personal business a secret just like you are keeping Mr. Perez and your romance a top secret." Pomedra asked Roselita what she had just said to her. "Wait a moment, what do you mean my romance affair with Mr. Perez?" Roselita answered, "Oh, Pomedra, how naïve you are. Face the facts. There was a leak that came from Mr. Perez when he told

Gerald and me that he hoped his wife never finds out about his three year love affair with you." Pomedra, being caught off guard by Roselita's approach regarding her secret love affair with the CEO of the company Mr. Perez, became startled, wanting to know all what Roselita and Gerald knew. "What? Do you mean Mr. Perez told Gerald and you about us?" Pomedra was now in denial. Pomedra was stunned that Mr. Perez would go as far as to tell their secret when they promised each other that nobody in the entire building should know. Pomedra hoped nobody would tell if some people found out the truth. Roselita went on to say, "Yes after our morning meeting on last Tuesday, Mr. Perez pulled Gerald and me aside to let us know he needed to talk with someone regarding your pregnancy." Roselita finished saying, "Listen, Pomedra, I don't know what you two are really up to but you're involved with a married man who has four lovely children and now maybe one on the way with you." Pomedra's eyes widened as she said, "I can't believe what I'm hearing. I thought Mark and I were keeping this under wraps, but I see it's starting to bother him."

Roselita said, "Yes and he doesn't even know if he's the father or not. Mark also mentioned that he isn't ready to be a father again." Roselita knew she now had Pomedra's attention. Roselita felt like rubbing the situation in deeper, which is just what she did. Roselita added, "So if I were you, and thank goodness I'm not, I would watch how I speak to people in this company. I would love to finish this conversation with you but I really do have a lot of work to get done since Norlina is out of the office today." Roselita also knew that revenge resolves nothing, but since Pomedra was always running her mouth and gossiping, she felt sometimes being revengeful means giving someone a taste of their own medicine." Roselita continued to speak, "Oh, and Pomedra just remember while you're running off at the mouth gossiping, just know that someone else could be saying something about you in return." Roselita walked away from Pomedra with a grin plastered on her face. Roselita felt good knowing that for once someone finally stopped Pomedra in her gossiping tracks and made her think about how she's been mistreating people throughout Welcome News Express Company. Roselita walked over to the elevator door and pushed the button. The door opened. Roselita was still grinning because she had never felt so good after getting back at Pomedra for her immature behavior. Roselita stepped off the elevator unlocked the Human Resource office and turned on the lights. Roselita locked her handbag in the electronic cabinet; as she sat down to continue the paperwork for the new hires. The laptop rang. It is Brandon calling to see how one of his favorite women was doing. Roselita thanked him again for the lunch date. Every time Roselita had spoken with Brandon she always felt that there was some chemistry between them. Brandon wanted to know if she had any plans for the evening after work because he had two tickets to go see the play "That Night We Fell in Love" starring Nan Hilliard and Julia Ernestine. Roselita was open for the event with Brandon Bright. Brandon informed Roselita that he would be picking her up around six-thirty p.m. followed by dinner and a drive throughout the city. Roselita finished talking with Brandon. Roselita gently hung up the telephone as the fax machine began to send faxes through. Roselita pushed back her chair stood up and walked towards the machine. Just as she was doing this, her high heel snapped on her right foot. Roselita reached down, picked up the heel and stood there wondering what was going to happen next. Right at that moment, the fax machine began to eat the paper by crunching it up while the ink leaked all over the fax paper coming out. Roselita felt this wasn't her day. First Norlina calls in sick. Then one of the new hire's became flirtatious and Brandon was interrupted during her lunch date with him. Back at the office Pomedra, the CEO's secretary, started a confrontation. Then her high heel broke and the fax machine ate the paper. The ink cartridge got messy. All Roselita could do is imagine how she hoped the day would end so she could go home to relax. Roselita's heart danced with delight because it was finally time to go home from work. Just before leaving the office and the building, Roselita made a cell phone call to her mother to see how things were going along with her since she had not spoken with her today. Roselita ended the call with her mother as she turned off the lights and locked the door to the Human Resource department. On her way to the elevators, she saw Pomedra doing what she does best at the company--gossiping about someone. Pomedra was talking to Carnella Mordorwalski, who works in the Internet Technology Department, Carnella is an Internet technician. Roselita proceeded to the elevator, shaking her head knowing that Pomedra just didn't know when to quit. Roselita also knew that sooner or later, Mr. Perez will probably terminate Pomedra after Mr. Perez takes a DNA test to verify if he is the father of Pomedra's unborn child. Roselita felt dolorous towards Mr. Perez, knowing that he had gotten himself in too deep with this young twenty-seven year old woman. But Roselita realized that Mr. Perez is the one who put himself through the storm and now if Mr. Perez had doubts, he could quiet it down. Roselita knew Mr. Perez should have thought ahead before having what may be a fifth child with a much younger woman. The baby is due on Mr. Perez's birthday, just a week before Mr. Perez's wedding anniversary with his wife of thirty years. Roselita didn't know Pomedra or her sister Bali personally but she did know that Pomedra was four months pregnant. Pomedra was a young woman who played her way to what she calls herself the playing love gamer. Pomedra would say if she can drop it like it's hot she could get any man she wants. Roselita knew Pomedra was very intelligent but wasn't too smart when it came to dealing with older men. Pomedra thought looks alone could land her a marriage with plenty of money flowing in her direction. Pomedra didn't consider that the money came from her own paycheck and the love came at the expense of a married woman with four children. Roselita also felt that Pomedra was looking for another father figure in her life because her own father walked completely out of her life earlier in the year. Mr. Hernandez started out living with Pomedra and her sister Bali, until he got too wrapped up in his own personal affairs. Then Mr. Hernandez moved out into his own apartment. This left Pomedra and Bali to live together. After a while, Bali moved in with her boyfriend, who ended up going to prison for twelve years, after which Bali became homeless. Bali met another man who then became abusive. This left their family distraught with their mother deceased and their father saying he disowned both of his daughters. Bali was the oldest. Bali lived in a woman's shelter, hiding from her abusive (second) boyfriend. Bali was hired to work at Welcome News Express first. Then her younger sister Pomedra joined the company later. Pomedra lived alone in the suburbs. Pomedra agreed to allow Mr. Perez to move in with her, despite knowing that he may be married with children. Pomedra also appeared to be older than what she really is. Pomedra kept choosing the wrong men. Roselita assumed that Mr. Perez would know that Pomedra was too young for him. Roselita felt that a desperate man would go out of his way only to please himself. Pomedra noticed Roselita leaving the building for the evening and walked over to her standing at the elevator. Roselita stood mumbling, "I wish this young chick-a-rouge would leave me alone. Pomedra needs someone to teach her the real world and what life really has to offer her instead of chasing older men." Pomedra said, "Hey Roselita. I knew that I could catch you before leaving the building." Roselita answered, "Yes, I'm all finished with my work. By the way, can I ask you a personal question Pomedra?"

"Sure you can ask me anything. What would you like to know Roselita?"

Roselita said, "I'm curious to know ... is Mr. Perez really your unborn baby's father?" Pomedra, being stomped by Roselita's approach, came at her defensively, saying, "Chile please! No! My unborn baby father's name is Corey Ryan. Why do you ask?" Roselita said, "Oh I was curious that's all. I just assumed that since you and Mr. Perez are living together and you are pregnant." Pomedra tried her hardest not to give Roselita the truth, even though Roselita already knew the truth that Pomedra baby's father is Mr. Perez—well, until the DNA results come back. Roselita wanted to know how Pomedra was going to answer her question since Pomedra loves to meddle in other people's personal business. Pomedra really didn't feel up to discussing her private romantic affair with Mr. Perez. Pomedra changed the subject by trying to become Roselita's new friend. Pomedra said, "Roselita, I know I've been hard on you lately but I was only asking about your male friend because you don't talk about your love life much?" Roselita said, underneath her breath, "I wonder why ... it could be because you know too much about everyone already, except you can't get any information from me." All of a sudden, Roselita could hear a small plea asking for her help. Roselita felt that Pomedra was ready to reach out to someone. The only one Pomedra felt she could trust is Roselita. Pomedra longed for an older woman role model since she didn't have her own mother with her. Pomedra asked if Roselita could be her mentor by helping her get through life dealing with older men because all she knew was older men seeing young women as prey. Pomedra felt that some men saw her as a walking beauty object or a mannequin, fake but loving to be dressed up and set out for display. At that very moment, Roselita's heart dropped. Roselita felt the peace. After that long conversation, Roselita left the building thinking of how Pomedra wanted Roselita to coach her throughout life. Roselita made it home and checked her laptop voice mail, hearing Brandon left a message letting Roselita know, he will be running five minutes late. But he'll be at her home soon. Roselita sorted through her mail, overlooking the junk mail and reading the bills. Roselita walked over to the kitchen cabinet, grabbing a box of wheat crackers to snack on and picking up a green apple. Roselita went upstairs to take a shower and get dressed for the play she is going to attend with Brandon Bright. Roselita put on some relaxing music while she slowed her pace down, leaving trails of scented peach-n-cream mixed with vanilla to circulate throughout the vents. Just as she is preparing herself to relax, the laptop telephone rang. "Hello Macalaonez and Macalaonez Express, how may I help you?" The voice on the other end said, "By telling me you'll be ready by the time I get there which is in five minutes?"

Roselita said, "Brandon is this you?"

Brandon answered, "Why, were you expecting someone other than me coming over to your house?"

Roselita said, "No, just you silly?"

Brandon responded, "Oh so it's like that huh, why do I have to be silly?"

Roselita became filled with joy as she said, "Brandon you know I'm playing around with you ... say, can we talk when you get here? I need to finish getting dressed--especially if a certain man expects me to be on time."

Brandon replied, "Ooh, that sounds nice; but it would be better if I didn't have to wait standing outside of the front door?"

"Wait a minute ... you mean, you are already over here?"

Brandon said, "Yes, now can a man come in or do I have to be a bad boy and go back to the car and wait until you are ready?"

"Brandon, you know you're wrong for this. I'm nowhere near being dressed and I haven't even showered yet?"

"That's okay; I'll just be waiting in the car until you are done."

Roselita said, "No wait. I'm coming down as soon as I cover up."

"Thanks, but that was too much information, letting me know that you don't have any clothes on, but I can handle that." Roselita laughed because she knew the only person who could cheer her up is Brandon. Roselita is still trying to figure out why she is so drawn to Brandon. Roselita knew that Brandon made her feel more complete. Roselita felt a deep love for Brandon, one that only he could fulfill. However, Roselita didn't allow her emotions to override their friendship. Roselita covered up herself with her robe and dashed down the stairs to let Brandon in. Roselita glanced through the peephole to make sure it was really Brandon and not some crazy stranger going from door to door. While looking through the peephole Roselita smiled, she hadn't realized how extraordinary Brandon could be since she last saw him dressed up for the Entrepreneur's Ball in a tuxedo. Roselita opened the door, gazing into his sexy brown eyes standing at five foot eleven with his broad shoulders, Brandon's shaped haircut, and shaved face. Roselita wanted to stand on her tip toes, reach up to Brandon, and kiss him. Instead Roselita kept letting herself know that they're only close friends. Roselita enjoyed Brandon's masculine scent of honeysuckle, sandalwood and balsam cologne. As Roselita stared at Brandon's blackened goatee. Roselita greeted Brandon saying, "I'm going to get you for showing up before your time, and by the way you look and smell good." Roselita closed the front door and quickly ran back up the stairs; leaving Brandon to make himself feel comfortable. Once upstairs, Roselita caught her breath as she leaned against her bedroom door, smiling than jumping up and down. Roselita danced around her bedroom while proceeding to get ready for their evening date. Walking into her master bathroom and turning the knob to warm, as Roselita stepped into the shower. Roselita wrapped a towel around her body, walked over to her walk in closet, and picked out a long off-the- shoulder Chocolate evening dress. The dress showed off Roselita's curvaceous figure, leaving something to the imaginative mind. Roselita glanced at her million-pairs-of-shoes collection, trying to decide which one would best compliment her wardrobe. Roselita picked black sleek high heels, making sure that her accentuating style would lead people to think she was a younger woman, a damsel in disguise. Brandon yelled out, asking if she is ready. Brandon felt Roselita was taking too long. Brandon commented, "Oops, I forgot. It takes a long time for a woman to get ready." Roselita left her bedroom and stood at the top of the stairs, saying in return, "Hum, you are too humorous, because as I recall, you were running five minutes late yourself." Roselita turned around and walked back into her bedroom relieved that she had gotten him back for his male chauvinism.

"Roselita, stop trying to play revenge now," Brandon retorted. Roselita laughed infectiously, "Brandon, you know I love you."

"Okay, Miss Smarty, must you have the last word in this conversation?"

Roselita said, "Well you know that a woman is always correct." Brandon responds, "You're right--in her dreams. But when it comes to reality, she hates to be proved wrong."

"Brandon, please give me a few more minutes and I'll be ready. Continue to make yourself at home." Brandon said, "Don't worry you don't have to tell me twice, I'm enjoying being comfortable." The laptop rang. Usually, when Roselita had company visiting her, she didn't like anyone answering her laptop telephone other than herself. But because she was pressed for time and didn't want to keep Brandon waiting any longer, she asked if he could answer the phone for her. Brandon opened the laptop as he answered, "Good evening. This is the Macalaonez residence." It is Roselita's mother calling to speak with her daughter. Mrs. Macalaonez is shocked to hear a male's voice answering her daughter's laptop. Mrs. Macalaonez thought she had reached the wrong number when she said in a calm but scared voice, "Um. Yes excuse me but is there a woman by the name of Roselita Macalaonez who lives there?" Brandon is overcome, wondering who is calling Roselita, so he kept speaking with her, "Yes, may I ask who is calling to speak with her?" Mrs. Macalaonez said, "This is her mother. May I ask who this is answering my daughter's laptop?" Brandon laughed with a deep chuckle as he greeted her, "Good evening Mrs. Macalaonez. This is Brandon Bright." Mrs. Macalaonez is still in shock to hear Brandon answering her daughter's laptop, but she felt relief as his voice softened while her laughter filled the laptop phone waves, "Hi, baby this is Mrs. Macalaonez. I am calling to speak with Roselita. Is she there?" Brandon said, "Yes, Mrs. Macalaonez. Roselita is getting ready. We're going to see a play tonight. Hold on for a moment. I will get her for you." Brandon yelled upstairs, letting Roselita know that her mother is on the laptop phone. "Roselita it's your mother on the laptop. Roselita thanked Brandon for answering the laptop letting Brandon know that she would take the call upstairs. Brandon transferred the call to Roselita as he walked over to her plasma television, turning it on to the sports station. Brandon walked into Roselita's kitchen and grabbed a bottled of water from her refrigerator, walking back into the living room to sit down and watch television. While a commercial was on, Brandon looked up at the mantle noticing all of her photos. Brandon saw one where Roselita and her father stood holding each other while on a family vacation. Brandon also saw another photo of both Mr. and Mrs. Macalaonez together in what appeared to be their happier times. His eyes came across Roselita's college graduation photo followed by a recent picture of Roselita working at Welcome News Express. All of a sudden, Brandon seemed buoyant staring at the photo, realizing how snazzy Roselita is. As Brandon turned around to sit back down, Roselita came down the stairs. Brandon's brown eyes noticed Roselita's star-studded off the shoulders long Chocolate dress with black sleek high heels. Roselita's hair was style was pinned up and her makeup, flawless as always, which gave her skin a golden tone. Roselita's perfume left Brandon breathless, filling his nostrils with the scents of magnolia, jasmine, peach and passion fruit. Brandon gave Roselita an assertive look letting her know she is beauteous as Brandon asked if Roselita is ready to go see a play. Roselita picked up the remote control from the table, clicking the off button as she placed her left arm underneath Brandon. Outside, Brandon opened the car door for Roselita and waited until she is seated properly before walking around to the driver's side. Once in the car Brandon's cell phone rang. Brandon said, "Who is this trying to ruin a perfect evening out on the town with you?" Brandon glanced at the caller ID from his cell phone and saw it is his mother calling, "Hello Mother. How are you doing?" Mrs. Bright sensed that her son isn't in the mood to be talking with anyone. Mrs. Bright continued in a sarcastic tone of voice, "Well, good evening to you too son, I'm doing well." Mrs. Bright said, "Well, since it seems like you're uncomfortable with me calling and ruining one of your many dates for the evening, I can call you later." Brandon apologized to his mother for his shrewdness. Brandon knew his mother is the only person who, if Brandon had gotten angry, Brandon would never take it out on her. Mrs. Bright said, "Son, the reason for me calling is to see how my son is doing. Is that okay with you?" Brandon respond, "Thank you, mother. I'm doing well, again sorry for my shrewdness towards you. I didn't mean to get you upset." Brandon concluded, "It's just that Roselita and I are going to a play."

"Okay, so what does your attitude have to do with your mother calling?" Brandon answered his mother by saying, "Nothing."

"Listen son, I'm going to let you get back to your date with Roselita since she has you acting giddy about your mother calling you?"

Brandon said, "Mother, Roselita has nothing to do with my shrewd attitude."

"Uh Huh...I see...Well get back to enjoying your evening and tell that darling Miss Roselita that your mother says hello. You two young folks be good and safe. Brandon I love you son."

Brandon said, "I love you too mother. I'll let Roselita know that you send your love."

"Thanks baby, good-bye Mr. I Am So in Love."

Brandon said, "Mother!"

Mrs. Bright said, "Well it's true, bye."

"Bye Mother." Brandon placed his cell phone in the holder near the dashboard as he laughed. Roselita looked over at him, "Are you okay?"

"Oh yes, I couldn't be any better since my mother called inquiring about my love life. By the way, she says Hi." Brandon continued to drive down Hampton Street until he exited unto Highway eighty-one going eastbound headed towards Chancellor Hall Theatre. While he drove, Roselita closed her eyes, taking a quick nap as Brandon thought about how his mother was right; his love for Roselita is strong. Brandon pondered on the last conversation that he shared with his mother when Mrs. Bright said, "She couldn't figure out what is keeping her son Brandon from proposing to Roselita, when Roselita is the only woman fit for her son Brandon Bright." Back at her home, Mrs. Bright felt concerned about her son Brandon. Mrs. Bright had wished that Brandon wouldn't take much longer in keeping Roselita in suspense about his true love towards her. Mrs. Bright felt comfortable being around Roselita. Mrs. Bright thought about all of the other females that her son had brought to her home. Most of the women range from thirty to forty-five years old. For instance, Mrs. Bright experienced this young woman in her early thirties who came to her home wearing booty shorts and a chopped up halter top showing more then she could carry in the cleavage area. The next young woman that Mrs. Bright met had a bad hair weave and awful bleached color. When the young lady smiled she appeared to be a gold-digger. Mrs. Bright met another woman who was so drunk; the woman peed on Mrs. Bright bathroom floor. While another woman who was used to being spoiled a lot kept looking at herself through her makeup compact. Then last but not least, there was a different woman who searched down Mrs. Bright home than later had her ex-boyfriend robbed Mrs. Bright home, only taking her thirty-two inch flat screen television and stealing her precious jewelry from Jane Wards jewelers that Brandon had brought for her as a Mother's Day gift. From that point on Mrs. Bright informed her son Brandon that enough is enough? Mrs. Bright didn't want Brandon bringing any more trifling women to her home again unless they were able to handle themselves respectfully. Mrs. Bright loved Roselita as if she is already her daughter-in-law. Mrs. Bright had known Roselita and her family for fourteen years now. This made Mrs. Bright feel very comfortable being around Roselita. After reminiscing about her son Brandon's love life, Mrs. Bright went into the kitchen to prepare dinner for herself. Mrs. Bright placed a load of clothes into the washing machine and finished doing house cleaning until her dinner is ready. Every now and then Mrs. Bright would stop in the living room to watch television and then resume cleaning. After eating dinner, Mrs. Bright would call her friend up to discuss the types of women that her son Brandon is choosing to date. Brandon shared with Roselita his plans for the evening. Brandon asked, "What is Roselita's favorite restaurant?" Roselita picked Le'Ricardo's Italian Restaurant that played jazz music in the exclusive blue room. Brandon agreed that Le' Ricardo's was an excellent choice for dinner followed by a night drive throughout the city. Silence filled the car as they drove to Chancellor Hall Theatre. Brandon pulled up to the front door as he and Roselita got out of the car. Allowing the valet to park the car, the usher passed out programs while another usher escorted them to the VIP room. The room turned into a balcony once the windows were opened overlooking the audience and the stage. Brandon walked around greeting and introducing Roselita to people from Constitutes Law Firm. Everyone continued to hold conversations until it is show time, while waiters came around carrying hors d'oeuvres and beverages. Jilla Handsberg, who has been in love with

Brandon ever since he started at the Firm, interrupted Brandon while giving Roselita piercing eye contact. Brandon turned slightly, whispering in Roselita's ear, telling Roselita how obsessed Jilla is with him and then assuring Roselita that there wasn't anything to be worried about. Jilla pretended to be friendly, sending an unpleasant smile Roselita's way, "Ah Brandon darling, so glad you came are you enjoying the evening so far?" Brandon didn't want to be bothered with Jilla's immature behavior so Brandon proved Jilla to be wrong every time Jilla spoke to Brandon in front of Roselita. Brandon kept grinding his teeth, managing to keep a fabricated smile on his face as he responded back. "Yes, you know, what better way to enjoy the evening then to share it with my woman?" Brandon continued, "Roselita sweetness, this is Jilla Handsberg and Jilla this is Roselita Macalaonez." Brandon gave Jilla a smirk as he escorted Roselita to the other side of the room. Jilla became frustrated as she pouted, telling her co-worker friends that if not now, then soon Brandon will be hers--but first she has work to be done. On the other side of the room, Roselita asked Brandon if he was going to be okay since his stalker is in the room with them. Brandon implied that he would be okay but he worried about Roselita. Brandon didn't want Roselita to feel uncomfortable being in the presence of Jilla Handsberg. Brandon tried to prevent drama at all cost. Unfortunately, Jilla isn't going to let Brandon escape from her too quickly, so she went after him every chance that she had following him throughout the evening. Jilla approached Brandon again for the second time. "Brandon, hey I'm sorry for interrupting you again but since the play hasn't started I figure we could chat some." Roselita gave Jilla a cold-hearted look without saying a word leaving it up to Brandon to handle the situation. "Listen Jilla I know the play hasn't begun but I would like to finish introducing Roselita to everyone if you don't mind." Brandon excused himself from being in the presence of Jilla and her tag-along friends from the office. Jilla thought of something quick to stop Brandon and Roselita from walking too far from her. Jilla said, "Brandon wait...I'm sorry but I just wanted to congratulate you. We'll be working as a team for the Co-Slashes Murder case next week." Brandon stopped walking, quickly turned, came close up on Jilla and said, "What do you mean we're teamed up next week?" Jilla broke into a wide, open smile, "Yes I know this could have waited until next week's morning meeting but why wait." Brandon is now furious, wondering why Jilla is doing this to him--especially in front of Roselita. In spite of the trouble that Jilla is causing, Jilla continued to add conflict to the situation, "Well Brandon, I can't wait until next week when we can exchange cell phone numbers since we'll be working together. Roselita leaned over to whisper to Brandon that he shouldn't allow Jilla's unacceptable behavior to ruin their magnificent evening and that he should remain calm. Brandon felt perspicuous realizing that Roselita was right. Brandon didn't need to become hostile because of Jilla's behavior. Instead he told Jilla, "We will have to see about this. But in the meantime, Roselita and I are going to finish socializing." Before walking away, Roselita said, "Jilla was your name right? Nice to have met you, I hope you enjoy the play." By this time, Jilla spat out the words contemptuously, "The nerve of that Brandon. He knows I'm supposed to be with him and not that loathsome woman named Roselita Macalaonez." Jilla walked away distraught because the man she's been longing for ended up escorting another woman to the play instead of her. Roselita noticed Jilla's mood towards her and sensed that Jilla wished she were the one on Brandon's arm. Brandon assured Roselita that Jilla's corruption wasn't pleasant; therefore Roselita shouldn't worry. It was show time. Everyone in the room found a seat as anticipation filled the building. The lights dimmed as everyone found their reserved seating. Brandon came across his seating arrangement that said, "Reserved for Brandon Bright and Guest." Roselita took her seat next to Brandon as he placed his right arm around Roselita's shoulder. Jilla watched from afar. Jilla felt she should be the one on Brandon's arm and not Roselita. Jilla stood up and walked over to her and Brandon's supervisor trying to swap seats with him and his wife but they refused to move. Jilla wasn't giving up too soon. Jilla kept going until she came across Mr. Reginald and his girlfriend. Jilla bribed him by paying two hundred dollars so her co-workers and she could sit behind Brandon and Roselita. Mr. Reginald took Jilla up on her kindly offer as he and his girlfriend gladly moved out of their seats. Jilla sat directly behind Roselita and kept kicking the back of Roselita's seat. Roselita could feel Jilla kicking her seat and realized how infantile Jilla was. Roselita leaned over and let Brandon know that Jilla was being absurd and that they should move from their seats. Brandon agreed with Roselita as they stood up and walked to the other side of the room where there was more seating available. Jilla wanted to follow but one of the co-workers con Brandon she that they were seat hopping too much and they wanted to stay seated right where they were. Jilla stayed seated, never taking her fiery eyes off Brandon and Roselita. Jilla made sure she watched Brandon throughout the play. Jilla became desperate, going to any measures to ruin what Brandon had called a lovely evening out with Roselita. During intermission, Roselita excused herself from Brandon as she walked toward the ladies' restroom, leaving Brandon seated. Jilla watched as Roselita left Brandon alone. Jilla figured this would be a good opportunity to make another move at Brandon. Jilla walked over to Brandon as she sat in Roselita's seat, trying to con Brandon that he was making a big mistake by being with Roselita's instead of her. Jilla realized that her persuasion failed. Brandon gave Jilla a dumb founded look and said, "Jilla, don't you think if I wanted you I would have been with you instead of Roselita? But that's not the case. Sorry I've chosen Roselita over you." Jilla's friends informed her that Roselita was in the ladies room. Jilla stood up quickly as she pranced into the ladies' restroom with her friends. They entered the restroom where they saw Roselita standing in front of the mirror, freshening up her makeup. Jilla walked over to the mirror as she stood next to Roselita. Jilla gave Roselita an edgy smile as she pulled out her makeup compact. Jilla brushed her pressed powder onto Roselita's small satin chocolate handbag, which is lying on the counter top. "Oops, I'm sorry. Your handbag has make up powder on it. Here let me get it off for you." Roselita looked at Jilla angrily, grabbing her handbag and faced Jilla saying, "Listen Missy, I don't know who you think you are, but you need to understand if Brandon really wanted you, he would be with you and not me. Roselita added, "Woman, get a grip and please grow up." Then Roselita turned to walk away, but suddenly stopped and said to Jilla, "Sorry for the harsh words, but if you think being trifling and dropping your make up on my handbag is going to solve something, well you've just proved nothing but only embarrassment to yourself in front of your friends." Roselita opened the door and smiled as the bathroom door closed behind her, leaving Jilla and her friends to ponder her remarks. One of Jilla's friends was in agreement with Roselita, letting Jilla know that chasing after Brandon would not be worth the effort. Back in the VIP room, Roselita sat down and explained to Brandon all of the unnecessary things that Jilla was putting herself through just so she could have him. They shared laughter as Brandon said; "Now you can see, Roselita, why I'm a magnet, everywhere I go women follow." Roselita said, "I'm glad that you're aware of these psycho women. Be careful, one of them might say you're their baby's father?" Brandon and Roselita continued to talk until the lights in the room went dim and the glass window slid back open. The audience quieted as the play resumed and Jilla and her friends returned to their seats. Brandon whispered to Roselita, "Did you smack her down?" Roselita answered back, "Now you know I'm not like that trifling woman, I'm a woman with class, dignity and spirit. Now let's finish enjoying the play." An hour passed and the play ended as the lights all over the building came back on. Brandon said his good-byes to his boss and co-workers as he escorted Roselita outside of the theatre. They stood there waiting for the valet to bring them the car. As they stood waiting, Jilla and her friends came outside making sure she said something to him. "Brandon I'll see you at work tomorrow, sleep tight I'll be sleeping about us." Roselita shook her head in dismay, "You would think that Missy got my message, but once you're from around the way, you are always from around the way." Brandon said, "Roselita don't let childish play get under your skin just remember when God starts blessing you that's when the devil tries to mess things up." Roselita was touched by Brandon's soothing words of comfort. Roselita realized that only kindness could kill an envious heart, piercing it until it doesn't want to fight anymore, knowing that there isn't anything to be challenged. The valet pulled up to the curve with Brandon's car, getting out quickly holding the door for Brandon as the valet ran around to the passenger side opening the door for Roselita to be seated. Brandon drove of turning on the radio to KLSX 107.8 FM, the smooth jazz station. Brandon slid back the sunroof, allowing the night breeze to seep into the car. The wind blew at Roselita's pinned up hair style. They made a right onto Albright Street, pulling up in front of Le Ricardo's restaurant and giving the valet the car keys as Brandon and Roselita entered the Italian cuisine restaurant. They walked to the palladium where the host stood and asked, "Good evening Sir, How may I be of assistance too you?" Brandon smiled, "Yes I have reservations here tonight." The host replied, "May I please have your name?" Brandon said, "Yes, Brandon Bright." The host called for the waiter to seat both Brandon and his guest. The waiter followed the host's instructions by saying, "Yes, please follow me Mr. Bright." Brandon and Roselita proceeded to walk behind the waiter as he showed them to their reserved seating. Brandon pulled out Roselita's chair as he took his seat after her. They both took a few minutes to review the menu before placing their orders. The waiter returned with a dozen of red roses in his hand. "Excuse me ma'am but these are for you. Here is a tall vase you can place them in." Roselita filled with astonishment as she read the card that is attached to the roses it said, "Thank you for being so wonderful. A strong woman who is also a good friend has stolen my heart. Love, Brandon." Roselita thanked Brandon for the roses. While Brandon and Roselita sat eating, talking, laughing, and enjoying themselves by having a good time, Jilla and her friends ended up at the same restaurant. Jilla and her friends were also having a good time when she noticed Brandon and Roselita sitting at a table. Jilla saw the vase of roses and instantly became irritated. Jilla couldn't believe that Brandon seemed as if he was enjoying Roselita's company and he gave her a bunch of roses. Jilla then turned towards one of her friends saying, "How dare Brandon do that, he's acting as if he's welcoming her presence with such excitement, Brandon never does that to me." Brandon looked around the restaurant noticing others enjoying themselves when his brown eyes focused on Jilla and her friends sitting at booth. They noticed each other looking in the same direction. Brandon leaned forward letting Roselita know that Jilla and her friends were in the restaurant also. Roselita said, "I guess no matter where you are trouble always seems to find you. Or is it already there, waiting on your presence?" Brandon quietly laughed, "Now I have to agree with you on that one, it is so true... you know we don't have to stay here if you don't want to. We can go." Roselita replied, "I don't know about you, but I refuse to let some trifling woman mess up my evening with a handsome man." Brandon's face lit up as a beam of light was shining directly on his face. "I love a woman who stands up for her man." Brandon tried to catch himself from allowing his true feelings to show, so he redirected his comment, "I mean I love it when a woman is strong and takes charge." Being overtaken, he felt stricken by his comment. He felt Roselita needed a better understanding. Roselita said, "Wait just a minute Brandon Bright. You mean you have had feelings for me all this time?" Brandon tried suppressing his emotions, but they seeped out, "Well not exactly... I mean okay, so I'm interested in you--but only as a friend, so let's not take it any further, okay?"

"Hey, that's okay with me, but it's good to know that you're finally coming out with the truth instead of being in denial."

"Okay, okay let's not get overwhelmed with the thought of me expressing myself."

Roselita said, "Yes, but I think it's so cute to hear that at one point you had no feelings towards me, all of a sudden Mr. Bright came out saying that he's interested in me." Brandon felt Roselita was putting on the spot said, "Okay, so now you know. Let's drop the subject and move onto something else."

"Okay, Mr. Smooth Lover I'll drop the subject. What would you like to talk about now?" Brandon and Roselita continued to have a conversation when they saw Jilla and her entourage make their way over towards their table. On their way to the table, one of her friends insisted Jilla had done enough destruction. She insisted that Jilla would be making another fool out of herself. Jilla allowed herself to become distraught by not taking the advice from her friends. They agreed she was being too rational. Jilla lashed out, "Listen here no woman will ever take what is supposed to be mine." Jilla kept walking towards Brandon and Roselita's table with her entourage as if she needed protecting. At the table Jilla said, "Well, look at what we have here, Good evening Brandon darling, how are you?" Keeping his composure, Brandon answered, "Good evening Jilla. What brings you and your protective entourage to Le'Ricardo's for dinner after the play?" Jilla leaned over whispering into Brandon's ear, "With your good looking self. I think you and I should get together. This weekend will be good." Roselita told Brandon she was having second thoughts about eating dinner. Roselita was feeling uncomfortable with Jilla and friends hovering over their table. Jilla continued to cause commotion. "Brandon, do you mind if me and my friends join you and your sister--that's who you are, right?" she smirked. Brandon decided he had enough of Jilla's childish behavior so he said, "Excuse me Jilla, but that won't be necessary. And by the way, this is my friend of fourteen years, Roselita. We're trying to have an elegant evening."

The waiter returned, ready to take Brandon and Roselita's order. Brandon informed him that he and Roselita decided to cancel their meal. Brandon stood up walked behind Roselita's chair, waited for her to stand up, took her hand and placed it underneath his arm as they exited out of the restaurant. Roselita realized she had left the vase of roses sitting on the table. Roselita walked back into the restaurant to the table. Jilla gave Roselita an envious stare before saying, "You may think you have my man now but just wait--revenge is always a payback and you'll get yours." Roselita didn't respond. She gently took the vase of roses and walked away as she thought to herself, "How psycho Jilla is. Jilla needs therapy. Roselita joined Brandon outside, filling him in with what went on inside the restaurant. Roselita explained how Brandon's co-worker Jilla Handsberg made a fool out of herself. Brandon laughed hysterically, "Very funny Roselita, that's real cute." Roselita continued, "Well she's such a nut case. What went down between the two of you?" Brandon began to tell Roselita how Jilla had became obsessed over him as they waited for the valet to bring them the car. Brandon said, "All I could remember was when our company had a conference meeting awhile back last month with our CEO. After the meeting ended, Jilla started giving me I'm interested in you, eye contact and smiling." Roselita wanted to understand Brandon as she tried to piece his story together, "Okay, so how did she get tied to you?" Brandon went on telling Roselita everyone than gathered in the break room for a birthday party; we sat around playing a game called "Guess who." Everyone was having such a good time that's when I sensed Jilla was coming onto me but I didn't think anything of it at that time. Brandon said, "I guess you have to be careful how friendly you get with people." The valet pulled up with Brandon's car and opened the car door for Roselita as Brandon gave him a twenty-dollar tip even though they didn't get dinner there. In the car he turned the radio to KLSX 107.8 FM as he sang along with the song playing. Roselita and Brandon continued to talk and share laughs as they both enjoyed the ride throughout the city. After all that they had been through with Jilla and her entourage, they both decided that they weren't hungry anymore. Roselita was ready to get home and relax. Roselita felt she had enough action in one night. The roses that Brandon gave her would make up for their adventurous evening. Brandon pulled up into Roselita's driveway, thanking her for a wonderful night, excluding the circus of Jilla Handsberg and her crazed entourage. Brandon opened the car door for Roselita, walked up to her front door and kissed her gently on the forehead and said, "Maybe we could try this again, but next time we'll have to pick a place out in the serene suburbs." Roselita laughed as she made a sarcastic comment, "Oh, Brandon you're so silly, Say, thank you for the lovely evening. Yes, next we'll have to go further out somewhere--unless we check with Jilla Handsberg first." Brandon didn't have anything else to say except goodnight and good-bye. Brandon hoped Roselita enjoys the vase of roses and hoped she would have a restful night. Roselita turned to unlock her front door, turned on the lights in the foyer, and placed the vase on her table by the front door. Roselita locked the front door behind her and glanced out the window, watching Brandon back out of her driveway Wanting him to stay and keep her company. Roselita knew that would lead to trouble, as their emotions would have run high (at least hers would have, knowing how extremely handsome Brandon looked tonight).

CHAPTER TWO

***

Roselita turned off the light and walked upstairs to her bedroom. Friday evening had finally arrived. All types of cars lined the side of the street. Friends and neighbors became nosey, wondering what is happening at thirty-two forty-five Dove Court. As the sun began to set, more people had arrived driving in cars. Some even stopped in the middle of the street to let passengers out, while other cars drove around looking for parking space. "Well hello there ... come in ... come in. Welcome to my party. I'm the hostess, Mrs. Macalaonez." The house was full of guests. Music blared as guests sat around mingling and eating. The doorbell rang often. Each time Mrs. Macalaonez answered it, greeting her guests. Roselita finally showed up with Brandon. Roselita wore a rose-colored halter-top, matching Capri pants and open toed mules. Roselita's hair was pinned up on top of her head as she wore bedazzled diamond earring studs that enhanced her beauty. Carrying a designer handbag with her name on it, Roselita removed her name engraved sunglasses as she leaned forward to kiss her mother on the cheek. Brandon looked astonished. As always, he wore denim long shorts and his name engraved on his sneakers. Brandon also wore a baseball cap and a fitted muscle Polo shirt that revealed the budges of his triceps. Brandon showed off the contour of his washboard stomach pressed against his black shirt. Brandon's claves were sculpted to perfection. Brandon's shoulders were firm and broad, creating a Roman statue. With his obsidian hair neatly shaped underneath his baseball cap, his face appeared smooth, giving him the appearance of a young twenty-six year old. His brown eyes glowed while his smile captured the hearts of women who noticed this attractive stud. Brandon's smile gleamed from the whiteness of his teeth. Mrs. Macalaonez is blissful about the turnout for her social gathering. Mrs. Macalaonez closed the front door behind Brandon as he and Roselita walked into the house. Mrs. Macalaonez is very excited that her daughter Roselita and her close friend Brandon Bright could make it to the party. Mrs. Macalaonez said, "How is my future handsome son-in-law doing?" Roselita said, "Mother, this isn't the time to be discussing things." Mrs. Macalaonez replied, "Oh Roselita I was just asking how my other baby Brandon is doing. Is that all right with you, Miss. Uptight?" Roselita leaned towards her, "Mother, now you know Brandon is not my man. Besides, he never asked me to date him. So can we please leave it at that?" Mrs. Macalaonez answered, "No. First, I don't know why you are so uptight about me having some fun at my own party. Second, Brandon needs to hurry up and make it official. Third, if you don't pick it up some ditzy woman will and I can't have that too good of a looking young man Brandon settling with some flimsy, non-cooking woman all over him." Roselita became frustrated, "Mother, will you promise me that from now on you will leave it up to Brandon to decide who he finds to be his potential mate?" Roselita was trying to make sense of the conversation, hoping that her mother would understand. Mrs. Macalaonez said to her daughter, "Okay, Miss Old Woman but you just wait and see. Oh you can't because you don't know if you are in love or infatuated. Watch out, sooner or later you will be thanking me, your mother, for the small conversation we are having at this moment." Roselita said, "Mother you are always trying to match me with someone."

"Yes, baby because obviously you don't know how to pick men well." Roselita responded, "Mother, you know I love you, Troy, and Brandon, but so far none of your love match makings worked. Besides, I have never said anything about when you choose to date Hayman, who could soon be my stepfather. Mrs. Macalaonez responded, "Oh baby, of course not because your mother knows how to catch a man and keep him, that's why I'm getting re-married again." Roselita became upset with her mother pouting like a child. Roselita kissed her mother and walked into the living room. Mrs. Macalaonez turned toward Brandon saying, "Well Brandon baby, it's your turn. I tried to make sense out of this but as you can see Roselita's being stubborn." Brandon laughed and said, "Mrs. Macalaonez you look lovely. Don't worry about your daughter. Roselita will be okay after she cools down." Mrs. Macalaonez laughed as she responded back to Brandon, "I hope so...well knowing Roselita she will be all right once she has time to think." Brandon caught up with Roselita grasping her left hand as if they were a couple. Roselita felt his firm hand take a hold of hers, feeling a sensual vibe flowing through her body and making her feel cold chills going down her spinal cord. Roselita looked down at their hands locking together as Brandon quickly removed his from hers. Brandon gazing into her bright brown eyes, wanting to pull her close and kiss her but instead she directed his attention elsewhere. Brandon said, "Roselita, are you okay?" Roselita was still so caught up in the moment of them holding hands that she didn't hear a word Brandon said so she answered, "Yes." Brandon noticed that her eyes were still dreamy so he changed the subject, hoping she'll come back to reality. Sure enough, Roselita came back from spacing out into nowhere land. Roselita smiled at Brandon as if he was the best man she ever had, only to remember that they weren't a dating couple (although Roselita wished they were). Roselita couldn't resist how handsome Brandon was. Roselita allowed her eyes to glimpse Brandon's sexy physique. Roselita tried to shake off her lustful thoughts--but that wasn't working. Suddenly Roselita saw almost every woman's eyes at the party staring at Brandon. Roselita felt like saying, "What are all of you staring at, I came to this party with him and I'm leaving with him!"

Then she noticed how silly she looked, knowing that other women had every right to be checking Brandon out. He's tall and his mocha au latte complexion makes women want to grab and kiss all over him. Who could resist his smile and polished white teeth? Roselita knew Brandon was one of those men who could draw crowds of adoring women wherever he went. Brandon had a look that could be easily mistaken for an elite athlete. Brandon looked like he could date more than one woman at a time but still maintain his cool and keep the ladies coming back for more of him. Roselita shrugged her shoulders, mumbling to herself, "Well, this is reality and he's not a top notch athlete--but he sure does have the qualities of being one. Roselita took hold of Brandon's arm, giving it a tight squeeze as she glanced at the woman staring at them. Roselita told Brandon, "I see you have hungry wolves that are waiting to devour you; I can feel their hot breath longing to see if we're a couple." Brandon laughed, "Well, if you must know, I came here with you and that means I'm leaving her with you. So get that silly notion out of your mind." Roselita smiled broadly. Roselita couldn't believe that he respected her and isn't picking up just any woman for the night. They walked throughout her mother's house, pretending as if they were a couple. Mrs. Macalaonez spotted her daughter and Brandon sharing moments together. While noticing them, Mrs. Macalaonez called her fiancé Hayman into the kitchen. They shared laughs as they watched how Roselita and Brandon carried themselves as they greeted the guests. They observed Roselita and Brandon from a distance, watching them laugh while trying to be a couple for only one evening. Hayman pulled his fiancée closer as he kissed Mrs. Macalaonez saying, "Now I know where Roselita wants all of the attention from." Mrs. Macalaonez smiled, "Just think, true love is in front of their eyes... but do you think the two of them can see it in each other and start dating?" Hayman said, "Not unless they want to believe it can happen to both of them." While Roselita and Brandon were making the party lively, the doorbell rang. This time Hayman answered it, "Hi, come in. My name is Hayman. I'm Mrs. Macalaonez Fiancé." An older woman spoke first, "Well it's good to finally meet you. I'm Mrs. Goldstone, Mrs. Macalaonez Mother." Hayman's face filled with delight. Hayman had always wanted to meet Mrs. Macalaonez family. Hayman was starting to worry that he wouldn't be able to meet them until the day of their wedding, but instead he was meeting them before they get married. Mrs. Goldstone stepped inside while her husband and the rest of the family followed. Hayman invited Mrs. Macalaonez family to join in her soiree and make themselves at home. Then he dashed back into the kitchen to tell his fiancée that her family dropped in. Mrs. Macalaonez is pulling another veggie tray out of the refrigerator when she heard the news. Mrs. Macalaonez gently the veggie tray on the counter top. "Hayman honey, are you serious? My family came all the way from the East to be here with us in the South West?" Hayman smiled in the kitchen doorway,

"Sweetie pie, I guess this is your day." Mrs. Macalaonez went into the living room. Mrs. Macalaonez couldn't believe that her family traveled all the way from the East to be with her. Mrs. Macalaonez said, "Mother it's so good to see you and dad. You both haven't changed a bit." Mrs. Goldstone became teary eyed and joyful. Mrs. Goldstone hadn't seen her daughter or grandchildren in five years. Mrs. Macalaonez father embraced her then hugged Hayman, welcoming Hayman into their family. Mrs. Macalaonez told her family to come in and join the party, insisting that they'd talk later. Mrs. Macalaonez wanted to make sure everyone had a good time. Brandon and Roselita were sitting outside on the patio socializing with her mother's friends when Roselita's relatives walked outside to see her. Roselita stood up, hugging her relatives as she introduced them all to Brandon and her mother's friends. Back in the kitchen, Mrs. Macalaonez and Hayman shared a quick moment together as they embraced and talked about how exciting it was that her family arrived. After they finished cuddling, they went back into the living room to visit with their guests. Just then the volume from the Mhzp3 stereo speakers out in the back yard blared as people gathered around to see the entertainment. Mrs. Macalaonez grabbed Hayman's hand as they walked outside. Mrs. Macalaonez laughed as her family members directed the guest to form two lines for dancing. Roselita stood behind her mother and told her that this was one of the best parties that her mother had ever thrown. Roselita whispered, "Mother, leave it up to Uncle Morales. Your party won't be lively until he gets it started!" Mrs. Macalaonez answered, "Roselita baby, now I'll have to agree with you on that one." While Roselita and her mother talked, Brandon walked up to Roselita, "Excuse me ladies, but would you like to join a sensual man for a dance, Miss Roselita?" Roselita said, "Yes, I would be delighted to join you for a dance." Brandon and Roselita joined the dance line as Hayman snuggled up to his fiancée. "Speaking of dancing, would my special lady care to join her man for a dance also?" As Hayman took her hand, Mrs. Macalaonez blushed and said, "Yes honey, I thought you would never ask." Everyone danced and laughed the night away until they got tired and eventually drifted home. Roselita and Brandon helped put the food away and clean the kitchen. While Hayman passed out the dessert, Mr. Goldstone, Roselita's grandfather, and Mrs. Macalaonez next-door neighbor mellowed the remaining guests with a jazz rendition of "That's my Baby." While Mrs. Goldstone, Roselita's grandmother, and her other daughter's, Roselita's aunts, cleaned the living room, Roselita's uncles took down the stereo equipment. Roselita and Brandon finished up in the kitchen. It was late and Roselita was tired. Roselita told her relatives that she and Troy would visit them tomorrow afternoon. Brandon thanked Mrs. Macalaonez for the party. They said their final good-byes to the remaining guests and to Roselita's family. As Roselita slid into the car, Brandon asked, "Roselita, would you like to go to Aroma Café to join me for a cup of café latte mocha?" Even though Roselita is really tired, Roselita didn't want the night to end too quickly. Roselita answered, "Sure that will be a good way to end our lovely evening." Brandon observed, "I didn't know that your grandfather could play the saxophone?" Roselita replied, "Yes, he used to give me saxophone lessons. I remember when I was a little girl and my grandfather called me from outside and said, 'Come here Rosy Cheeks, Grand-papa's got something more exciting for you to do than playing with your friends outside." Roselita continued, "I would tell my friends that I had to stop playing with them to go see what my grandfather had planned for me to do. I tell you Brandon, I was so excited I would burst through the living room door with dirt smothered on my clothes and on the bottoms of my shoes. I left trails of mud on the carpet rushing to get to my grandfather, thrilled about wanting to see the surprise he had for me. By the time that I reached him, I was out of breath from running. "We had a room that we called the library. The room was not only filled with books and thirty-two inch plasma television, but also a baby grand piano. Troy took all of his piano lessons in there, while our mother watched television and our father studied for his culinary tests. Anyway, I would enter the library and find my grandfather polishing his saxophone, stroking it back and forth with a smooth cloth. My grandfather changed the mouthpiece so I could play it. At first all I could do was blow air out. My grandfather would let out a laugh saying to me in his husky, deep voice, 'Oh Rosy Cheeks, practice makes perfect. After a while, the perfect will no longer need practice.' "So from that day forth I practiced and practiced--after school, after dinner, and on the weekends, until I perfected the notes, making sure they sounded as smooth as a silhouette. I played day in and day out until my mother entered me in a jam session contest and I won first place for my solo selection. "On Sunday afternoons after church, we ate dinner with my grandparents. After dinner, my grandfather would gather everyone in our home library for a jam session. Troy played the piano while I played the saxophone. I eventually played for my church until I stopped to pursue a journalism career." Brandon said, "You mean to tell me that you can jam like your grandfather?"

"Yes, but it's been a while since I've played." Brandon continued, "Could I hear you play someday?"

"I don't know Brandon, as I've mentioned it's been a while. I'm a little rusty on the reeds. Brandon added, "Okay, so why not give it a try. After all, what harm can finding out be?"

"Yes, I guess you're right. Say, I'll tell you what. How about I play for you this coming Sunday afternoon over at my mother's home?" Brandon answered, "Sounds like a deal to me. I'll take you up on it this Sunday afternoon Miss Rosy Cheeks," he laughed joyfully. They finished their coffee as they walked back to Brandon's car. Roselita thanked him for coming with her to her mother's party. Brandon took her hand and squeezed it tightly as he said, "That's what best friends are for--to share in the good times and bad." Roselita then told Brandon why she is so thankful for his company. Roselita had explained to Brandon that her mother acted like him by matchmaking her with someone from her mother's parties. Brandon laughed harder, "So this time you decided to invite me just so she wouldn't introduce you to one of her available male friends?" Roselita explained, "Yes, at every social party that she's had so far she's been trying to make a match. Either the men were too old, unattractive or money hungry--in other words, looking for a woman to support them." Brandon said, "Hum, I see. So what you are looking for is someone like me who spends his money on you, takes you to elegant places, and makes you feel like a woman should feel. You know, a man who appreciates you and who has been committed to you thus far?" Roselita's face flushed. She knew that's exactly the type of man she wanted; but she coyly hid the fact that Brandon was the perfect man for her. On Monday morning, at approximately nine o'clock, Brandon walked into the conference room at Constitutes Law Firm wearing a charcoal tailored suit and black shoes. His swift movements were full of grace and virility, his shoulders like a foot ballplayers. Brandon greeted everyone with stern attention as he focused on each person, making sure they gave him some respect. Every woman who worked in his department wanted him--even the secretary would come to work dressed to attack him. Brandon's cologne carried the fall-in-love scent of lemon, basil and lavender. Brandon's essence permeated the room as he walked over to his nameplate. Brandon opened up his designer "MV" briefcase and pulled out a black electronic tablet. Brandon closed his briefcase and laid it down next to his chair then poured himself a glass of water into the glass cup placed in front of his nameplate. He smiled as the room began to fill with several attorneys, including the Miss Jilla Handsberg, who just had to make her way over to greet him. Jilla wore vermillion open-toed heels and a sleeveless cinnabar blouse that showed her shapely triceps. Her miniskirt matched her top. Jilla stood at five foot six inches tall with black hair and golden brown highlights; her envious brown eyes watched Brandon as much as possible. Jilla leaned forward and whispered "Good Morning Mr. Bright" into his ear. Brandon's pulsing heart raced as he felt the comfort of her body against his shoulder. Brandon quickly tossed any lustful thoughts from his mind; even though he knew what Jilla was trying to do, he returned her greeting. Brandon whispered back to Jilla making sure nobody could hear what he said, "Nice try, but it'll never happen. Just face it--you and I will never be a couple." Brandon sat upright and grinned as she sighed heavily and walked over to her seat, mumbling to herself, "Brandon, not now--but soon--you will be mine and that Roselita Macalaonez woman won't exist anymore." Their boss entered the room and everyone took their seats. He said, "Good morning. I take it that everyone is thrilled to be working on the Co-Slashes murder case--one of the biggest cases in history, which could not only land this company and your employees some mega money, but could also help put Mr. Co-Slashes behind bars forever. I have called some of my good friends from Fossil Law, one of the finest law firms in the Northwest to join us. Before we get started, please welcome them." Everyone applauded as he introduced his friends from Fossil Law office. He continued, "Now as you look over the information placed in front of you, you will notice the name above your folder. This is your partner. Now we'll be handling this case from about four to eight months, so please inform all of your family and friends that you will be working long hours, including weekends. As we all are aware, Mr. Co-Slasher has committed several heinous murders, including killing some of his family members. His one sister remains in hiding. We alone know where she's hiding. Please remember that the media will try to come after you for information regarding her whereabouts. Know that this case is confidential; anyone who leaks information will be terminated and will have his or her law license revoked. Once this meeting is adjourned, I would like everyone to find their partners and get straight to work." While Brandon's supervisor finished giving instructions, Brandon glanced at the name printed on his hunter folder. It read Jilla Handsberg. Brandon sat back, pushing the folder away from him and remembered what Jilla had said to him on the night of the play. She was looking forward to working as his partner. Brandon dreaded the fact that he'd been teamed up with her, realizing how deep her passion ran towards him. The meeting adjourned and Jilla walked up to Brandon feeling exuberant because she finally got her chance to be near him. Jilla gave Brandon one of her business cards with every telephone number on it. Brandon returned her greeting with an unpleasant smile and said, "Thank you but I'll only be using one number and that's the office number." Jilla sighed with satisfaction while walking away, knowing that she had accomplished a deprecatory task. Brandon felt relieved to know that the meeting was over and that he could return to work without being bothered by Jilla Handsberg. In his office, he immediately dialed Roselita's number, letting her know that he was going to be very busy working on the Co-Slasher case. "Hello, this is Roselita Macalaonez, how may I help you?" Brandon sarcastically answered, "By helping me deal with Jilla Handsberg." Roselita giggled, "Ah, it seems like someone isn't feeling happy today." Brandon said, "No, and don't rub it in with your catty remarks."

Roselita replied, "Well Brandon, I'm sorry that your morning isn't going pleasantly like I'm sure you would have expected it to go."

Brandon said, "Yes, I can't believe it. Jilla Handsberg and I are partners on this case."

Roselita said, "So how long do you and your girlfriend have to work together?"

Brandon became irritated by Roselita's comment as he said, "too long!"

Roselita said, "What...about a month?"

Brandon answered, "No, try four to eight months."

Roselita said, "Now, that's awful... extremely awful."

Brandon said, "Yes, tell me about it. And the sad part is this includes working weekends."

Roselita said, "Oh my, Brandon! Will you be able to hold out working with Jilla that long?"

Brandon said, "Roselita, I hope not. Pray that I can get through this tragedy of working alongside Jilla Handsberg." Roselita decided to add humor to the conversation. She knew Brandon was already upset because he would be working with Jilla Handsberg. "Hum, I don't know about the two of you working together, but on the other hand Brandon, you might strike up something worthwhile." Brandon didn't take Roselita's humorous comment lightly. "Wait a minute Roselita, whose side are you on anyway--mine or Jilla's?" Roselita answered, "I'm on yours of course. But since you are such a smooth talker, you should be able to handle Miss Stalker Jilla Handsberg." Brandon said, "Yes--but four to eight months?" Roselita wasn't going to ease up on the humor. She enjoyed teasing Brandon about putting up with Jilla's behavior for such a long time. She continued, "Well look at it this way: That's enough time for you to build a relationship." Brandon said, "Roselita, would you please stop playing around. I need your help. I don't know how long I can take her obsessive behavior." He added, "You know how Jilla's mind plays love fantasy." Roselita's other line rang. She placed Brandon on hold while she answered the call. It was Jamos West. "Good morning, Welcome News Express. This is Roselita Macalaonez. How may I help you?" A low baritone voice on the other end of the telephone said, "Hi, Miss Macalaonez. This is Mr. Jamos West. Do you remember me?" Roselita said, "Ah, yes Mr. West. Can you please hold for a minute?" She clicked over to Brandon, informing him that Mr. Jamos West was calling to speak with her. Brandon then added his own sarcastic remarks, "Hum seems like I'm not the only one who is having problems. It sounds like someone else is busy working on things themselves?" Before returning to Mr. West's call, Roselita said, "Whatever Brandon. At least I can handle this. And besides, this isn't going to last four to eight months like yours will. I'll talk with you later. Good-bye." Roselita disconnected Brandon's call and finished talking with Mr. West. To her surprise, Mr. West wasn't giving up on trying to pursue her. He wanted to know if they could go out on a date. Once again, Roselita informed Jamos West that she doesn't mix business with leisure. Roselita's voice raised an octave higher than normal, "Mr. West, I will have to report you if this continues; that can lead to your termination." Mr. Jamos West quickly backed off letting her know that he didn't want to be terminated and that she had every reason to be upset with his intolerable behavior. "Mr. Jamos West, enjoy your day. And again, welcome to Welcome News Express." Mr. Jamos West thanked Roselita. She hung up the telephone, shaking her head and saying out loud to herself, "Goodness this man just doesn't get it. Oh well, it'll register with him sooner or later." A woman entered Roselita's office wearing a raven silk pants suit. The woman's blue-black hair was cut short and layered. The woman wore a white gold seven-carat wedding ring, fourteen karat diamond stud earrings, and eighteen karat wristwatch all sparkled. The woman walked up to Roselita as she introduced herself. Roselita stood up from her desk to greet the woman, who said, "Good morning Miss Macalaonez. I'm here because I was told you could assist me in getting a message across to someone." The woman continued to speak, "Oh, I'm sorry. My name is Mrs. Rehab Kingsley-Perez." Roselita extended her hand "Nice to meet you Mrs. Kingsley-Perez. Yes, I can be of some assistance to you; but before any work can be done, you need to sign an affidavit." Mrs. Kingsley-Perez agreed to sign the paper and any other legal policies. The only thing that was important to her at the moment was exposing her story to the public. While Roselita reached into the filing cabinet to get the papers, Mrs. Kingsley-Perez told Roselita who she was and explained why she wanted a print-up in the Welcome News Express newspaper blog. She said, "Well Miss Macalaonez, I'm not sure if you are familiar with Kingsley Jewelers Exchange." Roselita's head was buried in the papers as she said, "I'm sorry Mrs. Kingsley-Perez I haven't heard of that." Mrs. Kingsley-Perez explained," The owner is my husband. He also who owns several senior assistant homes and two golf courses—one in the United States and one in Egypt." His name is Mr. M. Perez. Roselita was finally done with looking for the paper work as she said, "Here you go Mrs. Kingsley-Perez. Now, what can I do to help you out?" Mrs. Kingsley-Perez sat down in the chair in front of Roselita's desk and slowly exhaled. She continued sharing information about her life. "Well, he has been having an affair with some young woman who is about to have his baby. She has been trying to talk him out of paying child support to our children." Roselita said, "Please continue, Mrs. Kinsley-Perez, I'm listening. What is it exactly that you want me to do?" Mrs. Kinsley-Perez said, "I would like you to type up a story that reveals that this young woman is having an affair with my husband." Roselita asked, "Mrs. Kingsley-Perez, please correct me if I'm wrong, but you want to seek revenge on your husband? Just to prove your point, you have decided to go public about your life?" Roselita continued, "Are you hoping your husband and his mistress will understand your message loud and clear?" Mrs. Kingsley-Perez answered Roselita, "Yes Miss Macalaonez. Now you are talking. I have already paid your supervisor nine hundred dollars to have you write the story for me." Roselita said, "Excuse me Mrs. Kingsley-Perez. To write and print a newspaper section doesn't cost that much." Kinsley-Perez said, "Yes, Miss Macalaonez you are right. But when I'm angry, I don't yell at people. I spend all of Mr. Perez's money." Roselita mumbled, "Well in that case let's get down to business." Mrs. Kingsley-Perez went over all of the information she wanted Roselita to type so that everyone could know how Mr. Perez had been treating his wife and their four children. Roselita jotted down all of information she received from Mrs. Kingsley-Perez, leaving nothing out. Mrs. Kinsley-Perez told Roselita that the more she gets back at her husband, the more energized she feels. Roselita considered revenge to be a pathetic waste of time. But she didn't care; she knew that her supervisor agreed to pay her half of the nine hundred dollars for the article. Roselita felt that Mr. and Mrs. Perez should have learned how to communicate instead of throwing away money. Roselita recognized this as the lifestyle of the rich and important—they carelessly waste money on vengeful newspaper stories. Roselita and Mrs. Kingsley-Perez talked and talked beyond office hours. Mrs. Kingsley-Perez expressed that she was still deeply in love with her husband. She even talked about how she envied his young mistress. Mrs. Kingsley-Perez felt old and no longer capable of keeping a man. Roselita felt she could somewhat understand Mrs. Kingsley-Perez's feelings as she remembered the rough times that her parents endured with her father's infidelity. The devastation took a toll on the whole family, especially after they found out that he died of AIDS. Roselita noticed it was getting late. Roselita ended the conversation by asking Mrs. Kingsley-Perez to return the next day. Mrs. Kingsley-Perez thanked Roselita for her assistance. Mrs. Kingsley-Perez was starting to feel a little better because someone listened to her and helped ease her troubled mind. Before Mrs. Kingsley-Perez left Roselita's office, she handed her two complimentary gift cards to Marlitio's Restaurant on forty-five and Central Avenue. Roselita thanked her for the gift. As she put it in her desk, she thought to herself, "Poor lonely woman. Mrs. Kingsley-Perez is a good woman but she must be so distraught. Mrs. Kingsley-Perez is literally giving away things from her marriage to unknown people like me." Roselita realized this was a way for Mrs. Kingsley-Perez to vent, to slowly let go of her past and start a new life for herself with her children. Roselita felt there were are some people who have experienced what Mrs. Kingsley-Perez is going through. Roselita thought about the people whom she knew that once hurt or are still hurting; like Pomedra Hernandez, who is hurting inside? Pomedra just wanted love and attention. Roselita saw the desperation of Jilla Handsberg fighting to win Brandon Bright's heart. Roselita saw the anger of her mother towards her father (deceased) when he was unfaithful. Roselita saw her brother Troy's weakness when he allowed his wife to drop out of his last year of college. Roselita noticed the emptiness in Brandon's soul as he searched for a mate despite failed relationships. Roselita saw strength in her mother's fiancé Hayman because he loved her mother for being herself and not for materialistic things. Roselita forgave her father even though he hurt their family. She wanted to ask God, "Why me, and why now? What is going on with my life and the people around me? Why are these strange things happening?" Roselita felt lost. Roselita remembered that her mother used to tell her that things happen for a reason and season. Only God knows the real answers. Roselita cleared off her desk, picked up her handbag, and walked to her office door with Mrs. Kingsley- Perez. Roselita turned off the lights as they both stood in the hallway. Roselita locked her office door. Mrs. Kinsley-Perez and Roselita walked over to the elevators, as Pomedra came up to Roselita and gave her a warm smile. Pomedra said, "Good night Roselita," Pomedra looked as if she had a lot on her mind. Roselita smiled back at Pomedra, wishing her a good night also. Roselita knew that counseling Pomedra had worked because she noticed an improvement in Pomedra. Roselita realized that sometimes a person just needs someone to guide them in the right direction. From that day forward, Roselita and Pomedra's friendship became stronger.

CHAPTER THREE

***

Saturday morning came and Roselita ran around her home looking for something to wear. The doorbell rang and she ran downstairs to answer it. To her surprise, it was Brandon's friends from his work: Lucinda, Myann and Yamilla. Roselita opened the door and said, "Good morning. Come in. How is everyone doing? I've been expecting you?" The three women walked in and answered in unison, "Good!"

"Well, have a seat. I was just looking for something to put on when the doorbell rang. Would anyone like something to drink?" Everyone answered, "No thank you. But thanks for the offer." Roselita let the women know she would be ready in a few minutes. Roselita turned the Home Coise Theater System to KLSX 107.8 F.M. Yamilla said, "Hey, they are playing my song." Lucinda responded, "Oh no, now we have to hear her sing along." All of the women, including Roselita, laughed. Roselita left them sitting in the living room while she finished getting dressed upstairs. While she was in her bedroom, the telephone rang. When she saw Brandon's name in the caller ID, she picked up the telephone.

"Hi Love. Did the ladies arrive at your home?" Roselita knew Brandon would be calling to check up on her. He sent some of his closest female friends to hang out with her. Brandon made sure that they treated her with the most utmost respect.

"Yes Brandon. Lucinda, Myann and Yamilla are here."

Brandon laughed because he had thought they wouldn't show up on time--especially Myann, who doesn't like to show up on time to events. Brandon knew she even shows up to church late--and she's definitely late to work. Brandon reminded Roselita to check yesterday's mail. He had sent her a package with his credit card placed inside, along with a note. Roselita went through her mail that lay on her desktop. She found Brandon's package and quickly opened it up to read his message. The note read, "Hi Roselita. This is for you. Do as you please. Max it out. Enjoy your free shopping spree, courtesy of me. By the way, don't worry--the statement is being billed to me. Love, Brandon. Roselita dropped the phone and started jumping up and down while Brandon was left hearing her rejoice. He smiled because he knew she would be happy. Roselita slowly calmed herself and picked the phone off of the floor, shouting out, "Thank you Brandon, thank you!" Brandon could still sense Roselita's excitement so he said, "Now go and have some fun with the ladies—I know you will--and call me later." Roselita wanted to know what Brandon was doing for the day. He said, "Not much. I'm going to work out for two hours. Then I'm going to wash my car and work on the case. That's about it." Roselita had forgotten that he would be working with his partner, Jilla Handsberg from work, so she rubbed it in. "So Brandon is Jilla coming over?" Brandon chuckled saying, "I don't think so. Besides, whatever she has to say she can say over the cell phone and I'll take note of it." Roselita let Brandon know that after being friends for fourteen years, she knew him well. Roselita knew that we wouldn't let anything come between their close knit-Friendship. Brandon told Roselita that he would give her a call when he is done with his errands. Roselita told Brandon good-bye and hung up the telephone. Roselita was wearing a light blue sweat suit with a matching chemise under her jacket. Her hair was pulled back into a ponytail. Roselita wore a designer "MV" baseball cap matching her designer "MV" handbag placing her George

Blitz sunglasses into her designer "MV" glasses case. As always, her neutral makeup was flawless. Downstairs in the living room, the ladies stood up as Roselita entered the room. "Well divas, shall we go make the malls look small?" Roselita asked. Everyone felt jubilant as they walked out the front door. Yamilla insisted that they all should ride with her since she had just bought a new car. Before getting into the car with Yamilla, everyone else made sure that their own cars were fastened. They piled into Yamilla's car and she pulled the sunroof back, allowing the sun to beam down on them. Yamilla turned on the radio to KLSX 107.8 F.M smooth Jazz. Everyone said in unison, "Jackson Mall, here the divas come." They talked and laughed while they drove, listening to the radio and singing to the tunes. Myann was overwhelmed by the radio announcer's voice, "Oh, have any of you ladies met him before?" Roselita laughing asked. "No, but I'm sure you are going to tell us," Myann said. "That cinnamon spice man is good looking; you ladies have to meet him. He is Nigel Stock, nicknamed Maestro." An outburst of laughter filled the car. They could feel Myann's enthusiasm towards Nile, and they knew she wanted to fall deeply in love with the man. Yamilla said, "Myann, you know we haven't seen the man, but I suppose you are going to give us the four-one-one on him." Roselita stopped laughing when she realized that the man Myann was talking about was the one she had met in the elevator at her work a while back. Roselita said to Myann, "Wait just one moment. What is his name?" Myann repeated herself, "Nigel Stock. Why, have you met him also?" Roselita then realized it was the same man that she met in the elevator; she knew he was too good looking to be true. Everyone except Roselita listened as Myann kept talking. Roselita tuned her out for a moment while thinking about how good-looking Nigel Stock was. Roselita closed her eyes and pictured him. Roselita finally opened her eyes just in time to hear Lucinda asking if she was okay. Lucinda noticed that Roselita seemed to space out on them. Roselita relaxed--she was having a good time hanging out with Brandon's female co-workers. Roselita found all of them to have a unique sense of humor. Roselita could sense closeness, because they were carefree about everything from politics to life issues. Roselita felt comfortable being around them--but not so comfortable that she could share her personal business with them. Roselita gave them straightforward answers when they asked her personal questions. Yamilla made a right turn onto Wellington Lakes Road. Roselita drove past Jumbo Seafood Restaurant, some fast food places, gas stations, and a Jack's grocery store. Yamilla by passed by Richwood Mall, making a right onto Jackson's Mall parking lot; she parked and turned off the car as everyone got out. Yamilla locked the doors when Myann said, "Well ladies are we ready to have some fun shopping?" Everyone laughed. Myann was the comedian in the bunch. Lucinda said, "Ladies, I was born for this kind of stuff ... shopping." Inside the mall everyone split up and met back up in the food court for lunch. Yamilla and Roselita walked around together first. Yamilla had an eye for stylish clothing. While Lucinda and Myann went separate ways looking for things to improve Roselita's wardrobe, Yamilla and Roselita came upon a store called "It's for you." When they walked in, a saleswoman asked them if they needed assistance. Yamilla said, "No, but if we need help, we'll call you." Then Yamilla led Roselita over to look at what was hot-- and what was not. Roselita tried on a few outfits that Yamilla felt she would look nice in. They went to several department stores, trying everything from casual wear to elegant evening wear. They finally found something that they agreed on. Yamilla picked a casual but elegant gold silk sleeveless midriff dress. Roselita was enraptured by the choice that Yamilla had made for her. Roselita picked two more outfits just in case they didn't turn out right. They then met up with Myann and Lucinda so they could switch shopping partners and take Roselita shopping for shoes, accessories and make-up. Myann was in charge of helping Roselita pick her shoes while Lucinda made sure her make-up would give her a radiant look that would entice not only Gordon Gem, but also every other single man. Lucinda also made sure Roselita's accessories made her look radiant. Roselita trusted Yamilla, Myann and Lucinda's expertise to work such wonders that even Brandon would be mesmerized by her splendor. He might even believe that he's the one for her, and not Gordon Gem. After several hours of searching, their eventful shopping day ended when everyone met at the front entrance of the mall. Lucinda suggested that they eat lunch at Marlitio's Restaurant. After being seated, Lucinda ordered a Caesar salad, fettuccini with thick creamy chicken sauce, and sugared iced tea. Myann ordered the barbecue chicken wings with French fries and lemonade. Roselita ordered rosemary red potatoes; honey glazed carrots and grilled salmon with parsley and lemon. Yamilla ordered the baby greens and bacon salad, red beans and rice, green beans and roasted herb chicken. After they enjoyed the delicious lunch, Lucinda ordered cappuccinos for everyone. They talked while sipping their coffee, but grew silent as they noticed Jilla and her friends. The waiter escorted Jilla and her friends to their table as they went past Roselita, Yamilla, Myann and Lucinda's table. Jilla interrupted the waiter, "Excuse me, but can you just show my friends their table? I see some people I would like to talk with for a minute?" Jilla then told her friends that she'd join them in a moment-- she was going to stop and greet some people she knew. Jilla looked at Roselita, Yamilla, Myann and Lucinda and said, "Well look who we have here if it isn't Lucinda, Myann, and Yamilla." Giving Roselita an envious stare, Jilla added, "And my--look who is hanging with the Jackson Law Firm crew! I'm sorry I forgot your name." Roselita wanted to lash out, assuming that Jilla remembered her name but hesitated to say it. "Ah yes, now I remember. Brandon told me it is Roselita Macalaonez." Myann became angered by Jilla's unruly behavior and defended Roselita by saying. "Listen here Jilla I don't know what it is that you want, let alone why you even stopped to speak, but you will never achieve whatever your stalking self wants." Lucinda said, "We put up with too much of your trash talking self at work and now that it is the weekend, we don't care to hear it anymore." Being the sensitive one, Yamilla told Myann and Lucinda that getting back at Jilla Handsberg wouldn't solve anything. Yamilla then asked Jilla if Roselita had done anything wrong to make her feel uncomfortable. Jilla's voice raised an octave, "Actually yes, she did do something wrong. She stole my honey Brandon Bright from me." Roselita couldn't take it anymore. Roselita said, "That's it! Excuse me ladies. Listen you delusional woman--I don't recall stealing anyone's man from her. As far as I can see, Brandon doesn't belong to you!" Myann acted irresponsibly and said, "Now that's what I'm talking about! If we can't put Jilla in her place, at least someone else is able to. Thank goodness for that!" Yamilla told Myann to be quiet and allow Roselita to express herself. Roselita continued, "Jilla, you and I don't know each other well enough for you to be approaching me in a manner that only teenage girls could understand." Myann glanced at Yamilla and Lucinda, smiling and nodding her head in agreement with everything. Roselita also said, "Furthermore, as I see it, this conversation will end here and now. Good-bye Jilla Handsberg!" Jilla, flustered by Roselita's bluntness, walked away and mumbled, "You may have my man now, but he is still mine." Roselita then realized that Jilla's problem was deeper than it first appeared. Roselita could see that Jilla was mentally insane. It didn't matter what anyone said, she would always have the notion that Brandon would be hers. Yamilla then said, "I feel awful. If only Jilla could stop listening to those so- called voices from inside her head, just maybe she would be okay." Myann added to Yamilla's comment, "Interesting, because I have never known Jilla to be on medication, but I know she sure could use some now." Roselita said, "She might not be on medication, but somehow she's been rejected too many times and each time it seems that she's searching for love that no man wants to share with her." Yamilla said, "You know, that could just be Jilla's problem. Jilla isn't content with herself and Jilla has never sought healing." Myann said, "Well, whatever seems to be the case, she still needs help and only a therapist has a remedy for it." Lucinda said, "Yes, whatever her problem, maybe we should pray that she be willing to seek professional help." Myann, with her humor, added to all of the comments that were said about Jilla Handsberg, "No, the one we need to pray for is Brandon's good looking self." Everyone at the table laughed because they knew Myann's humor could ease the tension of a moment like the one they just had with Jilla. Yamilla reminded everyone that both Jilla and Brandon would need their help to get through this difficult situation. The women stood up as Myann left the waiter an eight-dollar tip. As they walked to the door, Jilla passed them on her way to the restroom. Jilla smiled at Yamilla, Lucinda, and Myann, and made sure Roselita could see the chill in her darkened eyes. Roselita felt assertive and smiled at Jilla, hoping to convey that Jilla's schemes would not work on her. Yamilla, Lucinda and Myann noticed Jilla's gaze towards Roselita. Lucinda said, "Yes, poor Brandon. He has to work with the feisty one. But knowing our friend Brandon Bright, he knows how to put the flames out quickly." Myann said, "Lucinda please do not remind us. My stomach can't take much more it turns just knowing how true it is. Yamilla was laughing so hard she said, "I have to go the restroom, excuse me." Then Myann burst into laughter. Roselita said, "Oh yes, that's right, after Jilla's been stalking him, poor Brandon. What is he to do when he has to put up with her craziness for the next four to eight months?" Roselita tried to think of a way for Brandon to avoid working with Jilla Handsberg. Maybe he could ask to switch partners or see if he could work on the case by himself. Finally the women left Marlitio's Restaurant as they walked over to Yamilla's car. Yamilla drove them back to Roselita's home so

Lucinda and Myann could get their cars. Everyone got into their own car after they returned to Roselita's house. Roselita waved good-bye to them and walked into her home. She unlocked the front door, stepped into the house and locked the door behind her. She disarmed the security system, which she keeps the on ready setting on while she is home. Placing the shopping bags on the floor in her foyer Roselita walked over to her couch, took off her sneakers, and propped her feet on the couch to relax for a moment. Roselita picked up the remote and turned on KLSX 107.8 Smooth Jazz. She reached for her laptop and dialed Brandon's telephone number. Brandon answered, "Hello?"

Roselita said, "Hi, Brandon did I interrupt you?"

"No. Roselita, how are you doing?"

"I'm okay. I just got home from shopping."

"Yes, I dozed off for a moment while working on this case."

"Well I won't keep you from working. I can talk with you later."

Brandon answered, "No that's okay. I'm able to talk. So tell me all about it. How was the shopping spree?"

"Everyone is wonderful. The ladies were great, especially Miss Myann. She is a fun person to hang around."

"I can sense…she kept you laughing, huh?"

"Yes, the entire time--including when we ate at Marlitio's Restaurant for lunch."

"Excuse me big spenders, can a man have some of that money flowing around?" Roselita mentioned that while she and the ladies were out having such a good time, Jilla was also out having lunch with some female friends of hers. Brandon came to attention and said, "What Roselita? What do you mean Jilla was also there eating lunch?" Roselita felt Brandon's anger inflate as his voice went deeper; it felt like he was going to come through the laptop computer phone. Brandon said, "Carry on, Roselita!" Roselita realized that there wasn't any backing out of this conversation. Roselita had to finish letting him know the details. Brandon was in full alert, as he wanted to know what happened. Brandon wanted to know why Jilla made a scene that nobody cared to see. Roselita continued explaining what happened. Roselita said Jilla wasn't going to give up trying to win him over. Roselita mentioned that everyone agreed Jilla needs professional psychological help. Brandon agreed with the mental health issue, but he didn't think that was Jilla's real problem. He felt she desperately wanted a man to fulfill her dream of not being lonely. Roselita said, "Hum, that's interesting."

Brandon asked, "Why is that so interesting?"

"Because Myann, Lucinda, Yamilla and I agreed that she needs prayer and needs to be content with herself."

"I believe that prayer changes things, but she also needs professional help.

"Oh yes, there is one more thing. We ladies decided that you will need prayer while working with Jilla Handsberg." Brandon laughed, thanking Roselita as he wondered why he needs prayer. "What have I done for you to say that about me?" he asked. "Well, we felt that since you are her partner on the Co-Slasher Murder case, she will be bugging you all of the time."

"As you know, we made an agreement that we will only discuss things at work and it must strictly be about business." Roselita sensed that Brandon was starting to love Jilla because he quickly became so defensive that his voice kept going deeper. Roselita had never seen Brandon protect someone he had no interest in getting to know on a more personal level. Roselita knew that she went in too deep with Brandon by talking about Jilla Handsberg. Roselita realized that Brandon's temper was at a boiling point. Brandon became hostile towards Roselita for mentioning the whole thing about Jilla Handsberg. Roselita calmly asked Brandon why his anger was spinning out of control if he had no interest in Jilla. "Listen Roselita, I'm just tired of hearing about Jilla this and Jilla that. Yes, she is irritating me also." Roselita then noticed Brandon's voice slow down and become peaceful. She wasn't trying to get him worked up, but he did ask for the details surrounding Jilla's behavior. He didn't want Roselita omitting any information. Roselita just gave Brandon the news about how Jilla acted. But if Roselita had known that Brandon was going to get bent out of shape, she wouldn't have brought it up. "I flared up because I know I have to work with her and I really don't want to." Roselita suggested that Brandon talk with his supervisor about Jilla's obsessive stalking. Roselita continued, "If your supervisor knew what was happening, he might have a little compassion and replace her with someone else to work with. Or he might have you work by yourself." Brandon's attitude returned to normal as they continued to talk. Brandon thanked Roselita for her helpful advice. Brandon said, "Roselita I don't know what I would do without you." Roselita then told Brandon that everything would turn out all right if he would just trusts his instincts. Brandon said he was glad that Roselita had a good time with his female co-workers and that he couldn't wait to see the finale on the day of the conference. Brandon's telephone line clicked. Brandon asked Roselita to hold on for a moment because someone was calling him. Brandon clicked over, only to hear Jilla's voice. Just after he had calmed down, his temper flared again. Brandon put Jilla on hold while he returned to Roselita and letting her know that Jilla was on the other line, waiting to speak with him. Roselita laughed, "It is as if she knew we were discussing her. Jill knew when to call." Brandon excused himself from Roselita so he could talk with Jilla, knowing that if he didn't speak with Jilla now, his telephone would ring all night. Than Jilla would find a way to speak to him somehow, no matter what it would take. Jilla was becoming fractious by constantly pursuing Brandon—especially after he made it clear that he was not interested in her. Brandon and Roselita concluded that he would sooner or later change his mind and love her. Roselita, on the other hand, always felt that she didn't need to challenge another woman just to get the man she always wanted. She knew some things weren't worth getting--but when it comes to a man, it would be best to let him do the choosing. Roselita remembered what her mother told her, that a down-to-earth woman knows how to wait for a man while a foolish woman can cause a man to lose interest in her. Roselita knew that Brandon and she were already close friends. Roselita also knew that Jilla's unstable behavior would threaten any relationship. Roselita left the situation up to Brandon to handle, hoping that he would make the right decision to get rid of Jilla. Brandon was in his office on an important telephone call on Monday morning when Jilla knocked on his door. She said, "Excuse me. May I come in Brandon?" Without allowing him to answer, she walked in. Brandon was still on the telephone when Jilla sat down in the chair in front of his desk. Brandon asked the person he was speaking with to hold for a moment. Brandon looked at Jilla politely, asking her to step out of his office until he finished his important call. Still sitting there, Jilla said, "Your caller can wait because I'm more important to you than he or she will ever be."

Brandon stood up, walked around, and stood in front of his desk with eyes darting back at hers. Brandon said, "Listen Jilla, I don't know what it is that you want from me. I have nothing to give to you." Jilla sat upright on the edge of the chair as she said, "Brandon just face it. You know I'm too irresistible for you to keep ignoring me." Brandon stepped back, sat back down, and told the person he was speaking with that there was an emergency he needed to attend to. Jilla then leaned back and crossed her leg in a sexual gesture. Brandon hung up speedily, stood up, and placed both hands firmly on the desk. "This is it Miss Handsberg. I have had enough of you. This has gone too far. Now it's time to take legal action--and I can do that since I am a lawyer." An optimistic look appeared on her face, making him go into cold sweat. Brandon wasn't sure what Jilla Would try and do to him. So Brandon picked up the telephone and made a call. Jilla didn't hear whom, Brandon was calling at this point she didn't care all Jilla knew was that this was her opportunity to make her move. Brandon continued to talk on the telephone as she gave him a seducing look. Brandon smiled at her to make her think that he was interested; he knew he was playing with fire, but he was willing to take the risk. Brandon stood up and walked around to the front of his desk, sitting on the edge while still talking on the telephone. Jilla smiled exuberantly as she uncrossed her legs and pretended to pick something up off the floor. Jilla knew Brandon was watching, so she made sure he could catch a good glimpse of her cleavage as she slowly arose back up. To Jilla's surprise, Brandon didn't look at her as she tried to seduce him with her body language. Brandon knew his shortcomings; he knew that his heart wasn't into her. Why should he pay any attention to someone who doesn't have dignity or self-respect? Jilla continued to try to allure Brandon, this time she rubbed her neck as if she had cramp in it. As Brandon continued to sit facing Jilla, he smiled again without saying a word. Jilla felt that she had his attention now so she continued making sexual gestures, assuming he was enjoying her performance. There was a knock on his office door. Their supervisor entered with the building and escorted Jilla down the hallway into his office. As they were removing her from Brandon's office, his supervisor turned towards Brandon and thanked him for stopping Jilla's. Brandon's supervisor then left Brandon's office, following security back to his office where he served Jilla's termination papers. Brandon's supervisor explained that Constitutes Law Firm does not tolerant irrational behavior of any kind. Instead it helps the government protect citizens by defending human rights. This doesn't exclude the work environment or work related situations. This includes sexual harassment or exploitation. Jilla sat quietly as her supervisor continued to read the rules and regulations of the company policy. While she sat there vaguely listening to her supervisor talk, she just realized that when Brandon was smiling and talking on the telephone, he was talking with their supervisor at Constitutes Law Firm. He finally finished the paper work as he handed Jilla copies and said, "I hope you have learned a valuable lesson. I hope that wherever you go, you won't be repeating the same behavior. Thank you for working at Constitutes Law Firm." Jilla picked up her handbag, asking if she could clean her work station. He granted her request, insisted that security stay with her until she leaves the premises. On her way back to her workstation, she walked passed Brandon's closed office door. She rolled her eyes as she proceeded. Jilla mumbled, "So you think you have gotten rid of me Brandon Bright, huh? Well Mr. Bright, this isn't over until I say it's over?" One of the security guards overheard her talking to herself and asked if she was talking to him. Jilla replied, "No, but if I was, don't you think I would be asking you what you think about all of this that just happened to me?" The other security guard quickly glanced at his partner, signaling him to say nothing. He felt she had already done enough damage to the company and its employees now. What more could she do? Jilla cleaned off her desk as everyone in the area watched, wanting to cheer, but keeping a straight face. Jilla kept her head down until she finally finished. Jilla walked out of the work area, escorted by security back down the hallway past Brandon's office for the last time. Jilla turned her head, only to see that his office door was still closed. Jilla had hoped she could rewind things by making up for her obsessive behavior. Jilla knew it was too late, her walking papers were served to her just minutes ago and she knew she had blown her chance of pursuing Brandon. Jilla had reached the entrance to the building as one security guard returned to his post and the other one continued to escort Jilla to her car. Outside in the parking lot of Constitutes Law Firm, she looked up at the building and noticed Brandon standing in front of his window on telephone.

Brandon was looking across the parking lot; she saw Brandon but quickly noticed that he wasn't looking down in her direction. Brandon was focused on his telephone conversation. Jilla felt if she had another chance to say her final words to him, just maybe he would have a change of heart and want her after all. Jilla unlocked her car door with the security guard still standing there. Jilla placed her belongings in the car as she yelled up at Brandon's office window. Jilla said, "Brandon Bright how could you? After all we've been through? After all of those many nights that we spent making love--I knew you would love it!" Brandon finally looked down and saw Jilla looking up at him. He couldn't hear her because the office windows were bulletproof. He could only see her mouth moving but he couldn't hear what she was saying. He assumed she was making her last plea, telling her lies to the world. How foolish she looked right about now--with a security officer standing at her side. Jilla looked insane while yelling at the air with nobody but the security officer to hear her. Brandon then turned away from the window as he sat down to finish his telephone call. As soon as he hung up the telephone, it rang again. This time it was Roselita calling to see how his day went. Brandon answered, "Good morning Constitutes Law Firm. This is Brandon Bright. How may I help you?" Roselita asked if he was okay. He didn't sound like himself. Brandon said that he felt happy but also saddened. Being a softhearted man, he knew that he did the right thing, but his guilty conscience made him feel awful. Brandon explained to Roselita what had just happened between Jilla and him. He thanked Roselita for her advice. Brandon could now get on with his work and move on with his personal life without worrying about Jilla Handsberg threatening his family and friends. Brandon was especially concerned for Roselita, who meant the world to him and who would always be around for him, no matter what was going on in his life. Brandon realized that he allowed Jilla to affect his emotions; here he was feeling upset because he just had someone terminated because of harassment. Roselita told him that things would be okay as soon as he realized that his life could have been worse if hadn't done anything. Brandon snapped back to reality saying, "That's it Roselita?" Roselita felt lost—as if she had just made a mistake, she said, "What do you mean that's it?" Brandon began to pull his thoughts together, "That's it... Jilla's completely gone!"

Roselita said again, "What do you mean, Jilla Handsberg is completely gone?" Brandon answered her, "Jilla Handsberg is gone for good because I took the advice you gave me last night on the telephone."

"Okay and that was please, refresh my memory, Brandon."

Brandon said, "You told me that I should have a talk with my supervisor and have Jilla Handsberg replaced as my partner on this Co-Slasher Murder case." All of a sudden, a shocking discovery hit Roselita with full force, "Brandon, I know you didn't have her fired." Brandon laughed a loud and said, "Yes, I did--you have given me every reason to go through with it." Roselita responded, "Okay, so give me the details of what brought you to have her gone for good." Filled with glee, he said, "Jilla barged into my office while I was on an important phone call with a client. I immediately hung up because I felt things were about to become crazy, which they did." Roselita said, "Carry on I'm listening to you Brandon." As Brandon talked and Roselita listened to him, she felt that she had never meant for Brandon to have Jilla fired--she only wondered if he could switch partners. She thought maybe he could take on what he could handle and leave the rest up to his supervisor to deal with. However the situation went, he doesn't have to deal with Jilla Handsberg anymore. Brandon cut their conversation short because he had fill out paperwork on Jilla Handsberg and meet with his supervisor. Roselita went back to working as she did before, throughout the day Brandon stayed on her mind. Roselita felt that once all of this passed, Brandon would be okay and everything would go back to normal. Roselita finished typing before she went on her lunch break. Brandon was filling out the paperwork when supervisor called to see if everything was okay with him. Brandon mentioned to his supervisor that had never intended for Jilla to get terminated. His supervisor informed Brandon that he had to follow Constitutes Law Firm protocol. To stop Jilla Handsberg from injuring others, Brandon made the right decision. Brandon then remembered what Roselita and his supervisor said to him about things getting better since Jilla Handsberg is gone from the company. Brandon would be able to work without interruptions from Jilla Handsberg and her seducing, obsessive, psycho behavior. During his lunch break he saw Lucinda, Myann, and Yamilla eating in the cafeteria. He paid for his lunch as he walked toward their table. He said, "Excuse me, but is it okay if I join you ladies?" Wanting to cheer him up, Myann quickly responded, "Yes, have a seat... Um, hum you can always have a seat." Myann smiled at Brandon, lifting an eyebrow. Lucinda, Myann and Yamilla knew that, Brandon is the most attractive single, childless, never married. Good looking man who worked on their floor at Constitutes Law Firm. Everyone laughed because they knew Myann was the comedian out of the group. She could take a bad day and turn it into a fun one. He shared their laughter at Myann's invitation to join them for lunch. Lucinda leaned over and whispered to Yamilla something about how good Brandon looked. Lucinda looked at Brandon from head to toe. Noticing Brandon's tapered haircut, his manly scent, and his stylish clothing. Yamilla said, "If I was Roselita I would be trying to marry him, but I understand they share a close friendship." Myann asked, "Hey, no whispering at the table--well at least while Brandon is present." Lucinda said, "Oh we're not whispering about Brandon—just about womanly stuff." (Myann knew exactly whom Lucinda and Yamilla were discussing but Myann didn't want Brandon to find out.) Lucinda continued to answer Yamilla, "Skip the close friendship—let's go to the dating part and onto marriage plus children." Both women laughed out loud as they high fived each other. Myann was still rumbling about how she missed the conversation that Lucinda and Yamilla were so eager to carry-on. Brandon laughed at both Lucinda and Yamilla as he interrupted, "Is that so? Is that what you would do with me?" Lucinda looked over at Brandon and said, "Hum, you don't even know what we're talking about." Brandon laughed harder, "So do all of you feel I should skip being friends with Roselita and just ask her to marry me? Or should I pick one of you to marry?"

Myann, still being sarcastic, said, "Well it would never hurt for you to try marrying one of us. After all, I'm the prettiest out of the group?" Lucinda said, "Once again here we leave it up to Myann to save the day." Brandon replied, "Well at least she's honest and has humor." Lucinda answered, "Oh and I suppose Yamilla and I would be boring to date?" Brandon said, "Oops, I have said too much. I think I'll just sit here and finish eating my lunch without saying another word." Everyone laughed. Lucinda said, "Brandon, you know that you are just too good looking not to have a beautiful woman attached to you." If anyone wanted the four-one-one news flash, it was Myann, who knew how to work information out of people. Myann asked Brandon what went down earlier. Myann wanted to know why Brandon never asked Roselita to be his woman. Yamilla choked on her lunch because she knew Myann was taking things too far by being too personal with Brandon. Lucinda said, "Myann, he might not be ready to talk about what happened earlier between him and that wicked Jilla Handsberg. Besides, it's definitely none of our business to know either." Myann said, "Um excuse you Lucinda. Speak for you self! Besides, what is there to hide especially when Jilla walked out of the building being escorted by security?" Lucinda told Myann that she made a valid point. After all, Jilla was standing out in the parking lot yelling obscene things about Brandon. Yamilla said, "Sorry to interrupt, but I think Brandon has had enough in one day, so let's not get him going...please." Myann said, "Okay Mr. Brandon Bright. Have you had enough--or are you ready to get with me?" Everyone at the table burst out laughing. Brandon said, "Myann, I think that you and Jilla should be sisters because you are just as crazy as she is except you are able to make people laugh without getting angry at you." He went onto say, "If I did get with you, would you have promised not to manhandle me since you are such a forceful one?" Lucinda and Yamilla laughed. They were all happy to see Brandon back to his normal self, having a good time. Myann asked Yamilla if she had Roselita's telephone number because she needed to tell her that she's wasting time. Roselita better pick up Brandon before someone else does. Yamilla said, "Yes, I do have Roselita's number, and I'm not giving it to you. Besides, this is Brandon's personal business and not our concern." Lucinda said, "I guess you are right. You know how quickly he got rid of Jilla. You might want to see if you could be next, Myann." Brandon didn't like the direction their conversation was going so he changed the subject their shopping trip. Yamilla sensed he was getting tired of discussing Jilla so she joined him in changing the conversation. Myann was still waiting for answers, knowing that she wasn't going to be getting answers any time soon. Lucinda said, "I need to return to work, I'll talk with you all later." Yamilla kicked Myann under the table, sending her a message that now would be a good time for her to leave the table. Myann said, "Ouch... Listen Yamilla, if I leave the table I think you need to be going also." Brandon looked at both women, wondering what they were talking about. Neither one filled him in on their little spat. Brandon said, "Well if you both leave, I guess I'll be by myself." Yamilla laughed as she tried to be humorous, "Only if you are not finished eating and you like how I make you feel." Myann couldn't help but laugh, saying, "Yamilla, comedy isn't your career so don't quit your day job. It'll only make us upset if you quit working at Constitutes Law Firm to pursue a comedy gig." Myann continued. "Besides, Brandon just might want quiet time and I think we'll hinder his peace. After all, I'm sure he found your humor to be generic and rusty." They both stood up and said good-bye to Brandon as they left him to finish his lunch by himself. Brandon's cell phone rang. It was Roselita calling him back to see if he wanted to come over for dinner. Brandon gladly took Roselita up on the offer and apologized for his rational behavior. Roselita told Brandon he didn't have to explain. She knew he would be upset. He just needed to vent. His line clicked again. This time it was his mother calling to check up on her son. "Please hold on Roselita, I have another call coming through." Brandon clicked over to hear a sweet, loving voice, "How is Mama's baby doing?" A bright smile filled his handsome face as he sighed in relief, "It's good to hear from you mother. Can you hold on for a moment?" Brandon returned to Roselita sounding carefree knowing that the one person whose wisdom he appreciated is his mother's. Brandon told Roselita that his mother was on the other line so he'd have to call Roselita back later. Roselita understood, telling him to greet his mother from her. Brandon connected back to his mother. "So how have things been going for you, mother?" Mrs. Bright responded, "Oh baby, I'm doing well but what about you and this Jilla Handsberg woman?" Brandon was shocked to know that his mother already heard about him and Jilla Handsberg. He figured out the only person who could relate the message so quickly to his mother is Roselita. Brandon said, "Mother, before you get upset, I'm doing well also.... really." Mrs. Bright answered in her sweet tone voice, "Brandon baby why haven't you called me to explain what is going on in your hectic life?" Brandon knew that whenever his mother got upset with him, she wanted to know what the problem was. Finally he said, "Mother, there was a small problem--but it wasn't anything that I couldn't handle." Mrs. Bright still didn't believe that her son was telling her all that happened at work. Brandon got up and placed his serving tray on the counter top while still talking on his cell phone with his mother. Brandon walked over towards the elevators and waited for the door to open. Brandon's supervisor passed by, smiling at him as he walked towards the cafeteria with some important-looking people. Brandon returned the smile and continued to talk with his mother. The elevator doors opened. As he stepped in, a woman and her child entered also. The woman smiled at Brandon as he greeted them both. The little boy stared at Brandon with a chipper grin. Brandon looked down, noticing the woman's son staring up at him. Brandon watched the elevator numbers go up until they reached his floor. The little boy then looked at Brandon and said, "Look there's daddy." His mother bent down and said, "No, this gentleman isn't your father." Brandon had forgotten he still had his mother on the phone when the young boy made the comment. Mrs. Bright said, "Oh no! Not another woman with a child. Who thinks you are the child's father!" Brandon laughed, "Mother, you heard that through the cell phone?" The woman on the elevator looked at Brandon and said, "Oh, I'm sorry. Were you talking to me?" Brandon responded to the woman on the elevator, "No ma'am. I'm on my cell phone." Mrs. Bright was appalled that her son was talking with some woman whose child asked if Brandon was his father. Mrs. Bright continued, "Excuse me Mr. Giddy Lover man, Brandon Roman Bright. Do you hear me? Your mother is trying to talk to you?" Now feeling embarrassed by his mother and her reactions, he tried to take control of the situation by talking with both women. His mother then became upset, telling him that if he would keep his body part private and his mind from lurking, then just maybe she wouldn't be so belligerent. Brandon always knew he could count on his mother when it came to dealing with women. The little boy then said, "Ah huh. Watch daddy--would you hold my hand?" Brandon looked at the little boy saying, "Listen little fellow, your mother is right. I'm not your father." The little boy became apprehensive saying, "Then why did you keep smiling at us like you wanted my mother?" The little boy's mother suddenly interrupted, "Excuse me. I'm sorry, but my son can be a handful at times. Please forgive him." Brandon's mother said, "Umm son, are at your office floor yet?" The elevator rang as the doors opened. Brandon stepped off with the little boy standing behind him. Brandon turned around, noticing that the little boy stepped off with him. Brandon said, "Oh no, you can't follow me around. What happened to your mother?" Mrs. Bright is now angry because that woman allowed her son to follow a stranger off the elevator. Mrs. Bright started yelling through the cell phone, "Brandon baby, you need to find that child's mother right away." Brandon is wondering what to do, he couldn't concentrate with his mother pressuring him to find the little boy's mother. Suddenly he said, "Mother I'll have to call you back after I have found his mother." Mrs. Bright got angrier, "Oh no, you won't Brandon Roman Bright, I'm still talking with you... Now find his mother right away!" Brandon placed his mother on hold as he stood at the elevator door waiting for it to open. The door opened as the little boy's mother reached out to hug her lost son. "Oh thank you sir," The woman told Brandon. Then the woman started yelling at her son, "Now you see, this is why I don't like taking you anywhere because you don't know how to act." Brandon interrupted the woman scolding her son. "Sorry to stop your so-called disciplining, but if you would take time to give him love, just maybe he would understand right from wrong." The woman stood up and smiled at Brandon, "That's the nicest thing anyone has ever said to me. "Hi. My name is Nadine Appleton and this is my son Nate. Say 'hi' to the gentleman." The little boy said, "Hi" as he squirmed while his mother was holding his arm still. Brandon smiled at Nate, bending down to give him a handshake as Nate smiled back at Brandon. The woman thanked him for returning her son to her. Nadine took a hold of her son's hand as she waited for the elevator door to open. They entered the elevator. Nadine looked out of the elevator door, hoping he would place his foot in between the door to keep it from closing so that he could ask her to call him sometime. Instead the door closed as he walked toward his office. In his office he released the hold button on his cell phone, asking his mother if she would call him back on his office phone. Mrs. Bright called him, this time speaking in a tempered voice, "I hope you are not going to give that desperate woman, in search of her son's daddy any of your home, cell, and work phone numbers." Brandon's voice became husky, "No mother, I'm not giving any numbers out. Besides, I'm done chasing women for now." Mrs. Bright laughed, "Baby, you think I'm supposed to believe you on this?" Brandon sensed that his mother didn't believe he was telling the truth. Brandon went on to say, "When I get married, will you believe me then?" Silence followed as Mrs. Bright realized she just insulted her son Brandon. Mrs. Bright also noticed that when Brandon said, "He was done messing around with women; he meant that he only wanted stable women." Mrs. Bright felt that her grown son Brandon was mature enough to make his own decisions. Mrs. Bright apologized for her shrewd behavior towards Brandon, explaining that she only wanted the best for Brandon and that she supported his decisions. Brandon melted after hearing his mother's forgiveness as they shared a quick laugh and continued to talk. "I suppose you heard the news about me having Jilla Handsberg terminated." Mrs. Bright said, "Yes. Roselita called to tell me what happened this morning between you and that irresponsible Jilla Handsberg woman. Mrs. Bright continued to say, "Son, you may not realize it, but sometimes the woman for you is the one who really cares for you." Brandon respected what his mother was saying, but he felt that he was too wild to be with Roselita. Brandon knew he could never love Roselita in spite of their fourteen-year friendship. Besides, Brandon felt Roselita deserved someone who was ready to get married--Brandon wasn't ready yet for that type of commitment. Mrs. Bright said, "Son, I know that sometimes you want to stay single because you can have as many women as you want, but after a while, chasing those hopeless women who don't strive for anything leads you nowhere. They sometimes try to hold you back from going forward." Brandon made it known to his mother that not all women are hopeless--they just might be comfortable where they are in life. Brandon continued to say, "Some might be empowered to do good while others may find that just being themselves is good enough." Brandon continued, "I'm really not looking for a woman who has to prove she's a super woman. However, I'm looking for a woman I can share an interesting conversation with or someone I can agree with about life." Brandon went unto to say, "I want a woman who can be herself and smile, knowing that the world's standards cannot change the woman that God has made her to be." After listening to her son express what he wants in a woman, she realized how deeply he wanted to find the right woman to settle down with someday. Mrs. Bright said, "Son, it's okay to cry and allow a teardrop to fall at your desk." Brandon said, "Mother, real men don't cry." Mrs. Bright said,

"Oh yes they do. It's the ignorant ones that don't show pain." Mrs. Bright added, "They try not to show it, but baby trust me--that only lasts for a moment because when they're alone, the tears roll down hard." Brandon became more and more attentive as his mother spoke words of wisdom, filling his heart with joy, knowing that everything was going to be all right. They finished up the conversation and his mother said, "Son you know I will always love you. I know that you're smart enough to know what's best for you." Brandon said good-bye to his mother, placing the phone back on its stand. Brandon turned on his computer and began working. As Brandon worked, he was called to his supervisor's office. Brandon stood up pushed his chair backward and walked down the hallway to his supervisor's office door. As he closed the door behind Brandon, his supervisor said, "Ah Mr. Bright my man, please come in here and have a seat." Brandon felt nervous, wondering why his supervisor had a crazed look on his face. Brandon sat motionless, wondering what he did to end up in his supervisor's office. Employees at Constitutes Law Firm go to the supervisor's office only for morning meetings. Brandon's supervisor asked Brandon if knew of anyone who is in search of a new job, since Jilla Handsberg is gone. Brandon looked at his supervisor gave him a stern look and said, "No sir I don't have anyone in mind." His supervisor surprised Brandon by revealing, "Ah I see. Well, Miss Jilla Handsberg has already been replaced by a woman named Nadine Appleton." Brandon couldn't believe what he is hearing. Brandon tried to ask reasonable questions of his supervisor. "Excuse me sir, but does this Nadine woman have any children?" His supervisor answered, "Why yes. She has a handsome little rascal named Nate. What? Have you two met before?" Brandon replied, "Yes. I met both of them this afternoon as I was coming from my lunch break." Brandon's supervisor stood with one hand in his pocket and the other looking at Nadine's credentials. He sipped his coffee as he walked over to Brandon and said, "Please treat her with respect, because she's my niece and the little squirt is my great nephew." Brandon's eyes became bright with merriment as he imagined making Nadine feel comfortable at Constitutes Law Firm. Brandon left his supervisor's office and sprinted back to his desk. Brandon felt he could fulfill his duties and not become flirtatious with his supervisor's niece. Brandon was sure that his lust wouldn't go beyond his imagination. At five-thirty pm, Brandon left the office and started for home. Once at home, he rushed up the stairs to his bathroom, turned on the cold water, dropped his pants, shed his shirt, and admired his perfectly sculptured washboard stomach and toned round buttocks. Brandon grabbed his towel as he stood in the shower, allowing the cold water to drizzle all over him. Brandon lathered his golden brown body and curly black hair with soap and cooled his body temperature. Then the phone rang. Brandonnt wrapped a towel around his waist, walked into his bedroom from the shower, and answered the phone. His friend Royston Friends was calling to see if Brandon had checked out his new team partner, the supervisor's niece Nadine, who would be starting next week. Brandon laughed while talking with Royston. Brandon said, "Royston, Nadine is off limits because I made a promise to our supervisor that I would watch out for her." Royston said, "Yeah man, she may be off limits to you, but not to me or the rest of the single men in the office." As Royston talked, Brandon's thoughts drifted back to the conversation he had with his mother when he promised he would change and not get involved with Nadine. Then Brandon snapped back to his call with Royston and said, "Hey man, she's all yours! There's someone else that I want for my forever love." Royston is curious to know why Brandon isn't going after Nadine, "My friend Brandon, what's going on with you? I hope it's not that woman Jilla Handsberg, because she's history." Brandon laughed hysterically. Brandon knew that just because Jilla and he had to work together didn't mean he wanted to sleep with Jilla. Brandon didn't allow her behavior to affect his gentle compassion. Brandon isn't going to let Jilla ruin his opportunity to finally express his true love towards Roselita Macalaonez. Brandon said, "Man! What is it with Jilla Handsberg, first my Mother, then Roselita, Yamilla, Myann, Lucinda and our supervisor, and now you?" Royston said, "Man, you know how it is when a man and a woman are assigned to work together; you know everyone is going to have their suspicions." Brandon answered, "Man, I see... A man can't work with a woman unless he gets physical with her--and that's horrendous." Royston affirmed, "Man--and you know that!" Brandon replied, "Well it's sad to see men like you who have no respect for yourself, or the women who you use?" Royston became explosive with Brandon, "Now hold on Brandon. You can't be saying this because everyone has been used at least one time by someone." Brandon answered Royston back, "Yes, but after a while, the game gets old as you get older you than began to get tired." Royston said, "Oh--I see Mr. Bright is slapping down his chasing women game, huh?" Brandon responded to Royston, "Say man, when will enough be enough for you.... when you realize that you're not worth it anymore and nobody wants you?" Royston became aggressive, "Listen here Brandon, you may have had all the beautiful women and you may have played your game, but don't go around dogging on one who hasn't experienced it yet." Still calm and reserved, Brandon said, "That's my point. You'll never understand it because you can't even understand yourself, player...player." Brandon continued to smooth his body with peppered lemon and lime scented lotion. Exuding sandalwood and musk, Brandon walked back into the bathroom lathering his face with shaving cream of the same aroma. Brandon put his cell phone, which is mounted on the wall in the bathroom, on speakerphone. Brandon picked up his white gold electric razor and began to shave. Brandon and Royston kept talking about women. Royston is still fired up about Brandon's comments and tried to explain to Brandon that one doesn't change his mind in a day and decide to stop chasing women. Brandon said, "It's a habit that can be broken--but it will take some time." Brandon understood where Royston is coming from, but if a man isn't raised on playing mind games with women, than dating women may become a little easier to that man. Royston said, "What does upbringing have to do with anything? And where did that come from? I wasn't getting prudish with you." Brandon said, "See, if a man is raised with good morals, yes he might want to play the game, but in actuality his shallow intentions are just temporary. The man would definitely know that playing games could get someone hurt." Royston said, "I'm trying to understand you--Brandon. So what you're saying is that if someone is raised by a single parent that would make a difference too?" Brandon replied, "No, because one parent can train children as well as two parents can." Royston explained, "It's up to that man; whenever he feels he's ready to stop playing mind game, he'll stop. But on the other hand, if a man never seeks healing, then he'll never know when to stop. Man, Brandon, you have some deep issues going on with you. So you just gave up because it's not right? Brandon replied, "Royston, now you're talking. Besides, who wants to keep playing an old love game over and over again until you've proved yourself to be wrong each time?" Brandon continued, "You know, back in history that game sounded good--but it ended up killing thousands and tearing families apart. Men have—and continue to--use and abuse women because they are angry with themselves." Royston said, "Brandon, I have to hand it to you, being a player does get old; some of these young wannabe smooth talking men have a lot to learn." Royston added, "You know, I'm wondering if some of those men could picture their own daughters receiving this abusive treatment. Man Brandon, what's really going on in today's society? Speak to me please." Brandon said, "Listen Royston. Man, I'm not sure about other men, but I know Brandon Bright is done and done for good playing mind games with women. Brandon continued, "Hey Royston, I would love to finish chatting with you but I have some business to take care of. I'll talk with you some other time or when I see you at work." Royston answered, "Yeah, well thanks for your advice Brandon--and just because you quit playing mind games, doesn't mean you have to lose your charm for the ladies." Brandon laughed, telling Royston he'll be sure and keep it. Brandon released his cell phone conversation from Royston and dialed Roselita's number.

Roselita answered, "This is Roselita."

Brandon said, "This is Brandon."

Roselita continued, "Hi! How are you, Brandon?" Brandon sensed a warm welcome. "I'm doing well--and what about the lovely Miss Macalaonez?" Roselita was in the kitchen stirring the tomato-basil sauce for the sausage, thyme and rosemary ravioli when chills went through her body. Roselita enjoyed Brandon's romantic talks with her, even though Roselita knew Brandon is playing around with her. Roselita responded in a skittish way, "I'm doing well." Still in a flirtatious mood, Brandon said, "Oh really? So is Miss Roselita Macalaonez ready to have company come over?" Roselita started screaming through her laptop telephone with anticipation saying, "Brandon you better not! Are you standing outside of my home again?" Brandon chuckled, "No, not this time. But I'll be there in fifteen minutes if you can keep the food hot until I come over."

Roselita almost fell to the floor. Roselita allowed herself to be caught up by Brandon's smooth talking. Brandon said, "Wait. But then again, it would be nice if a man could come inside instead of standing outside." Roselita said, "Brandon, are you serious?" Brandon said, "Okay... I'll stop and be serious. I'll be at your home in fifteen minutes--more like ten minutes now." Roselita began to get nervous because she felt Brandon is almost at her home. Brandon said, "Ah ha... I got you again, Roselita. Calm down, I haven't even put my clothes on yet." Roselita said, "Okay that's more than a woman needs to know--but not having any clothes on sounds good to me." Brandon said, "Now you see, I play an important role in your life because I said the same things to you on the night of the play you and I had attended at Chancellor Hall theatre." Roselita said, "Yes, I'm attentive--just as you are Mr. Bright." Brandon wanted to know what their evening would involve, so Roselita gave him a brief description of the dinner menu. Roselita said, "First, we meet and greet each other. Second, we have a toast to our lives. Third, we'll eat dinner--followed by Chocolate Mousse topped with a chocolate peppermint sauce and whipped cream." Brandon said, "Wait a moment woman--what's for dinner? You haven't said that yet, you just started with dessert." Roselita was caught up with the dessert. Roselita forgot to mention the main course. Roselita said, "Oh yes, let me back up and start at the main course. We are having sausage, basil, thyme and rosemary ravioli with a basil-garlic marinara sauce, toasted garlic Panini and grilled parmesan chicken salad topped with croutons and raisins, served with olive oil balsamic vinaigrette. We'll be drinking a smooth red wine from Sisal's Vineyard. Brandon, overcome by the elegant evening he was anticipating, wanted to get over to Roselita's home quickly. Roselita ended the conversation, "Now that's all you need to know." In a baritone voice that made Roselita quiver, Brandon said, "Ah, mi Amor, Roselita." (Ah, my love Roselita) Roselita had no idea that Brandon could speak eight languages. Brandon is able to speak in these languages; English, French, German, Portuguese, Somali, Spanish, Greek, and Australian. Roselita spoke only English, but from time to time, Roselita would test the Spanish that she had learned in college. Roselita swooned, saying, "Okay how about this: let me see if you could guess what I'm saying Brandon, "Por favor venir mi Amor." (Please come my love) Brandon's laughter sounded carefree and full-hearted as Brandon said "Eso fue excelente Miss Macalaonez. Yo, Amor Como tienes habló español" (That is very good Miss. Macalaonez. I love how you spoke Spanish) Brandon is thrilled that Roselita knew some Spanish also. Roselita continued talking through the intercom of her laptop as Roselita finished preparing dinner. Roselita is wearing a white diamond necklace and matching bracelet. Roselita's shoes are black one-inch mules showing off Roselita's French pedicure toenails. Her nails had a French manicure. Roselita's translucent make-up revealed her smooth skin. Roselita's hair was styled elegantly. Roselita lit a honey-almond, and a spicy nutmeg and cinnamon candle. Roselita placed a white and orange rose bouquet on the table as a centerpiece. Roselita pulled out her gold-trimmed china, wine glasses, and her formal flatware and placed each piece carefully on the table. Roselita then returned to her kitchen island and sliced fresh lemons, which she dropped into a crystal pitcher filled with filtered water. Roselita also stirred the sauce and checked on the bread and the chicken salad. Roselita kept the salad chilled in a bowl of ice, which remained in the refrigerator until dinner is ready to be served. In the meantime, Roselita paced back and forth; making sure the kitchen was spotless. Roselita rinsed her hands as Roselita took a final look around. Roselita left the kitchen and walked towards the living room, stopping by her guest bathroom to check herself in the mirror. Roselita fluffed her hair with her right hand and smiled at herself, showing her brilliant smile. After marveling at how beautiful she looked, Roselita turned off the bathroom light and walked over to her jazz CD collection in the living room. A fanatic of the smooth-jazz world, Roselita placed a Monte' CD in the player. The sound from her home theatre system created a live concert rhythm on the instrumental song, "Only Love." Roselita fluffed the pillows on the couch and sprayed the room with a soft mist of tropical rain room spray. Roselita walked back into the kitchen to complete the dinner. Roselita poured herself a glass of water, added a twist of lemon, and wondered to herself, "Why am I cooking a romantic dinner for Brandon Bright and myself?" Knowing that Brandon was just a close friend and remembering that he hadn't asked her to date him, Roselita felt whatever was going on between the two of them would work itself out later, down the road. Roselita turned the stove down, allowing the food to simmer. Then the telephone rang; it was her mother calling to see how she was doing. Roselita answered, "Hello Macalaonez and Macalaonez Express.

How may I help you?" Mrs. Macalaonez responded playfully, "Ah, yes I'm looking for a pretender named Miss Roselita Macalaonez?" Roselita was surprised by her mother's comical talk. Mrs. Macalaonez continued, "I'm just calling to check up on my daughter." Roselita said, "I'm doing well--just waiting for Brandon to show up." Mrs. Macalaonez is lost in amazement. "Baby what do you mean you are waiting on Brandon to come over?" Roselita forgot that once her mother started lecturing, there was no stopping her, especially if it pertained to Brandon Bright. Mrs. Macalaonez loved Brandon dearly. She had been waiting for him to ask her daughter Roselita to marry him. Roselita said, "Mother, Brandon has been having a hard time at work. He had to terminate a co-worker." Mrs. Macalaonez said, "I understand baby, but what does his problem have to do with you?" Roselita became defensive over Brandon. She explained to her mother the purpose of the evening she had planned for the two of them. "Mother, I just felt it would be nice to cook Brandon dinner and let him know that no matter what he faces in life, he always has me as a friend." Mrs. Macalaonez didn't accept her daughter's reason for having an evening to show appreciation for his friendship. Roselita was upset with her mother but she knew that her anger wouldn't last. "Mother yes, I'm cooking Brandon dinner to reinforce our friendship." Mrs. Macalaonez said, "Now let me get this clear—you're cooking Brandon a romantic dinner because he's under pressure from work and you appreciate having him in your life?" Roselita said, "Yes mother. Is that a problem? Or are you trying to make it a problem?" Mrs. Macalaonez continued, "Hum. Seems like this is a touchy subject for a thirty-eight year old woman named Roselita Macalaonez who, it appears, is in love with Brandon Bright, her close friend of fourteen years." Roselita realizes how she over reacts at times; she knows where her behavior comes from. Roselita had hoped that she could breakthrough to her mother, but felt she needed more time to conBrandon her mother. Instead of going over and over this topic, Roselita changed the subject. "Mother, how is Hayman doing?" Mrs. Macalaonez answered, "He is doing well. Stop trying to move the topic away from Brandon Bright and you." Roselita knew she couldn't reason with her mother so Roselita told her exactly what she wanted to hear. Roselita said, "Okay, so Brandon is coming over to dinner because I'm interested in him. I've been interested in him since the first day we met at Constitutes Law Firm." Mrs. Macalaonez voice shot up an octave; you could hear glee surge through the telephone. Mrs. Macalaonez said, "Now see there, I knew you'd come around to giving me a better explanation." Roselita knew her mother had the upper hand; her mother was very intelligent and could tell when she didn't get the full scoop. Roselita sighed and mumbled, "I will say anything just so she'll get off the telephone--that was smart thinking on my part." Mrs. Macalaonez advised her daughter to allow Brandon to decide when he's ready for a committed relationship. Roselita took her mother's advice and wished her a good night. Just as she placed the telephone on its cradle, the doorbell rang. Roselita quickly glanced around the house, making sure everything was intact. Then she walked to the front door and spied through the peephole. Roselita saw Brandon holding a boutique of flowers, looking good as usual. Brandon is dressed splendidly in a "MV" designer black suit that accentuated his gray shirt and matching black and gray polka dot tie. Brandon's name is engraved on his dazzling cuff links. Brandon newly shaved face glowed with a handsome smile. When Roselita finally opened the door, Brandon wanted to embrace Roselita, but he kept his composure and instead just marveled Roselita's beauty. Roselita was enthralled with his masculine scent of cedar, leather and peppercorn. Roselita noticed that his black and white gold designer wristwatch matched his outfit. Brandon still wanted to feel the comfort of her softness pressed against his body; his heart raced a mile ahead of his mind, tempted by her sweet perfume. Roselita told him to have a seat in the living room while she added a special touch to the table arrangement. As Brandon took a seat on the plush down sofa, he looked around; noticing the romantic atmosphere Roselita had created for the evening. Brandon said, "It smells wonderful in here--I can't wait to eat." Roselita rushed into the kitchen and leaned on the refrigerator door, swooning over how good Brandon looked. Roselita collected herself and walked back into the living room, smiling as she said, "You look nice Mr. Bright. Dinner is ready when you're hungry." Brandon thanked her for the compliment and added, "You look radiant yourself. Everything looks great." Brandon didn't know what else to say, he was so caught up in the moment. Brandon repeated himself, "Yes, Miss Macalaonez you're stunning also." Roselita laughed a little hysterically, saying, "Thank you." She sat on the sofa next to him as they silently stared into each other brown eyes, as if they were two children meeting for the first time. Roselita finally stood up and put a CD into the music player. The soothing sounds of jazz filled her entire home. When Roselita again joined Brandon on the sofa, he told her how magnificent she made her home look and asked what would happen next. Roselita was so mesmerized by his appearance that she had forgotten to ask if he wanted something to drink. Before he could answer, his cell phone rang. Brandon wondered who was calling to interrupt this lovely evening with a radiant woman. Roselita's eyes flared as she also wondered who was intruding on their special evening. Brandon took the call. "Hello, this is Brandon." Without checking his caller ID, he heard a woman's voice. Brandon didn't recognize the voice, so he continued to talk. "This is Brandon Bright. How may I help you?" The woman said, "I'm calling to apologize for my behavior." Brandon still didn't know whom this voice belonged to, so he checked his caller ID The name showed up as Unknown. The woman finally said, "This is Jilla Handsberg, how are you?" Brandon finally realized it was Jilla. He thought he had gotten rid of her, but she still had his home phone number. After two rings, Brandon's home calls are forwarded to his cell phone. Being a gentleman, he didn't hang up on her but instead continued to speak with her. Roselita threw both of her hands in the air shook her head and said, "I don't believe this ... that deranged woman just doesn't get it, does she?" Brandon continued talking to Jilla while Roselita walked towards the kitchen, still shaking her head in dismay. Roselita wanted to grab his cell phone. Instead, she kept her cool and ignored them both; Roselita felt Jilla needed a mental institution. Brandon said, "Thank you Jilla, but I'm busy right now and I would appreciate it if you wouldn't call this number anymore." Jilla's voice trembled as she sensed Brandon wasn't in the mood to talk to her. She decided that no matter what, she wasn't going to give up on him. Jilla felt that deep down inside, Brandon wanted her. Jilla assumed Brandon was just too scared to admit that he needed some time to think things over and that after a while; he'd be ready to fall passionately in love with her. Jilla said, "Brandon, I know things haven't been the best between us. I know that I smothered you too much—that's why I'm calling to apologize." Brandon became aggravated because Jilla didn't understand that he didn't want anything to do with her. Brandon now agreed with Roselita, Yamilla, Lucinda, Myann, his mother, Mrs. Macalaonez, Royston and his supervisor, that Jilla needed to be hospitalized. Brandon sensed her loneliness, desperation, hurt, discontentment and jealousy, and knew Jilla just wanted to be loved. Brandon saw that Jilla is an older woman in search of a man, not willing to wait for a man to find her. Brandon guessed that Jilla was scarred by many years of rejection and torn relationships and that she would attach herself to the first man who showed her affection. Brandon wanted a renewed woman who could overcome her past failures -- not a woman with emotional baggage. Brandon thanked Jilla for her concerns and said, "Jilla, this has to end here. I'm sorry if you've wanted more than a business relationship." Then Jilla said, "Brandon, I know you love me just as much as I love you. I'm not going to let you get away from me that easily." Roselita came from the kitchen and stood in the living room, staring at Brandon. She gestured that would be pointless to try to reason with a confused woman who needed professional help. Roselita knew that Brandon was a gentleman who didn't want to hurt Jilla; he would try to let her down easy. Roselita grew more frustrated as Brandon kept talking to Jilla. Hoping to end the ridiculous phone conversation, Roselita schemed to make sure Jilla could hear her talking to Brandon in the background. Roselita shouted, "Brandon honey, your dinner is ready!" Roselita smiled at him and Brandon returned the smile. To Roselita's surprise, instead of hanging up, Jilla snapped at Brandon, saying, "Brandon you said you were busy ... but not with some woman!" Now Brandon began to get impatient. He said, "You know, I don't have to tell you my whereabouts. You and I aren't in a relationship so I owe you nothing." Brandon continued, "Listen Jilla, I'm going to do both of us a favor." Jilla interrupted him, "Brandon, so you do care about me!" Brandon knew he didn't love her but wanted Jilla to get professional help. Brandon said, "You know what Jilla? I think we could make this work. I'll tell you what--tomorrow I'm going to take you to a special place, a place you'll love." Roselita raised one eyebrow and glared at Brandon, wondering why he was filling Jilla's head with lies. Jilla bubbled with hope and told Brandon she didn't care if he was busy with another woman, she knew he was all hers. Brandon hung up his cell phone and said to Roselita, "I know you are upset with me for what I have said to Jilla about tomorrow, but I need you to work with me on this one, please." Roselita raised one eyebrow at Brandon and said, "Now just what kind of plan, do you have for Miss Jilla Handsberg if you don't care to be bothered with her?" Brandon said, "It's definitely not a love thing here ... not ... that I don't care for her, you have understand I know Jilla is mentally insane--but this is why you and I are going to help take care of this issue." Roselita wanted to know what Brandon has planned for Jilla; Roselita also wanted to know why Brandon has a suspicious smirk on his face. Brandon said, "Roselita, I'm going to tell Jilla to pack some clothes for a couple of weeks, allowing her to think she'll be spending some quality time with me." Roselita raised both eyebrows this time and said, "Okay Mr. Clever, what if your plan doesn't work and she refuses to follow your resolute planning?" Brandon laughed, "Once again Miss Macalaonez, you have lost your trust in me. Right now I need your support, but you keep on doubting that this won't work." Roselita said, "No, I'm just thinking that it's a big step to get Jilla to pack two weeks' worth of clothing. Especially when your plans consist of being longer then you intend it to be." Brandon said, "Okay, I'm talking about having her stay--but whatever the issue, I need you to help me out." Finally Roselita gave Brandon a supportive look as she slowly removed her raised eyebrow from her face. Roselita agreed to help Brandon if he told Jilla the truth. They walked to the kitchen, forgetting their plan about checking Jilla Handsberg into mental institution. In the kitchen, Brandon could smell the dinner simmering. He adored Roselita's lovely beige and black table arrangement. Brandon followed Roselita over to the stove where he stood directly behind her. Roselita's heart sped as Brandon leaned forward, placing his arm underneath hers to help her stir the tomato sauce. Roselita closed her eyes, imagining Brandon holding and caressing her with his strong hands. Roselita imagined Brandon gently kissing her perfumed neck and then her lips. She allowed her mind to wander freely, envisioning both of them embracing for hours until the sun rose. Brandon noticed that Roselita was overcome by his gentle touch so he stepped back walked towards the dining room table and left her to relish the sweetness of love; it seemed as if Roselita was long overdue to be held. Roselita kept her head tilted and her eyes closed while enraptured by her own fantasies of Brandon loving her. Brandon sat at the table, amused at how she was caught up in her own dreamland. Brandon didn't say a word. Instead, Brandon watched Roselita tilt her head from one side to the other as Roselita smiled happily. Placing her hands on the counter, Roselita continued to smile with her eyes; closed thinking Brandon is still standing behind her. Brandon wanted to laugh hysterically but he sat there watching her emotions run freely. Suddenly Roselita's laptop rang. Roselita opened her eyes as Brandon burst out laughing, "I was wondering how long you would drift in Roselita's own world of happiness." Roselita threw a dishtowel at Brandon as she answered the telephone. "Good evening. This is Macalaonez and Macalaonez Express." The voice on the other end laughed. It was her brother Troy. He is surprised to hear his sister answer the telephone with that greeting. Roselita's brother Troy overheard a man's voice in the background laughing and he wondered why Roselita answered her laptop telephone as if she were running a company. Troy said, "Hey sister, what kind of greeting is that? I see you want your own business someday." Roselita angrily said, "No, silly. I always answer the phone like this in case someone unfamiliar calls." Roselita continued, "Remember I live alone so I have to be careful at night. You know, there are perverted men out there who sometimes get a kick out of hearing a woman answer the telephone." Troy agreed with his sister, "Yes, you're right. That's why it's my job to call often to check-up on you and make sure you're all right. From the sounds of it, I don't need to ask if you are all right--it seems some other male is already taking care of you." Roselita laughed, "Troy, don't be silly. That's Brandon you hear laughing at me." Troy said, "Well in that case, let me stop talking with you. I truly understand that Brandon is taking the place of your big brother; Brandon seems to have things under control at your place." Troy then put all joking aside, saying, "Well at least you've learned well from what Mother taught you about answering the telephone when a man isn't in the home." Roselita calmed down as she softened her voice. Roselita could feel her heartbeat return to normal after Troy's sense of humor riled her. "Troy, I would love to chit-chat with you, but I don't want to keep my company waiting too long." Troy started teasing her again. "Well excuse me for ruining your romantic, lustful, desperate and sizzling hot evening with Mr. Sexy Love, Brandon Bright." Troy knew his sister Roselita barely went on dates, so Troy told Roselita to tell Brandon that he said,

"What's happening?" Roselita answered, "Yes, now disappear." Just before she could hang up the phone, Troy said, "Listen here. You need to stop getting smart with me, Miss. Macalaonez, or I'll come over there and destroy your so-called romantic evening with Brandon." Roselita knew Troy loved being the older one. Roselita ignored his comment as she said, "Brandon ... Troy says 'Hi.' Okay Mr. Troy, off the telephone now. I am wasting my evening by talking with you." Roselita resumed talking to Brandon, "Now what was I doing?" Brandon said, "You were caught up in a wonderful moment that took you to your own Fantasy Island." They laughed as they discussed Roselita's reactions to his help in the kitchen. Roselita placed everything on the table as Brandon pulled her chair out for her to sit down. Then Brandon took his seat. Roselita asked if Brandon could bless the food. They held hands, bowed their heads, and closed their eyes. Brandon said, "Thank you Lord for this tremendous meal that you have allowed Miss Roselita Macalaonez to prepare and thank you for the hands that touch it. Bless us both and don't allow things to get heated physically after we enjoy this meal." Roselita opened one of her eyes as she looked up slightly and wished he'd take back what he said about lovemaking. Roselita acknowledged her lustful thoughts. Roselita whispered a quick silent prayer to herself: "Lord, allow us to enjoy our meal and help me to keep my mind focused. But Lord, Brandon is too good-looking not to be touched--why now and why tonight?" Roselita went back to listening to Brandon pray as he concluded, "Amen ... shall we eat?" Roselita served Brandon the ravioli with tomato sauce. She placed a slice of garlic Panini on his plate with the tossed salad. Brandon poured the wine while they both enjoyed their elegant evening. Brandon asked Roselita if she was okay alone with him--or if she felt like she would explode in his presence. Brandon wasn't ready to take their friendship to the next level, which meant being serious. Roselita longed for his stroke, wanting his commitment to her--but she knew that only time would tell when the timing would be right for them. They talked throughout the night while eating dinner--including Chocolate mousse fluff for dessert--followed by a movie on Satellite television. It is three o'clock a.m. when Brandon stood up from the sofa, put on his suit jacket, and slipped his shoes on. Roselita gave him a sad face and wanted him to stay longer, but Roselita knew if he did, things would heat up.

Roselita felt the moment was perfect to let Brandon know how she really felt about him, but instead she kept her comments to herself. Brandon wanted to kiss her and make love to her, but he knew he would risk his chances of truly loving her, so he resisted and instead left her with fond memories. Brandon said, "Well, Miss Macalaonez, thank you for the scrumptious dinner and dessert. I have enjoyed spending quality time with you. We must do this again." Brandon kissed Roselita on the left side of her cheek and then exited her front door. Roselita closed the door behind her and leaned against it, awestruck after spending what she felt was her best evening with Brandon Bright. Roselita stood there for a moment or two, picturing them as a couple. Roselita could imagine how perfect her life could be, if only she wouldn't suppress her true feelings. Roselita realized that sooner or later, Brandon might become curious and wonder why she behaves mysteriously at times.

CHAPTER FOUR

Roselita closed her eyes and remembered how they have grown attached to each other. Roselita felt she and Brandon should be dating after fourteen-years of having a good friendship. Roselita envisioned spending quality time traveling around the world with Brandon. Roselita hadn't loved anyone else as much as she loved Brandon Bright. Roselita always felt that she and Brandon belonged together but were too afraid to let their feelings show. Day in and day out Roselita longed for her and Brandon to be a couple and get married.

* * *

Friday Morning has arrived it is nine o'clock a.m. at Jack's Plaza Hotel, Gordon Gem said, "Good morning everyone. We have a busy day, so let's get started." Gordon was walking nervously, checking on the details of his conference when he received a telephone call. His secretary, Katie who appeared to be five-nine with short black hair, walked swiftly at Gordon's side. Katie is dressed in a beige and black skirt suit and carrying a striped yellow note pad. Gordon walked tall and gracefully while his secretary Katie jotted down his instructions. Katie carried a cell phone and took all business and personal calls while Gordon planned the details for his conference. All of a sudden the cell phone rang. Katie answered, "Good morning, Gordon Gem's office how may I help you." Brandon Bright was calling to inform Gordon that he was running five minutes late. Gordon's secretary

Katie took Brandon's message as she continued to walk down the hallway. A concierge said, "Excuse me, Mr. Gem. You have some guests who are down in the lobby waiting to meet with you." Gordon thanked the concierge and started walking towards the elevator with his secretary, who was still writing as she followed him. Gordon pressed the down button as he continued to talk; Katie wrote more instructions on the tablet. The elevator door opened, Gordon pressed L for the lobby, and the elevator moved slowly down from the fifth floor to the fourth, third, and then second floor where it stopped for more people. Gordon moved over to make more room for a fetching full-figured woman with golden brown hair sleeked and pulled back into a tidy bun. She is wearing a sophisticated business suit jacket with a gigantic black flower pinned on the top of her left shoulder. Her face glowed, showing off her nut-brown skin. She smiled demurely at Gordon and shifted her eyes towards the floor of the elevator. Gordon smiled and said, "Hello my name is Gordon Gem. I'm holding a "Build Your Future" financial networking conference on the fifth floor. It would be nice if you could stop by. Here is a ticket." The woman looked up, thanked Gordon, as she continued to wait for the elevator to stop on the floor she wanted. Gordon smiled at her with his signature smile; after speaking with the woman Gordon made sure he looked into her eyes as left her with a pleasing smile. The elevator finally stopped as the woman had gotten off. The woman kept smiling as she walked with confidence, knowing that Gordon had her attention. Gordon joined the other conference speakers in the lobby. Everyone greeted Gordon, who is the conference host with a warm welcome. Mr. Gem's secretary Katie had stopped taking notes when she walked over to the check-in desk. Katie handed the receptionist a paper with a list of names and instructions. As Katie turned around to meet up with Gordon Gem and his guests, Brandon saw her. Katie smiled, "Ah, Mr. Bright. So glad you could make it. Mr. Gem is expecting you." Brandon kissed her on her cheek and smiled at her. Brandon approached Gordon, who was seated with his guest. Gordon said, "Ah yes, speaking of Brandon Bright, here is the man who started it all." Gordon stood as he introduced Brandon to his guest and they all took a seat in the lobby. After Gordon conducted a quick meeting, his secretary Katie walked toward the elevators to finish taking care of business. Gordon and Brandon chatted some more; Gordon wanted Brandon on his panel to discuss excellence at Constitutes Law Firm. Gordon wanted to promote Constitutes Law Firm for those in need of legal assistance. Gordon had reserved a suite, including room service breakfast, for Brandon on the twenty-second floor. Gordon told Brandon to call him at his suite two floors up on the twenty-fifth floor if he needed anything. When Gordon and Brandon entered the room, the hotel staff was still setting up tables draped in white linen. In another room, a disc jockey was setting up his equipment when he noticed Gordon and Brandon entering the room. He called over to Gordon, "Hey, Mr. Gem, tonight is the night and the party starts out right!" Gordon waved his hand to the jockey, laughing while rhythm and blues filled the room with smooth grooves. Gordon patted Brandon on the back and said, "This is where you can meet some beautiful women who want to have a good time." Brandon smiled as both men checked out the preparations. A man approached both men, handed Gordon a bag, and shouted above the music, "GOOD MORNING MR. GEM! THIS IS THE BAG FOR THE DRAWING FOR A NEW CAR." Gordon said, "YOU DON'T HAVE TO SHOUT, because I can hear you with the music blaring." The man lowered his voice, "I'm sorry for shouting at you sir." Gordon laughed in a husky voice, "There's no need to apologize--it's all right." Brandon chuckled at Gordon and the man's conversation. Gordon invited Brandon to follow him as they checked on the evening meal preparations in the kitchen. "Mm, it smells good in here," Gordon said as he walked around the kitchen. He and Brandon sampled the food, including the sumptuous dessert Gordon smiled and said, "Man this is wonderful! Everything is looking good my man. Soon it'll be show time!" Agreeing with an assuring smile, Brandon said, "Gordon, I must say you put on a spectacular conference." Gordon agreed, "Man this is only half of how I like to party. I love to go out in style." They shared a laugh and Gordon added, "Well Brandon, I'm sure you want to relax in your suite before we get started later." As Brandon walked towards the elevators, his cell phone rang. "Hello this is Brandon Bright. How may I help you?" The voice on the other end is his mother's. Mrs. Bright said, "By telling me you're going to marry that woman named Roselita Macalaonez." Brandon threw back his head and let out a great peal of laughter, "Why, hello mother, and how are you doing?" Mrs. Bright said, "I'm doing well. So have you decided when to propose to that beautiful woman named Roselita Macalaonez?" Brandon continued laughing. He knew that he could count on his mother to cheer him up with her dry humor. Brandon said, "Mother, haven't we had this talk about my marriage proposal to Roselita before?" Mrs. Bright said, "Yes, and you are going to hear it again and again until you marry that precious woman!" Brandon mumbled, hoping his mother didn't hear him say, "I need to find a man for her so she'll leave me alone." Mrs. Bright said, "Brandon Roman Brown, I heard what you said! As a matter of fact, I have a man now. You need to find a woman you can settle down with!" Brandon knew he couldn't reason with his mother so he changed the subject, telling her that he was staying at Jack's Plaza hotel for three nights, courtesy of Gordon Gem the founder and owner of Gordon's Global Network Systems and E- Biz Web Design and Hosting Programming. Mrs. Bright was proud to hear that her son was keeping himself busy. Mrs. Bright reminded Brandon to stay focused on the Co-Slasher Murder case while speaking at Gordon's Conference. Mrs. Bright told Brandon again that she prayed he would remember to include Roselita in his marriage plans--she wanted nothing but the very best for her son. Brandon was the fourth oldest of eight and it was sometimes hard to get him to change his stubborn mind. The other line rang; it was Roselita. Brandon placed his mother on hold and told Roselita that he was talking to his mother and would call her back. Brandon clicked back over to his mother. Mrs. Bright said, "Brandon baby, I don't know about you, but sometimes you act like your stubborn father. Bless his soul as he lay in his grave." Brandon was tired of his mother always comparing him to his father. At times he could feel his mother's bitterness over the way his father treated her. Ever since his father died of cancer, Mrs. Bright took most of her frustration out on her sons. Brandon realized that his father could have improved in some areas of his life. After so many years, he hoped his mother would let go of the pain from the past. Brandon wanted his mother to live in the here and now. Unfortunately, Mrs. Bright always brought up painful memories targeting her sons, blaming all of her sons for being like their father. Brandon sometimes got angry as he tried to assert his innocence. Brandon never told his mother how he felt because he knew it would break her heart. So Brandon kept his anguish inside and only spoke comforting words, assuring his mother that everything would be all right. Brandon told his mother that someday he would settle down and marry--but marriage just isn't in his immediate plans. Mrs. Bright loved her son Brandon dearly as she said, "Baby, I understand. But don't wait too long because while you are sorting out your life's problems, someone else is watching for permission to snatch that precious woman from you." That's when Brandon thought about how he was going match his best friend Roselita Macalaonez with Gordon Gem. Mrs. Bright words blurred as Brandon realized that the one woman who was really for him was about to meet Gordon Gem and fall in love. This means if Brandon doesn't make his love interest towards Roselita soon. Gordon Gem could very well end up being the one married to Roselita Macalaonez. Brandon continued holding a conversation with his mother as Mrs. Bright said, "Baby, I can sense something is wrong--what's going on in that powerful brain of yours?"

Brandon didn't want his mother to be worried over his emotions. He said, "Nothing is wrong mother. I just forgot I needed to figure out what I'm going to speak about tonight, that's all." Mrs. Bright said, "Well, let me get off this phone so you can think. I love you and I'll talk with you later." Brandon told his mother he loved her as he disconnected the cell phone from his ear stepping into the elevator, pressing the button for the twenty-second floor. The elevator bell alerted him when he reached his floor. Brandon unlocked the door and walked into the room as the door automatically closed and locked behind him. Brandon placed his briefcase and suitcase near the desk in the room, checking out the amenities. Brandon walked into the bathroom and turned on the shower, allowing warm water to run and heat up the shower while he sat it on the bed. Brandon opened his suitcase and took out his "MV" travel kit with his shaving cream, toothpaste, toothbrush, shower gel and mouthwash. Brandon took off his clothes and stepped into the shower, allowing the warm water to run down his tapered short black hair and drip over his goatee. The water poured into his mouth as he grasped for air. Brandon reached for his "For Men Only" shower gel. Brandon squeezed the bottle working up a good lather with his hands. Brandon rubbed each curve of his manly body while thinking of Roselita. Brandon had wished Roselita could join him in the shower. However Brandon felt that would jeopardize their friendship. His thoughts became heavy as he envisioned holding Roselita and calling her his wife. Brandon reminisced about how close he and Roselita had become as he tried shaking Roselita from his thoughts as he showered. Yet Roselita's face appeared clearer and clearer! Brandon now realized that he longed for Roselita; he thought he might be lusting for her. Thoughts of Roselita now completely controlled him as Roselita's face stayed brightly in his mind. Brandon thought about everything his mother had ever said about settling down with Roselita as his perfect soul mate. Brandon didn't know why this was happening; he assumed his mother was probably right--he needed to think about settling down. Brandon needed to be monogamous instead of chasing after gold-digging women who only wanted to use him as a trophy. Brandon's head felt as if it was going to explode, so he finished showering. Brandon stepped out of the shower, drying his body and wrapping a towel around his waist. Brandon then lathered the shaving cream on his face and put toothpaste on his toothbrush. After brushing his dazzling teeth, he swished his mouth with mint-flavored mouthwash. Brandon smoothed his face with his electric razor and splashed it with aftershave cologne. After Brandon finished pampering himself, as he picked out his tailored suit for the evening. Brandon then walked over to the window, opened the blinds, and allowed the sunset to flood the room. With the remote control, he flipped on the sports channel and relaxed on the bed with the towel still wrapped around his waist. Cool air from the air conditioner dried Brandon off as he watched television. Room service interrupted his repose to ask if he wanted a wakeup call and breakfast. Brandon requested a wakeup call plus breakfast. Brandon then pulled out his law books and laptop as he began to work on the Co-Slasher murder case, until he felt sleepy. Brandon had gotten up from the table where he is working set the alarm clock for seven p.m. and pressed the snooze button. Brandon laid across the king sized bed, as he fell asleep; he began to dream of Roselita. Brandon saw himself on one knee, holding Roselita's left hand while placing a white gold engagement ring on it. Brandon pictured Roselita standing in amazement. Brandon could hear Roselita say in his dream "Oh, Brandon thank you! This is what I have longed for and now my dream has come true!" As Roselita kissed Brandon she would proclaim, "Yes I would love to be your wife ... Mrs. Roselita Bright." Brandon smiled in his sleep as the two of them danced, celebrating their eternal love. Brandon saw the joy in his mother's face as she affirmed that her son chose the right wife. All seven brothers making Brandon number eight would fete his proposal to Roselita Macalaonez. Her mother, Mrs. Macalaonez, soon to be stepfather Hayman, and brother Troy would also join the festive affair. Brandon pictured himself at the altar standing tall, wearing a "MV" designer suit with his hands clasped in front of him. His brother would stand next to him awaiting the blushing bride. Brandon saw his mother dressed in a Ping Wong designer dress, wiping tears of joy while the other guest patiently awaited Roselita's entrance. Brandon glanced over at Roselita's mother the soon to be Mrs. Macalaonez-Rome showing excitement on her face. Brandon felt he couldn't have picked a better woman; Brandon knew he made the right choice. Brandon smiled at the Reverend as his hands became sweaty. Brandon couldn't be any more nervous. His best man, Royston Friends, gave him a handkerchief to wipe his brow. The next time he looked out at the crowd, everyone stood as the doors to the sanctuary opened. Brandon's heartbeat raced as if he were running for a marathon. His eyes filled with tears when he saw how radiant Roselita looked. His heart feel at peace when he saw the four flower girls waltz in front of the bride, each one dropping pink rose pedals on the carpet of the church. Brandon wondered why it took so long for him to make this unforgettable decision. Brandon could see the triumph on Roselita's soon to be stepfather Hayman's face as he walked Roselita in. Brandon could feel his pulse rising as Hayman kissed Roselita before joining Roselita's hand to Brandon. Before Hayman sat down, he shook Brandon's hand and said, "Roselita is finally all yours, enjoy my man." The ceremony continued as Brandon and Roselita exchanged vows and rings. At the reception, Brandon's best man, Royston Friends, told the story of how Roselita could have been his at the Entrepreneur's Ball that Brandon, Roselita and He attended awhile back. But God had other plans that flourished into something worthwhile; his buddy, Brandon Bright, was meant to have the most beautiful woman." Everyone laughed as Royston wished the newlyweds the best in life. The music played as the disc jockey called everyone to the dance floor for the newlywed's first dance together. The wedding party then invited their guests to join them in dancing the night away, surrounded by people they loved. Brandon slipped deeper into his dream as he saw them open the door to the new five-bedroom home they bought for their growing family. While Roselita had quit working for Welcome News Express to become a stay-at-home mother and entrepreneur, Brandon continued working at Constitutes Law Firm. Brandon is eligible to be promoted for the company's CEO position when his supervisor retired. This meant that Nadine would become Brandon's secretary. Nadine married her son's father and then they had a little girl. Brandon felt everyone was now happy with his or her life except one person. Brandon wondered how Jilla Handsberg is doing after he put her into a mental institution. Brandon was about to go deeper into his dream when he heard beep, beep, and beep ... it was the alarm clock alerting him that it was time to get ready for the first night of Gordon Gem's conference. Brandon placed his bare feet on the carpet next to the bedside and stood to get himself dressed. Brandon's cell phone rang. It was Roselita calling to see how things were going for him. Brandon talked with her for a few minutes until he was completely dressed. Brandon promised to a call Roselita later. Brandon turned off the lights in his hotel room as the door closed and locked behind him. Brandon walked over to the elevator and waited for the elevator to arrive at his floor. Brandon stepped it to an elevator filled to capacity with people who were also attending the conference. The bell rang as the door of the elevator opened and people quickly stepped off, walking towards the ballroom. At the entrance, Brandon saw Gordon's private room. Gordon's secretary Katie came over to him as she directed Brandon to the VIP room. When Katie and Brandon entered the VIP room, Gordon was chatting away with some other VIP's as his secretary Katie and Brandon walked up to him. Katie said, "Excuse me Mr. Gem, here's Mr. Bright." Brandon turned to thank Gordon's secretary Katie for the escort as she walked out of the room, leaving Brandon to get acquainted with some of Gordon's closest friends from over the years of partnering with him. Gordon talked and laughed as he introduced Brandon to them, Brandon smiled as he greeted everyone. Gordon then walked Brandon over to some beautiful women who were standing around chatting as well. Gordon informed Brandon that he could have anyone of those women as he leaned over to whisper to Brandon saying, "They are all single and have no children, and they range from thirty to fifty years old." Brandon gave Gordon a smile, but deep inside he didn't find any of them to be interesting. Gordon walked away, leaving Brandon to explore them. One of the women approached Brandon as he said, "Good evening?" She smiled, giving Brandon a sharp seductive stare and returned his greeting, "Good evening." Brandon felt, "Here we go again." Brandon knew he couldn't go through with meeting another woman--and he surely didn't want to deal with another Jilla Handsberg. Brandon introduced himself as the woman made sure she is appealing to him, hoping that her seduction was working on him. Brandon sensed she was coming on too strong, so he immediately backed away from her by excusing himself as he quickly walked to the other side of the room. While Brandon stood on the other side, a waiter walked passed with a platter of hors'd oeuvres. Brandon picked up a small plate from the platter with shrimp cocktail on it. While Brandon stood there eating the food, he noticed another attractive woman looking in his direction. After eating the shrimp cocktail, Brandon pulled out some breath mints. Brandon stood attentively and gave the woman a macho walk, showing his sternness as both of his arms swayed back and forth. Brandon introduced himself, "Good evening, my name is Brandon Bright?" The woman stood five foot six inches wearing an extravagant citrus orange halter mini dress. The woman wore dazzling diamond matching orange open toed high heels, which showed, off her French pedicure. The woman batted her eyes, hoping that Brandon was single and available. The woman is over taken by his subdued voice that let her know that he was very interested in her. The woman said, "Nice to meet you Mr. Bright, my name is Sandy Rockwell." Brandon, now jubilant, felt this could be the one woman for him instead of Roselita. Brandon hadn't felt this way about a woman since he was in love with Roselita Macalaonez. He wasn't going to make any moves towards Roselita until he got a better opportunity to know this Sandy Rockwell woman. Brandon then extended his hand to shake Sandy Rockwell's. Just as they were greeting each other, Brandon couldn't help but notice Sandy Rockwell's irresistible perfume. The smell of Rose pedal powder filled his nostrils, causing him to drift away. Brandon knew that smelling a woman's perfume made him weak in the knees.

Brandon tried to stay focused. Brandon took a glass of Red pinot wine from the waiter as he passed by Brandon and Sandy Rockwell while they talked. Brandon asked Sandy Rockwell if this is the first time that she had attended one of Gordon Gem's conferences." Sandy Rockwell said, "Yes, and how about you? Is this your first time also?" Brandon answered, "Yes, this is my first time. Excuse me but if you don't mind me asking you, what do you expect to get out of this conference?" Sandy Rockwell laughed bashfully as she responded to his question. "Well, I own my own telecommunication company and I felt that Gordon would be able to give me some pointers on how to network by enhancing my technology." Brandon was stunned to hear how interested Sandy Rockwell was in expanding her company. Sandy Rockwell wanted to connect resources within other countries and make her business more successful. They continued to talk and share common interests by having Brandon lead most of the conversation. Just as the two of them Brandon Bright and Sandy Rockwell were getting to know each other, the conference is about to start. Everybody began to clear the private room while Brandon escorted Sandy Rockwell into the ballroom, which was filled to capacity. When Sandy Rockwell and Brandon Bright entered the ballroom, they saw Gordon holding the cordless microphone on stage, preparing to say something. "Good evening to everyone I'm so glad all of you wonderful people could make it to my sixth Annual Global Network Conference." Gordon smiled as he glanced at the crowd, noticing old acquaintances and new friends to make. "If some of you are wondering who I 'am, my name is Gordon Gem, the CEO and owner of Gordon Global Network, also E- Biz Web Design and Hosting Programming Welcome and enjoy the event." The audience applauded Gordon as he handed the microphone over to the Master of Ceremony for the evening. Gordon stepped off the stage and walked around greeting and meeting his guest. A woman on stage asked everyone if they could take their seats so they could get started discussing new techniques for their businesses. Gordon then left the room. Brandon and Sandy Rockwell took their seats as they sat next to each other. Sandy Rockwell pulled out an Eco-carbon paper notebook with Eco-embroidery on it. Sandy Rockwell also pulled out her Applet II computer tablet. Brandon looked over at her, "I'm astounded! At least someone came prepared." Sandy Rockwell gave

Brandon a surprising look as she said, "Oh. So you don't come prepared yourself?" As the evening progressed, Brandon and Sandy Rockwell stuck together, going from booth to booth and checking out the latest and greatest information. Brandon's cell phone rang. It was Roselita on the line, wanting to know how things were going so far at the conference. Brandon was having such a wonderful time with Sandy Rockwell that he wasn't in the mood to be talking with Roselita. Brandon politely informed Roselita that he would have to give her a call later because he was caught up in the moment of getting to know a woman by the name of Sandy Rockwell. Roselita pretended to be okay with Brandon talking to another woman other than her, but she felt like crying. Roselita felt she had put too much of her time into pleasing Brandon. Roselita's heart sank as if it were a ship, slowly sinking under pressure of its weight. Roselita wanted to know where she had gone wrong. All of sudden another woman could be replacing Roselita by dating Brandon Bright. Roselita became upset, knowing that Brandon had never missed the opportunity to talk with Roselita, no matter what he is doing. Roselita sensed this woman was going to take her close friend Brandon Bright from her. While laughter echoed in the background, Roselita heard blissful energy from Brandon as he told Roselita he would call her back later. Brandon's voice gave way to the exciting moment he was having enjoying the first day of the conference while meeting Sandy Rockwell. Roselita listened to Sandy Rockwell talk as Brandon quickly ended his conversation with Roselita so he could resume his attention back to Sandy Rockwell. Roselita then heard a click as she looked at her laptop telephone and said, "Oh, I know Brandon didn't just hang up on me without saying good-bye like that?" Roselita is now feeling hurt because she wanted to be more than just friends with Brandon, even though she tried to conBrandon herself that they were just friends. This shouldn't matter whom Brandon sees or wants to date. Roselita walked upstairs into her bedroom and entered the bathroom, filling the tub with warm water and lighting scented candles. Roselita put on some jazz as she placed her left foot in the tub followed by her right foot. Roselita slid her body into the warm water, resting her head on the pillow made just for the bathtub. Roselita began to wonder what went wrong again. Why was she so overtaken by Brandon? Roselita closed her eyes, allowing the water to relax her body while the aroma of the scented candles eased her startled mind. Roselita saw her life flash before her eyes, thinking about what her mother had said to her about Brandon Bright. Roselita then pictured Brandon's mother, Mrs. Bright, telling Roselita how much her son Brandon had always loved Roselita and that Brandon wanted to marry her but was too scared to let Roselita know the truth. Roselita could envision her brother Troy James saying that she would be silly if she waited around praying, wanting Brandon to be her husband. Roselita heard both of her grandparents Mr. and Mrs. Goldstone, plus her step father Hayman say to her sometimes when you're looking for love its right in front of you; just don't ignore what your heart beats for. Roselita then opened her eyes and she looked up towards the ceiling saying, "Lord, would you please give me a sign or tell me what's happening between Brandon Bright and me? Why have I been feeling this way? I understand that it isn't lust but what you desire for me to have as my husband." Roselita quickly opened up her eyes for a moment then she closed them again as she saw Brandon's face flash before her. Roselita saw Brandon standing at the altar, looking handsome as always dressed in a "MV" designer tuxedo. Standing next to Brandon is his best man, his buddy Royston Friends who once tried to date her. Roselita imaged her mother and brother along with her relatives and friends waiting the joyous occasion. Roselita saw everyone stand as the church became quiet. The big beige doors to the sanctuary opened as Roselita stood holding her step father Hayman's arm. Roselita was wearing an exclusive sleeveless flared white gown with a vintage open back. Roselita saw herself walking down the aisle gracefully as she smiled, showing the whiteness of her teeth. Standing at the altar waiting to make her the new Mrs. Bright was Brandon. Roselita noticed his handsome features. Roselita was breath taken by his five-ten height, his raven hair and darkened goatee. His tuxedo was tailored to perfection in her favorite colors: black with a gray shirt matching the wedding colors. His cuff links matched his suit and his handkerchief was neatly tucked into the pocket of his tuxedo jacket. Roselita could hear herself mumble the words "Lord, thank you for blessing me with this good looking Toffee man. Roselita continued, "Thank you for allowing me to wait; even though it took years, Brandon is finally my husband." Roselita made it to the altar as her face continued to light up as if it were the Fourth of July and the fireworks were exploding. Roselita felt nervous as she clinched harder, holding Hayman's arm and causing the blood supply to slow down. Hayman lifted her veil, gently kissing her cheek as he released her arm and took her hand and joined it with Brandon's hand. The wedding ceremony turned out as lovely as Roselita had imaged. When Roselita finally opened her eyes, she realizing she was dreaming. Roselita finished bathing. As Roselita stepped out of the bathtub to dry off, all Roselita could do was think about how Brandon would never have refused to talk with her for any reason. For this one reason, Brandon didn't want to talk with her because he was too busy enjoying the warm, windy evening at Gordon Gem's Conference. Roselita knew she and Brandon weren't dating each other but she felt that their friendship made it feel that way. Roselita left the bathroom walked back into the bedroom and lay across her oversized bed with her body positioned on her back and her face looking up at her ceiling. A tear rolled down as Roselita released her emotions, thinking it was her fault for being too pushy with Brandon. Roselita erased that feeling, realizing that she didn't need to blame herself for Brandon not wanting her. Roselita stood up from the bed as she began to pace back and forth, thinking of how she was going to fix this problem. Roselita felt that just because one man didn't work doesn't mean there isn't another man out there waiting to marry her. Roselita felt there could be a billion more men in this world willing to be her friend and wanting to marry her. Roselita had questions and was looking for answers. Roselita wanted to know what Sandy Rockwell had going for herself that Sandy Rockwell drew Brandon's attention to her. Roselita wondered if this other woman had a bigger chest than her. Is this woman smaller or taller? Did the woman have long or short hair? Is the woman fat or skinny? Is the woman attractive or unattractive? Roselita paced back and forth, trying to figure out who the woman is and why the woman is occupying her friend Brandon's time. Roselita knew Brandon is having a good time but she didn't think he'd have that much fun. Roselita worried that this other woman would steal her close friend Brandon Bright from under her. Roselita began to tire herself out pacing back and forth and worrying about something she hadn't any control over. Roselita realized that Brandon was being himself and hadn't any intent to settle down with Roselita.

She returned back to her bed lying across it once again this time staring at the ceiling trying to free her mind. Roselita felt like crying as her face flushed with anger; her brown eyes swelled and turned red with water forming in the corner of her eyes. Roselita squeezed her pillow tightly as her anger flared up, wondering what went wrong. Not one moment past with her realizing that she was making unrealistic excuses for herself. Roselita knew her negative thoughts caused more damage then what she perceived to be going wrong. After a while, Roselita fell asleep for the remainder of the night. Roselita awoke the next morning, rejuvenated from last night's tossing and turning because she was envisioning her wedding day involving Brandon Bright. Roselita walked around with her chemise lingerie on all day as she called into work claiming she is feeling sick. Roselita is causing herself to be sick because she has the Brandon Bright love blues. Roselita let her voicemail take messages as she screened her calls, watching the names appear on the caller ID. Roselita tried reading romance books and watching the romance channel on satellite television, hoping that it would help cure her emotional sickness. Roselita baked chocolate chip cookies and made cinnamon rolls, spreading the glaze evenly and imagining Brandon was caressing her. Roselita made pink lemonade to help cool her hot flashes. Roselita sat on the couch, at times crying as she thought about Brandon wondering how this could be; why didn't he call her? When her telephone rang, Roselita jumped off the couch, reaching over the coffee table to see who was calling her, sighing when she saw it was her mother calling to see how her baby was doing. Roselita inhaled a deep breath and released it, hoping the caller was Brandon. Roselita spoke in a soft but mellow voice "Hello, mother how are you doing?" Mrs. Macalaonez noticed that her daughter isn't her normal self. She was curious to know why Roselita didn't show up for work. Mrs. Macalaonez asked," Roselita baby is everything okay?" Roselita felt like crying because she had never felt so in love before-- especially when she tried to conBrandon herself that she could never get emotional again about a man, "Yes, mother I'm alright. I'm surprised you'd call." Mrs. Macalaonez said, "Well I called you at work several times, but when your answering machine said that you would be out of the office, I got worried about you." Roselita said, "Thank you mother, but I'm really okay?" Her mother still didn't believe that her daughter was telling her the truth. Mrs. Macalaonez continued to talk with her daughter until Roselita gave up and told her mother the real situation. Roselita knew her mother was persistent. Mrs. Macalaonez isn't going to hang the telephone up until she had gotten information about what was really going on. Right at that moment, Roselita broke down and started crying because she couldn't bare the pain anymore. "Mother, the reason I stayed at home is because I've been affected with the love bug." Mrs. Macalaonez laughed as she became bewildered. Mrs. Macalaonez couldn't believe what her ears were hearing. Mrs. Macalaonez continued to laugh, "You mean to tell me you didn't go to work or do anything else because your heart has allowed you to fall in love?" Roselita didn't really want to share her true feelings with her mother because she knew her mother would do exactly what she was doing now by laughing at her. Roselita said, "Mother, I'm serious. I have the love bug?" Her mother, still stumped by her daughter's interest for falling in love again, finally stopped laughing. "So who is this handsome man that has my baby so wrapped into him that she can't pull herself together to go to work or do anything else except lay around and mope?" Roselita said, "It is Brandon, mother. Yes I'm actually in love with Brandon Bright." Mrs. Macalaonez laughed harder through the telephone saying "Baby, I'm not a bit surprised by you finally admitting that you are interested in wanting a committed relationship. Because I have been telling you that for years but have or did you listen to what your mother was trying to tell you? See I knew sooner or later one of you two were going to give in and real feelings would be created. This is why I stated that a man and a woman couldn't become friends because one of you is going to start liking the other." Mrs. Macalaonez continued, "Roselita baby, it's okay to fall in love. Does Brandon know how you feel?" Roselita said, "No, I haven't told him yet because I'm afraid he'll only bring the same thing up, saying I'm too much like a sister to him." Mrs. Macalaonez felt sympathy for her daughter. Mrs. Macalaonez responded, "Oh baby stop being so negative. You don't know his real feelings towards you." Roselita said, "You are right mother, but Brandon is such a loose man he is always with some woman."

"Oh, Roselita baby, you feel as if he needs to be with you. Well how is the man supposed to know this, if you haven't told him?"

Roselita answered, "Mother, throughout the fourteen years that Brandon and I have been friends, it's easier said than done."

"Yes, that's why he needs to know as soon as possible before another woman fills your place completely." Roselita said, "I understand. It's just that I'm nervous."

"Well baby, just don't take too long because after so long a mind does lose interest." Roselita said, "Yes but if he loses interest in a woman quickly, doesn't that mean she wasn't interesting from the beginning." Mrs. Macalaonez said, "Yes baby, that's also correct. But if you let him know up front, that will give him more time to put things into perspective." Roselita responded, "Okay mother. So what else do I need to know about love?" Mrs. Macalaonez said, "Well just remember in order to give love you have to first Love yourself, by respecting yourself?" Mrs. Macalaonez continued, "Once you have accomplished this task, then things should be able to fall into place." Roselita continued to listen to her mother's advice when suddenly her telephone clicked. Roselita asked if her mother could hold on while she clicked over to see who was calling to speak with her. The caller spoke in a tone filled with gladness and respect, "Hello Roselita." Roselita pretended as if she wasn't excited to hear his voice, after all she went through last night, crying and wondering who this other woman was that kept him occupied all night long. Roselita took a deep breath as she embraced herself by collecting her thoughts. Roselita sighed in relief before she spoke. Roselita said, "How are you doing Brandon?" He could sense something wasn't right with her. "Brandon before you speak, can you hold on for a minute?" Roselita clicked the receiver by connecting back with her mother. "Mother, it's Brandon on the other line, but I can let him go so you and I can finish talking?" Mrs. Macalaonez felt it was important for her daughter to talk with Brandon. She told Roselita she would always be around if she needed comforting. Roselita said, "Thank you mother I know I can count on you because you are here to help me work things out. Roselita clicked the line over to finish talking with Brandon. She said, "Okay, Brandon I'm back. Thank you for waiting until I had cleared my other telephone line. Brandon said, "How, are your mother and Hayman doing?" Roselita responded, "They're both doing well." Roselita didn't hesitate to ask about the conference before they talked about anything else. "So how was the first evening of the conference--and don't leave anything out." Brandon could still sense that there was something wrong because the tone in Roselita's voice appeared shaky and impatient. Brandon knew that wasn't Roselita's normal tone of voice whenever they speak to each other. Brandon ignored Roselita's behavior as he explained the details of how Gordon visualized the entire event. Roselita wasn't really interested in hearing about the details of the conference, she was mostly interested in knowing about the woman whom Brandon had meet and what made him so fascinated by her. Finally after talking about the event, Brandon mentioned that he met a striking woman named Sandy Rockwell. She had captured Brandon's mind and took his breath away. Her beauty mesmerized him. Sandy Rockwell seemed elegant and lady like, Brandon loved the way she smelled and how she spoke with intelligence. Roselita felt like screaming! Roselita could feel her temperature rising because for a moment that was all Brandon talked about. Sandy Rockwell this, Sandy Rockwell that, and how Sandy Rockwell made Brandon feel needed. I'm glad I've met Sandy Rockwell. Roselita realized that this Sandy Rockwell woman infatuated Brandon and that she lost her close friend to this woman named Sandy Rockwell. That's when Roselita interrupted Brandon to let him know that she was busy working and she wanted to finish what she was doing. Brandon paused for a moment, trying to figure out why Roselita was sounding so edgy. Brandon wondered if it was something that he didn't mention. Brandon said, "Hum, that's interesting that you were busy doing something because I felt you had the time to talk with me?" Roselita quickly responded, "You know I felt that I had the time to talk to you, unfortunately, I really do need to get back to my work." Brandon didn't say any more after Roselita's fierce attitude, "Well, don't let me keep you from taking up too much of your busy time?" She said, "Okay, then I'll be talking with you later." Roselita disconnected from Brandon as she paced back and forth, once again wondering why she allowed Brandon to distance himself from her. Roselita wanted to be the only woman in his life, even though they weren't a couple. Roselita felt confused. She picked up the telephone, dialing her mother back. "Hello, this is Mrs. Macalaonez." Roselita started crying aloud again. She couldn't bare the fact that she longed for Brandon. "Hi, mother it's me Roselita." Her mother responded, "Hey baby, did you have the chance to talk with Brandon and tell him how you felt towards him?" Roselita said, "Not really mother." Mrs. Macalaonez replied, "Well why not--after all of your pouting?" Roselita answered, "Yes, I know, but I didn't want to ruin his happiness." Mrs. Macalaonez felt sympathy towards her daughter while trying to embrace her by saying, "Well, don't worry yourself. There will come another time that you will get the chance." Brandon walked over to the television, turning it on to the sports channel while sitting on the edge of the bed, wondering what was wrong with Roselita. The telephone in Brandon's hotel room rang. It was Gordon asking if he could meet with Brandon to go over some notes for the conference. Gordon continued to ask Brandon if two-thirty P.M would be okay, immediately after Brandon finished talking with Gordon Gem on the telephone. Brandon's cell phone had ringed, Brandon hoped it was Roselita calling back to say she wanted to finish talking. When Brandon looked on his cell phone caller ID, he saw it was his mother. Mrs. Bright said, "Hi, mother how are you doing?" Mrs. Bright said, "I'm doing well baby." Her voice had a sweet calming tone that could relax you. "Baby, I know that you're at that conference. The reason why I'm calling you is because I can't get Roselita Macalaonez out of my mind. Brandon became surprised that his mother had called to tell him that she was thinking about Roselita. Mrs. Bright said, "I'm cooking a big Sunday meal of your favorites, a mixture of collards, turnips and mustards with green cabbage. The meal will include some black-eyed peas, Marlito's and cheese, corn on the cob, baked lemon-pepper fish, fried chicken, and sweet yams. We will also have cornbread, and peach cobbler for dessert. I'm serving pink lemonade or sweet tea to drink. I'm also making a chocolate mousse fluff cake in case someone doesn't like eating peach cobbler. Mrs. Bright continued speaking with her son, "Brandon, I would like for you to invite that beautiful woman, Roselita Macalaonez, and her family over to my home for dinner on Sunday." You know that your brother will be coming in town, so I want everyone to be together. Brandon laughed in triumph letting his mother know that he and Roselita weren't doing too well. As far as the communication between them goes, Mrs. Bright wondered what the problem between her son Brandon and his close friend Roselita was all about. Here Mrs. Bright was thinking that her son and his close female friend were having such a good time being friends. "What went wrong?" Brandon didn't know himself why Roselita was acting the way she was, but he was going to get to the source of the problem. "You know, I'm not sure what happened or why all of sudden things went wrong, but I'll find out and let you know later." Mrs. Bright told her son that she hoped everything would be all right; she'd be praying that things would work out for them again. He said, "Mother, you are acting like it's the end of a marriage between us. I'm sure she just needs some time to think things through." Mrs. Bright said to her son, "Yes, maybe you are right. We wouldn't want to keep pressuring Roselita Macalaonez. After all, it takes time to think about making a big step towards marriage." Before Brandon could respond to his mother's comment,

Mrs. Bright continued, "I mean Roselita can't be putting my son Brandon on hold too long. There are other women who are waiting for the chance of a life time to have my son." Brandon laughed, saying, "Mother you know that I love you, but don't you think you're moving a little too fast? I mean, I need to make sure this is what I want and this is best for Roselita." His mother said, "Oh son, don't be so foolish. You and I know what's best for you and I am the only woman who knows you better than Roselita." Brandon said, "You know mother, you and I could drag this conversation out all day, but I need to get dressed and find something to eat before meeting with Gordon Gem." Mrs. Bright said, "Okay, son. I understand you need to attend to business, but can you please do a favor for me by keeping the idea of marrying Roselita in your mind?" Brandon said, "You know mother, sometimes I feel this marriage thing is more for you than me?" Mrs. Bright said, "Son, as your mother I have my concerns and I don't want to see you end up wild like your brother." Brandon told his mother that he loved her as he ended their conversation on the telephone. Brandon walked into the bathroom of his hotel room and stood looking at himself in the mirror, observing his features. Brandon looked at the way his face was shaped to the specks of gray hair growing on his face. He looked down, noticing how strong his hands were from exercising. Brandon then turned the shower knob to warm as he stepped inside of the shower. Brandon reached for his scented men's fragrance body wash, squeezing a small amount of soap from the bottle onto his blue scrub. Lathering his toned physique, he washed himself and shampooed his hair. Back in the room, he dried off as he placed his casual blue dress slacks and a matching shirt across the bed. Brandon put on after-shave, and then patted his body with the scents of cedar, pine and balsam, leaving the room filled with a fresh aroma. Brandon pulled on his dress socks and put his watch on. As Brandon finished drying his hair, he pulled out his shoes and finished getting dressed. Brandon hotel room telephone rang. It was Sandy Rockwell calling to thank him for spending such a wonderful evening with her. Sandy Rockwell said, "Hi, is this the handsome man that I met last night named Brandon Bright?" Sandy Rockwell's voice sounded fragile because she didn't know how Brandon felt about her calling up to his hotel room. Brandon answered saying, "Yes, it definitely is" as Brandon continued to speak with Sandy Rockwell. Brandon said, "Is this the radiant woman named Sandy Rockwell that I also met on last night as well? "Brandon felt perplexed. He was glad Sandy Rockwell called wondering how she had gotten his room number. Brandon continued talking with Sandy Rockwell, "Ah yes, Miss Rockwell how are you this morning?" Sandy Rockwell said, "I'm doing well. Thank you for asking me." Brandon said, "Did you enjoy yourself on last night at the conference?" Sandy Rockwell said, "Yes. Say, I know this might come as a surprise, but I was wondering if you would like to join me for breakfast this morning." Brandon said, "Yes, I would love to join you for breakfast, I'm just finishing up. I'll call you when I'm fully dressed. By the way, what's your room number?" Sandy Rockwell laughed, assuming that Brandon already knew what room she was staying in. "Oh, I'm sorry, excuse me; I thought I had given you my room number already." Brandon now felt ebullient. He didn't know how to react, knowing that he was going to join Sandy Rockwell for breakfast. Brandon hung up the telephone as he leaped for joy, prancing around the room. Brandon put his pants on followed by his shirt, tie and shoes. Brandon took one final look in the mirror. Brandon took his right hand and swiped his eyebrows, making sure they laid flat. Brandon sprayed cologne on his hands as he rubbed his body down, patting his face while grinning at how good he looked. Brandon smiled at himself in the mirror as he said aloud, "Brandon baby, you've got that man's touch. Now go do your thing and knock yourself out having some fun." Brandon picked up the remote to the television, turning it off. He grabbed the room key card and placed it in his brown leather wallet; he turned off the lights in the room. Just outside of his hotel room, Brandon saw the cleaning ladies. They were in the hallway going from room to room. Brandon noticed them huddle, giggling in his direction. He smiled at each of them as they giggled more. Brandon began walking towards them until one of them spoke to him. A Latina woman with a heavy accent who could barely speak English said, "Excuse me sir would you like to have your room cleaned?" Brandon smiled and replied, "Yes, that would be okay." The woman turned around to face the other cleaning women as she spoke in Spanish. Brandon didn't mean to be rude so he interrupted their conversation, "Excuse me, I don't mean to interrupt your meeting but may I ask what you have said to them?" The Latina woman returned a pleasant smile to Brandon and said, "Sure, I was asking which one was going to clean your room and they all wanted to clean it, but I only assigned two of them to clean it." Brandon was intrigued by how they all wanted to clean his hotel suite. He then asked the Latina woman if four of them could clean his room. The woman said, "Yes, all four woman could clean the room and would get right to the job." Brandon then asked if she was their manager, because she conducted business well and the women followed her commands. The Latina woman answered that she was their team leader and that each floor has one team leader. The Latina woman went on to say that she was the team leader for the floor that they were standing on. If any customers have any major complaints about the room service, they report them to her--and if it's something that she can't handle, she reports it to their head manager. This can sometimes jeopardize her position and could lead to expulsion. Brandon let the woman know that he understood the rules and regulations of room service policies. Brandon didn't want to step over any boundaries by getting any one of the employees in trouble. He changed his mind and stuck with the two who were already assigned. Brandon gave a final smile as he walked towards the elevators, pressed the button and stepped inside, pressing the Letter L for the lobby. The bell rang as the elevator door opened to the lobby. Brandon walked over to the dining room where he met up with Sandy Rockwell. She had on an indigo strapless mini dress with a white rose attached to it. Her two inch black high heels made her look taller. Sandy Rockwell's make up was very light with earth tone colors and a touch of cocoa color to cover her formed full lips. Her hair filled with spirals that gently fell to her shoulders. The scent from her perfume graced his face, leaving him smiling. Brandon's pulse began to beat rapidly after seeing how lovely Sandy Rockwell looked. Brandon Bright and Sandy Rockwell greeted each other as he pulled her chair out; Sandy Rockwell took her seat as Brandon walked around the table to have a seat. The waiter came to the table with two menus. Brandon let the waiter know that they would need a moment before placing their orders. While Brandon and Sandy Rockwell got to know each other better, Brandon's cell phone rang. It was Roselita calling back to apologize for her unacceptable behavior. "Hi Brandon, it's me, Roselita. Did I call you at a bad time?" Brandon, caught off guard, hesitated before he said, "Oh no, I was just having lunch with a friend. Why, what's happening?" Roselita knew that he wasn't just having lunch with any friend. She assumed it was with his new friend Sandy Rockwell. Roselita acted out in a way that would only make her feel more foolish, "Say listen Brandon, don't let me keep you from your special guest. I know you'll be busy for the rest of the day." Brandon then realized that Roselita was upset because he wasn't spending enough time with her. Brandon sensed Roselita's jealousy because he wasn't paying any attention to her like he normally would be doing if he didn't have Sandy Rockwell on his mind. Brandon said, "Roselita wait don't go." Brandon placed his hand over the receiver as he told Sandy Rockwell he would be right back he was on an emergency call. Roselita heard him say this to his guest, but she had no idea that his guest was a female--and not just some female but Sandy Rockwell. Roselita over heard a woman's voice say, "Okay, Brandon but don't take too long or your food will get cold." Brandon returned back to speaking with Roselita and said, "Are you still there?" Roselita abruptly said, "Yes." Brandon excused himself from the table because he sensed Roselita's anger was about to burst. Brandon walked out into the lobby to finish talking with Roselita, "Say Roselita, are you okay?" Roselita pretended as if everything was still going smoothly between him and her. "Yes, I'm okay. Why are you asking?" Brandon said, "Because I've known you for over fourteen years now and I can tell when something isn't right, all of a sudden you are starting to shut me out from your world." Roselita tried to act as if Brandon wasn't telling the truth, since he noticed her immature behavior. "Oh and what makes you think that there is something wrong with me? Why are you analyzing me?" Brandon laughed, "Roselita, now you know all is well and that I'm not trying to analyze you, but I do want to know what's wrong with you?" Roselita still wasn't budging. Roselita stayed stern with questions and answers. "You know Brandon, we could drag this stuff back and forth all day, but I really don't have the time." Brandon's tone went from happy to serious. Brandon was beginning to dislike the fact that Roselita stopped him from having lunch with a beautiful woman, especially when it meant having an argument with Roselita. Brandon said, "You know Roselita, you are right. Maybe it was a mistake to accept your phone call. You know what from now on when I see your name appear on my cell phone caller ID and at home, I'll be sure and let the voice mail pick up." Roselita now frustrated because she felt Brandon was giving up on her completely. While Brandon focused all of his attention on his new found friend Sandy Rockwell. Brandon continued to speak with Roselita saying, "Well if you don't have anything else to say. Have a good day Roselita." Brandon quickly quit talking and hung up the phone. Roselita now realized that Brandon was fed up with her game playing, that it made her blood pressure rise, leaving her angry with herself. Roselita wondered how she had allowed this to happen. Roselita wasn't able to speak with Brandon anymore because of their misunderstanding. Brandon walked back towards the dining area to finish eating breakfast with Sandy Rockwell. Roselita slammed the telephone down, saying aloud and "The nerve of that Brandon Bright. How dare he not speak to me anymore?" Roselita stomped her right foot on the floor as she placed her right hand on her hip then began to pace back and forth this time more uncontrollably. Roselita became enraged, which caused her not to think straight. Roselita didn't know what was next. Roselita realized that she was starting to fall head over heels for Brandon and all of a sudden, what Roselita felt was a perfect picture of her and Brandon became hazy. Roselita picked up the telephone and dialed nervously, hoping that her mother would be available to talk. Mrs. Macalaonez answered, "Hello." Roselita said, "Hi mother, it's me, Roselita. Do you have a moment to talk?" Mrs. Macalaonez said, "Yes baby. What's going on is everything okay with you?" Roselita hesitated before she finished speaking. Roselita pretended that everything was going okay as she spoke in a calm voice. Roselita tried not to give any leaks wanting her mother to know that something was bothering her. Roselita said, "Oh yes mother everything is okay with me." Mrs. Macalaonez knew that her daughter is up to something because Mrs. Macalaonez could sense that her daughter isn't being her perky self. "Mother, can you tell me why it is so hard to get a man?" Mrs. Macalaonez laughed saying, "Oh baby I can't give you an answer for that, but I will say patience means everything." Roselita wanted to fill her mother in about Brandon but she felt that her mother was going to say that she was being too harsh on him. That's when her mother said, "Baby, is there something that you're holding onto?" Roselita decided she couldn't hold out any longer so she said, "Yes, mother I just finished talking on the telephone with Brandon and we got into a little spat." Mrs. Macalaonez isn't surprised by the argument between the two of them. She knew that Roselita liked to start them at times. "So tell me what happened." Roselita's tone of voice began to sound shaky as she continued to explain how she was feeling jealous of this other woman named Sandy Rockwell. She told her that when she called to speak with Brandon last night, he told her he was busy. She mentioned that he was having so much fun that he didn't want to talk to her. Then when they spoke just a few moments ago, he was having lunch with some friend. Mrs. Macalaonez felt Roselita is taking things too far because Roselita spent too much time worrying about Brandon Bright. "Oh baby, when someone says that they don't have time to date or they don't have any feelings towards a certain special person it doesn't mean that they are not interested, it just means they are busy at the moment." Mrs. Macalaonez continued, "It seems to me that they are also having a change of heart. After all, this doesn't mean that they don't care because if they didn't they wouldn't waste time dwelling on things, worrying about other affairs." Roselita was expecting her mother to get even with her by using her owns words that she strictly went by meaning that a woman is and will always be smarter than a man that's why God created woman to help man understand. Roselita became furious saying, "Mother whose side are you on, mine of Brandon's?" Roselita listened to her mother giving good advice as she wondered how her mother was so wise and good at giving a person almost the correct answer. "Now baby you know that I'm on your side but sometimes you depict things by not trying to get clarification on what's behind the situation?" Roselita felt that no matter what she says her mother is right. "Mother, Brandon always talks to me of informs me that he dating someone else, but never has this happened to me throughout our fourteen years of being close friends." Mrs. Macalaonez felt that her daughter is taking things too far and not allowing Brandon to go about his own life. "Listen here baby I know how much Brandon means to you but he is a grown man that doesn't need another mother or some woman trying to run his life for him." Roselita then realized that she wasn't going to get far with receiving advice from her mother she told her mother the same line she told Brandon. "Mother I would love to continued our conversation but I have some unfinished things that need to get done." Being the wiser one Mrs. Macalaonez knew that her daughter didn't want to face the truth when she told her about herself. So she told Roselita to finish whatever it is that she is attending to and she'll get back to doing her household chores, all day she had Brandon on her mind. Roselita tried leaving the house to go shopping than going to see one of the latest movies that was playing at the movie theatre. Roselita stopped at Social Books and Coffee Café as she walked in a woman standing behind the counter said, "Hi, welcome to Social Books and Coffee Café my name is May Lee Voss and if you need anything I'll be glad to assist you." Roselita thanked the woman as she walked toward the Romance section she found an interesting book entitled… "When our mind says yes, but your heart says you're not ready for commitment." Roselita sat down and opened the book to the first page as she read how a person's mind might think that they are ready to commit to a serious relationship but their heart isn't feeling the rush to settle down. Roselita continued to read as she took memory notes in her mind she realized that the book was describing her unbalanced emotions towards a man who hasn't committed himself completely to her. It was four-thirty PM when she noticed that she needed to be getting back home to fix herself some dinner. As she stood to go return the book to the shelf, Sally Voss passed by her asking if she needed any help to let her know again. After helping out a customer Sally Voss let Roselita know that if she found the book to be of interest she should buy it, all reading material is half price. Roselita said to Sally Voss if she brought the book it wouldn't do her any good because it would be sitting on her bookshelf collecting dust. Sally said to Roselita, "I'll tell you what since you think it's not worth the time to purchase the book and finish reading it how about I cut you an extra ten percent including the half off price." Roselita agreed with Sally Voss, they made a deal for Roselita by making the book a reasonable price. Just as Roselita finished paying for her book sitting across the room she saw Jilla Handsberg talking and laughing with some man. Roselita wondered how she was doing ever since Brandon talked her into living at the mental Institution. Roselita saw that Jilla seemed much happier and looked well she noticed that Jilla was sitting socializing with some man. Roselita grabbed her plastic bag that her book was in and quickly excited out the building without Jilla noticing her being in the bookstore. Roselita arrived home turned on the lights and went into the kitchen to prepare her dinner. Roselita poured herself a glass of Pink Lemonade as she walked back into the living room. Roselita flopped on the sofa allowing her arms to dangle on the floor. Roselita prompted both of her feet up as she stretched her body out, reaching for the remote control. Roselita clicked on the television turning to a movie already in progress just as she was making herself feel comfort the telephone ringed. Roselita reached over picking up the Cell Phone saying, "Hi, Macalaonez and Macalaonez Express may I help you?" The person didn't say anything for a while, she kept saying,

CHAPTER FIVE

"This is Macalaonez and Macalaonez Express, may I help you?" The voice was deep and husky as he said, "By telling me what man do you love the most, man number one or man number two?" Roselita still didn't recognize the baritone voice so she hung up the telephone just when she hung up the same person called back and said in his same deep voice said. "Tell me you want me, and then he started laughing." Roselita quickly checked the caller Id and saw that it was brother Troy playing around with her making her think he was some stalker coming after her. Roselita continued talking with her brother Troy until she started to get sleepy. After awhile Roselita hung up the telephone and went to sleep.

***

It was Friday morning and Brandon knew he had to break the ice between him and Roselita. It was the night for the conference he promised Gordon Gem that he would introduce him to a sophisticated close woman friend of his. Roselita was typing away at work when the telephone ringed, "Good morning Welcome News Express this is Roselita Macalaonez and how may I help you?" The voice on the other end made her heart skip a beat as Brandon said, "By taking my forgiveness and joining me tonight for the last night of Gordon's Global Network System Conference?" Roselita felt overjoyed because here she had felt the man that she was starting to have feelings for didn't want anything else to do with her. Is making a plea, she couldn't believe what she was hearing this early in the morning. Her close friend is asking her for his forgiveness Roselita wondered what happened to Miss Sandy Rockwell she wasn't good enough for him. Roselita felt Sandy Rockwell didn't know how to treat Brandon just right unlike she did. Deep inside of her heart Roselita always believed that there wasn't any other woman who could fit his type that he was really interested in settling down to marry. Roselita was the only one who knew Brandon personally except for the women in his family. Her Mind wandered on what made Brandon decided to come back as if he was begging for her affection once again. Roselita's head began to swell with pride knowing that Brandon wanted their friendship back to normal. Roselita triumph realizing that without her, Brandon would collapse; Roselita knew Brandon wanted her to be a part of his world that is filled with happiness. Brandon waited for her response, "Miss Macalaonez would you accept my apology and will you still accompany me for the conference?" Roselita finally came to herself as she accepted his apology and answered with a yes she will be joining Brandon for the conference. Roselita heard a sigh of relief come from Brandon as if asking for an apology was to get to this point. Brandon said, "Roselita thank you for having a change of heart towards our argument and thanks for accompanying me." Roselita let out a gentle laugh expressing that she was glad they resolved everything. Roselita felt as if a heavy burden had been lifted from her mind. Roselita informed Brandon that she still had the evening dress from when she went shopping with his friends from Constitutes Law Firm Yamilla, Myann and Lucinda. Roselita now bubbling with excitement inhaled as she released her worrying tension. After hanging up the telephone with Roselita, the secretary Sally entered Brandon's office. His office door was opened when she lightly knocked on it saying, "Good morning Mr. Brandon Bright, I have the Co-Slasher report files that you've requested." Brandon thanked the secretary Sally as she laid the hunter file folders neatly on his desktop making sure he sees them. As Sally walked away he asked if she could make a telephone call to the Beautiful Boutique Flower shop. Brandon ordered arrangement of summer set Boutique which is his favorite knowing how beautiful they would look sitting on

    Roselita's desktop. The secretary Sally did as she was instructed returning the bill to Brandon to be paid. Brandon flipped through the Co-Slasher files as he paced back and forth studying the case. While Brandon reviewed the reports the secretary Sally paged, saying there is a telephone call for him. Brandon told the secretary Sally to send the call through, "Good morning this is Brandon Bright?" The voice on the other end appeared to be soft spoken but crackly as if they were afraid to speak, "Hi, this is Brandon Bright is anyone there?" The person didn't respond for a while as Brandon continued trying to get a response from his greeting. Finally a woman spoke, "Brandon, hi its' me Miss Harris?" Brandon didn't say a word until he had more clarity of who this Miss Harris was. He said, "Hi, Miss. Harris do I know you and have I done business with you before? Who referred you to me? The woman became startled because here she was being put on the spot. Jilla didn't know what to expect so she remained calmed and kept the tone of her voice moderate. She said, "Yes, Brandon I use to work at Constitutes Law Firm as a matter of fact I once was your team partner, no you haven't done any business with me before? And nobody referred me to you." Brandon was now inexpressible he was well aware that he was speaking with Jilla Handsberg. Just when he felt that things between them had finally subsided, here she was calling him again. Brandon wasn't in the mood to talk with her so he kept the conversation to a minimal making sure he wouldn't give too much information. "Oh, hi Jilla how are you doing?" Jilla's voice sparked a happy feeling knowing that Brandon is welling to hold a conversation with her for a while; he took a break from his work as they talked. The first thing Jilla wanted to know was what happened to him and her. Brandon stopped pacing and walked over to the oversized office window marveling the scenery outside placing his right hand into his navy pin stripped pants pocket. Brandon explained to Jilla that they were only having a partnership relationship not a mutual love affair, he added, "I never had any romantic feeling towards you, Please don't get me wrong Jilla I think you are a beautiful woman but my heart longs for another woman." Jilla's heart started to weaken thinking that Brandon would forgive her. Brandon finally expressed his true feelings towards Jilla Handsberg letting her know that things will never be the same between the two of them and he just isn't that into her. Jilla darted back at Brandon, "So you mean to tell me that when we teamed up to work together you didn't feel an ounce of compassion towards me?" Brandon said, "That's correct and if I did, trust me, I would have made it known." Jilla Handsberg tried to contain herself from getting angry, "I see so what you are saying is that we dealt with things on a strict business matter." Brandon repeated, "That's correct, listen Jilla there are plenty of other men out here who would be willing to date you it's just I'm not the one for you." Jilla said, "Well Mr. Brandon Bright I don't believe you because the way you used to look at me by smiling told me that you wanted me?" Brandon laughed as he said, "You know Jilla now I can see were this conversation is headed to." Jilla responded, what direction might it be going into Brandon?" He said, "Funny that you should ask because you should know that answer a long time ago when you saw that it wasn't going far." Jilla replied, "Hum, that's interesting that you should say that because you always invited me into your personal life." Brandon became temperamental saying, "Alright Jilla you have now crossed the line, I don't know how much of that Mental Institution is working with you but I'm hoping that it is helping you to find some common ground." Jilla wasn't easing up on Brandon so she tried to provoke him more by not realizing that she is jeopardizing her chances at winning him over. The more Jilla made herself sound foolish the more Brandon became filled with rage, the more his dislike towards her hardens. Brandon said, "Listen Jilla I will no longer be expecting telephone calls from you, I can't help the fact that you have been hurt in the past but I'm hope that you will recover from all of this." Jilla answered with a disturbed attitude, "Well, you can save yourself because I'm not the one who needs deliverance, it's you who won't accept the truth and I understand telling the truth can hurt sometimes." Brandon said, "Jilla the conversation ends here.... Thank you for calling...good-bye!" Brandon slammed the telephone down as he began to pace back and forth worrying that Jilla is going to try something crazy. Such as trying to become an outpatient letting the ward see that her behavior is sane. Brandon shook his head releasing the tension by placing his right hand around his neck and gently rubbing it. Memories of Jilla's Psycho-self played as a recorder with her voice embedded into his brain causing him to be confused and frustrated by her insane behavior. Brandon poured himself a glass of water from the crystal pitcher that is placed on his meeting table as he drink the water he felt it would help clear his troubled mind. Brandon sat back down at his desk as he finished reviewing the case files. Brandon picked up the telephone calling over to his friend Royston Friends whose cubicle is located across from his office. Royston is chatting with another co-worker when he heard his telephone ring. Royston rushed to see if it was one of his female dates calling him at work. Royston glanced at his caller ID seeing Brandon's name appear Royston picked up the telephone, "Hey Man, what's happening Brandon?" Royston continued "What good news do you have to share with me today?" Brandon and Royston were best buddies; they would play basketball and double date at times. Royston knew that the only time Brandon called him on the office telephone is when he needed to have a man-to-man discussion about women. Brandon said, "Say Royston, man I need your help I'm stuck in a rut I had to beg Roselita to forgive me. Which I'm sure her head swelled up. Secondly, "I just finished talking with Jilla Handsberg?" Royston made an outburst laugh saying, "Aw man Brandon you have been busy by juggling to women, first Roselita Macalaonez with her sexy looking self then you dealt with Jilla Handsberg and her Psycho self." Royston continued, "Man Brandon what's really going on, you can't decide which woman you want, as he laughed." Royston added onto his comment, "I don't know Brandon but you are the man, I'm not mad just glad that I'm not you, although it would be nice to have Roselita Macalaonez but Jilla Handsberg I don't think so that woman is a lunatic." Brandon returned Royston's comments with laughter, "Man Royston that's what I'm talking about you always have a humor side especially when I could use some." Royston replied, "Yes well anything to help my lost buddy out it seems you stay lost speaking of lost what's with that Brandon, you have got to get yourself together...man." Brandon answered, "I know but it seems like every time I do something woman always show up on the scene pleading that she needs me or is desperate for me." Royston said, "Man, Brandon I will agree on that it's as if these women carry radar detectors tracking your every move." Brandon responded, "Yes, I know so are you going to help a man out or do I have to seek counseling from a Therapist." Royston answered, "I'll try my best to help you and no you don't need to see a Therapist what you need to do is find a good woman who can help keep you together." Both Brandon and Royston shared a moment of comedy once the humor faded away the seriousness kicked back in. Royston added, "Honestly Brandon man what are you going to do, you have two women to deal with well more like one Roselita Macalaonez." After laughing Brandon then realized that he was stuck trying to figure a way to let Roselita know that she's the one for him. Brandon didn't have much concern for Jilla Handsberg because he knew she is living in a Mental Institution. Brandon wanted everything to be somewhat perfect between Roselita and him. Making sure nothing else comes between them. Brandon felt what they have been through is too good to be lost forever. Royston asked Brandon if he needed to set up a romantic evening for them so they could start a relationship. Brandon felt that would be a good idea but if anyone is going to surprise Roselita it had to be him. Just then Brandon almost had forgotten that he told Gordon Gem he would introduce him to Roselita. Brandon described Roselita as a charismatic woman who walks with her head up, she's not ashamed of who she is and loves to be sophisticated. Royston felt Brandon is giving Gordon too much details concerning Roselita Macalaonez especially if he is trying to keep her for himself. That's when Royston said, "Brandon that was too much information to hand off to another man especially if you are the one who is looking forward to having Roselita forever." Brandon agreed with Royston realizing his best friend would help guide him through this situation. Brandon said, "Now that Gordon already knows something about Roselita, what's next?" Royston laughed, "Man you're on your own I can only suggest things but you're going to have to pull this off by yourself." Brandon said, "I know, it's still good to hear advice from a friend." Royston replied, "Brandon, all I could say is be careful that hearts aren't broken and make sure Roselita is the one who you really want?" Brandon said, "Royston for the first time in my life I have finally found my true love." Royston said, "That's good to know Brandon I hope everything goes smoothly for you. I also hope that you'll make Roselita Macalaonez your wife and give her the best love life that she deserves." Brandon said, "Royston I'm going to work hard at getting Roselita to except my marriage proposal." At that moment Brandon remembered what his mother had been telling him, that Roselita is his lifelong mate. Brandon always knew it in his heart, but couldn't get himself to believe it by making it happen. After fourteen years of being friends, it's time to end their friendship and start a Romantic relationship.

CHAPTER SIX

***

Roselita said, "Oh no it's going on six-thirty PM and Brandon will be here in twenty minutes. I've got to shower, powder, straighten and perfume up it's a good thing I went to the beauty salon and gotten my hair done earlier this morning. The telephone ringed...ring, ring, and ring. She said, "now who could this be I really don't have time to be talking to anyone at this moment. I should let the voice mail pick up, but it could be my mother calling, Troy, Yamilla, Myann, Lucinda, Hayman, Pomedra or Brandon calling. She continued to talk aloud, "Well, I do have a little time before Brandon gets to my home. Roselita picked up the telephone and said, "Hi, Roselita speaking." The woman on the other end of the telephone said, "Hi it's me Yamilla were you busy?" Roselita answered her saying, "Yes, I'm getting dressed for the last night of the conference." Yamilla said, "Oh, I'm sorry I didn't mean to interrupt you getting ready for the event on tonight."

"Roselita replied, "No, its okay I'm running a little late on being fully dressed. She added, "However, Brandon informed me that he will be at my home in twenty minutes. Yamilla said, "Well don't let me stop you from getting all Dazzled up."

"No, that's okay I have a time before he arrives what's going with you Yamilla?" She said, "Well the reason why I called you is because Jilla had called Brandon today talking about her unusual psycho nonsense." Roselita laughed saying, "Oh really so I see she's not easing up on him, huh?"

Yamilla told Roselita that she had talked with Brandon earlier this morning and he mentioned that Jilla Handsberg isn't, she still thinks that he and she will be dating each other soon. Yamilla continued to say, "Even though she's in a Mental Institution you still should be careful you know sometimes they do let psycho people out to get fresh air." Roselita said, "Yes, she's supposed to be in there for a long time besides I'm sure Brandon was stern with her." Yamilla was in agreement to Roselita as she responded back to her comment. Roselita said, "Yes, you are right maybe he had a good long talk with her explaining how he's not interested in her." Roselita's voice became low as a soft laugh cam bursting out, "Yamilla I don't know what with her but she just doesn't get the message does she."

"Now come on Roselita you know that the woman has a mental illness and we should be making fun of her." Roselita said, "That's true Yamilla but after a while you would think she would get tired of telling lies." Yamilla never cared for being friends with Jilla Handsberg so she added some humor to her and Roselita's conversation, "Now come on Roselita, from what... not being sane?" Roselita and Yamilla shared a laugh as they continued to talk about Jilla Handsberg and Brandon Bright. Roselita's other line on her laptop ringed as she said, "Yamilla can you hold for a moment someone is trying to reach me." She understands knowing that she had called Roselita at a busy time where she needed to finish getting ready for enjoying an evening with Brandon. She assumed it is Brandon calling to speak with Roselita so she waited until Roselita informed her that he needed to take the call it was important. Roselita said, "Hi, Macalaonez and Macalaonez Express." As a deep seductive male voice spoke with compassion, "Hi, my love, are you ready to dance the night away and feel the rhythm of the music." Before she could answer she hurried up and clicked back to Yamilla. Roselita said, "Yamilla, I'll have to let you go and you are right Mr. Debonair is on the other line waiting for me to return back to speak with him." Yamilla's voice carried with excitement, "Well, Miss Macalaonez don't keep the man waiting, I'll call you later, better yet how about if I call you tomorrow?" Roselita said, "That will be okay besides I'm sure you want to know the details?" Yamilla's laughter was rich and cheerful, "You know it, but that's only if you feel like discussing the juicy details. Now go have some fun and enjoy the evening with that too of a good looking man named Brandon Bright." Roselita said, "Okay, I will be talking with you on tomorrow" as she said good-bye to Yamilla. Roselita's heart began to fill with anticipation she couldn't wait to see Gordon Gem again, as pleasant thoughts filled her mind. Roselita realized that she is going to be sharing the evening with two wonderful men. Clicking the laptop dial key back over to Brandon, "Hi, how are you still here waiting on me to speak with you?" Brandon spoke in a soothing baritone voice saying, "Yes, my love where have you been, I have been waiting my entire life for you as he laughed playfully." Roselita being caught up into Brandon's romantic passes towards he didn't realize the seriousness of how he was beginning to fall for her. She placed him on the speaker while she finished getting dressed he asked if he is on the speaker." She became Daphnean by responding, "Oh Brandon you are so silly. I can tell you like to watch the romance channel also?" Brandon asked how she knew he enjoys watching those old romance classics. He said, "As a matter of fact I can't wait to see how romantically you look." She became flattered by his telephone etiquettes she couldn't believe that he took the time to call her and say kind things about her, which made the night, seem to be more fascinating. They talked and laughed until she realized if she didn't stop talking with him she would never be ready when he showed up. "Brandon you know I would love to chat with you some more but I really need to finish getting ready." He sighed heavily knowing that she was enjoying this moment, he could hear her breathing calmly as she spoke softly to him. He then said to her that he would talk with her once he gets to her home. Roselita walked into her amber and beige bathroom as she placed a towel around her head and twisted it tight. She removed her make-up by giving herself a quick facial than she removed her clothing as she turned the knob on the shower to the warm water. After turning on the water, she took one foot from her beige and amber tiled flooring and stepped into the shower. Roselita picked up a clear bottle of shower gel as she squeezed a small amount of soap on to her bath sponge and lathered her body. The fragrance of Orange Spice and Orange cream filled the air leaving the bathroom with a fresh aroma sending the scent into the vents of her home. Roselita closed her eyes and imagined she was drifting on an Island. Kissed by the golden bronze and orange sun while reclining her feet on soft sable sand. Roselita could hear the sounds of silence while gazing upon the crystal blue ocean. While Roselita sipped on Pineapple, Orange, Lemon and Lime non-alcoholic drink. As she lay relaxing on Roselita a beach chair with her designer sunglasses on a dark shadow crossed her sight. Standing in front of her was Brandon but he had the face of Gordon's she quickly leaned forward removing her sunglasses. She blinked several times in astonishment noticing Gordon's face hovering as he smiled at her. She could hear him say, "Roselita, my love oh how I've longed for a woman such as you." Suddenly, her imagination faded as she resumed back to showering. She walked near her bed as she blotted her body rubbing scented lotion and spraying some perfume called memory. She gently slipped into her evening dress adding some accessories to it. She is now fully dressed as she stood in front of her mirror smiling at how beautiful she looked. The doorbell ringed, it was Brandon standing outside waiting to pick her up for the evening. She left her bedroom walking downstairs to the living room dressed in splendor. Roselita picked up her house keys as she walked over to the front door, seeing Brandon standing outside her door ready to greet her. She placed her left arm underneath his as they proceeded to the car. While in the car they talked about a variety of things from Politics to everyday issues such as how their day at work went. After holding a lengthy conversation for quite some time Brandon decided to turn on the radio to KLSX 107.8 F.M, which is the smooth jazz station. Roselita leaned back in her seat to relax as she enjoyed listening to the music play. Brandon started up another conversation with asking if she felt nervous to be meeting Gordon Gem. Roselita sat up returning his question, "No, just curious to see how he is going to feel about me." Brandon laughed as he said, "Well, once you meet Gordon Gem all of your worries will disappear." Brandon continued saying, "Roselita just trust me on this one, I'm sure you will be hugging me later." She mumbled, "I wish I could do more than that to you, but I guess hugging him for now will have to do." She looked at Brandon and smiled as she noticed how intriguing he looks and the scent of his cologne-smelled good she wanted to kiss him right there. But instead she turned her head as she stared out the window. She continued to image if only Brandon knew how she felt about him she would call the meeting with Gordon Gem off. But she saw how excited Brandon seemed assuming she had found the right man for her. Roselita watched people and cars pass by while the soft music flowed through her ears. After a while she asked Brandon how did he feel about Gordon and her meeting and could possibly end up dating each other or getting married? Brandon turned his head quickly as if he saw something and he didn't want to miss out on it. He said, "What do you mean how do I fell about match making you and Gordon?" His face became emotional wanting to be upset because the only right woman for him is Roselita. He felt bewildered because she had did reverse psychology on him. He tried to mustard up all of his emotions as he said, "I feel Gordon and you are going to be perfect." Roselita then took her attention off from sightseeing as she directed back to him. Roselita said, "Brandon I know you the last time you tried to fix me up with someone your heart felt weak because you didn't like how he treated me." She added, "You also became jealous and started to prove that he wasn't any good for me." Brandon laughed harder, "You are right, I did become weak because I saw that you were really enjoying yourself until he started to disrespect you, and Roselita I wouldn't call a man disrespecting a woman as being jealous which you were referring to me." Roselita didn't say another word she sat in her seat and remained quiet. Roselita hadn't realized how much Brandon really cared for her and loved her. Brandon glanced at her as he asked, "What made you so quiet all of a sudden?" Brandon went onto say, "Just a few moments ago you were fired up and now you switched gears by going neutral. Roselita responded, "Oh it's nothing I just stopped to think about something that's all." Brandon leaned over to kiss Roselita on the cheek. Brandon said, "I know you were upset because you felt I hated on you but instead you were wrong and I just proved that to you." He continued to say, "Roselita, you know I'll always love you and you'll always have a place in my heart as long as I live you are my diamond in the rough." She smiled as he focused his attention back to the driving. She felt a warm sensation come over her while she leaned back and relaxed once again. Roselita closed her eyes as she said a quietly prayer, "Lord how much longer must, I endure this of not being able to have this handsome man named Brandon Bright as my husband." She went onto say, "Why couldn't we just handle this situation now and move forward." She opened back up her eyes and sat there finishing her sightseeing of the city night skyline. While on the hand Brandon went into his own quiet prayer, "Lord how much longer must I have to endure of not making Roselita mine I want this just as much...as she probably does but I promised Gordon Gem we could meet her and if he looks her they should date and possibly get married." Brandon added, "Lord you know my heart's desire is to have and make Roselita Macalaonez my wife but how do I go about turning things around from Gordon Gem wanting to date and make her his wife." Brandon continued to keep his eyes on the road as he pressed his foot down on the accelerator picking up more speed. He turned up the radio as the personality played both of their song called, "Dream Friends.... by Debra Jacobs." Brandon finally pulled up to the curb of Jack Plaza Hotel as the bellman opened the car door for Roselita. She placed her right foot onto the sidewalk as she stood up, while the bellman closed the car door from behind her. She looked around at her surroundings while she waited for Brandon to give the car keys to the valet as he step up onto the sidewalk. He placed Roselita's arm underneath his the bellman opened the door to the entrance of the hotel as they both entered. Standing in the lobby was Gordon Gem secretary, Brandon walked over to greet her as he introduced Roselita to her. Gordon's secretary than gave both of them a program to which room had venues in them while she directed them to the main ballroom where the party is being held. Brandon thanked her as he and Roselita smiled making their way towards the elevators. While waiting on the elevator they glanced around the lobby noticing the overflow of people from different ethnic backgrounds. Finally the bell to the elevator ringed as the door opened. Brandon and Roselita stepped inside with the other guests who were going to the event as well. Just as the elevator became crowded Brandon gently pulled Roselita closer to him as they made room for other to aboard. Roselita felt Brandon's arm snuggle her close to him wanting to smile assuming this is the perfect moment to be standing next to her best friend. They reached the fifth floor as the elevator door opened; they stepped off into the hallway of the ballroom area. They walked towards the room where several hosts and hostess greeted everyone as they picked up their passes before entering the ballroom. Once in the ballroom they looked around.

Brandon and Roselita begin to walk over to the buffet table. While they walked through the line Sandy Rockwell showed up to greet Brandon. He was startled because he felt Sandy Rockwell would disrupt the moment. Sandy Rockwell said, "Brandon, Hi how are you doing?" Both of the corners of his mouth turned up as a grin covered it from cheek to cheek. Brandon said," Hi Sandy Rockwell it's so good to see you once again after our last meeting." Sandy Rockwell smiled as she said, "Oh Brandon you know that was just a week ago when we had breakfast together." Roselita didn't say a word she give Brandon a vindictive stare, in hopes that he could stop blushing so much. He finally took his eyes from gazing at Sandy Rockwell. He introduced the two women, "Roselita this is Sandy Rockwell I met her on the first night of the conference." Brandon didn't realize that Roselita would feel awkward. Roselita sensed that he was interest in Sandy Rockwell instead of her. Sandy Rockwell stretched out her hand to shake Roselita's as she smiled. Roselita became jealous seeing how beautiful Sandy Rockwell is standing at five-seven showing off the slimness from her waistline. Sandy Rockwell's golden bronze complexion seemed to cause her beauty to shine her hair nicely styled in a flip up; her smile accentuated her face leaving a glow of happiness on it. She shook Sandy Rockwell's hand then quickly removed it leaving Sandy Rockwell to feel animosity between them. Brandon stood in amazement he marvel the two women. He asked Sandy Rockwell if she would like to join them as they paced the ballroom. All of a sudden Roselita's eyes became furious and sharp as she looked into his brewing brown eyes. Roselita felt like saying…. "Now hold on Mr. Lover Brandon Bright, isn't this supposed to be our night?" But instead she remained silent welcoming his open invitation for Sandy Rockwell to join them. Sandy Rockwell could sense her presence being not wanted from Roselita. She redirected her answer to Brandon's question, leaving him stunned. She politely excused herself as she spoke calmly to Brandon saying, "Oh Brandon I feel that would be too much to have a third party tag-a long." She continued… "Thank you for the offer but I'll pass." She then turned her head to face Roselita as she said, "Roselita it was nice to have met you." Roselita softened her fierce face as she calmly said in an unperturbed tune, "Yes, it was good to have met you also Sandy Rockwell." Brandon stood astound not being able to read

Roselita's psychological statement he didn't understand why Roselita became so edgy then quickly transformed her energy to neutral. He felt whatever the problem was; her vibes were immature and unpleasant. He over looked her recognizable behavior as he told Sandy Rockwell it was nice to have seen her again. Sandy Rockwell smiled one last time as she walked away, Sandy Rockwell felt that is the last thing she would want to do is break up a happy knit friendship. Both Brandon and Roselita walked away from the buffet table looking for a place to eat their dinner. Brandon spotted an empty table; he placed their plates upon the table while he pulled the chair out so she could have a seat. Just as he was helping her to be seated, Gordon Gem's secretary came to inform Brandon that once he is finished eating Mr. Gem would like to see him. As Brandon and Roselita sat enjoying their dinner, silence filled the air between them. After a while of silence he came out to ask her if she felt some interest for him. She stopped eating her food as she pretended she didn't understand what he was talking about. She said, "What do you mean...do I have some type of interest for you?" Brandon placed his fork on the plate as he looked into her beaming brown eyes. "Well, I've been noticing your rudely behavior lately, which has me assuming you're interested in me." Roselita gasped saying, "Oh Brandon you're incandescent you feel you know my behavior pattern?" His voice filled with laughter as they continued their minimal conversation. After they finished eating they walked a crossed the ballroom when they spotted Gordon Gem having a conversation with his guest. As they approached Gordon, he was caught off guard. He noticed the intriguing woman who is accompanying Brandon. Gordon politely excused himself from the conversation as he welcomed Brandon. His face lit up with delight as he said, "Ah, here is the man of the hour... Mr. Brandon Bright." Gordon and Brandon exchanged handshakes while embracing each other with a friendly hug. Gordon continued... "It's good to see you here Brandon, and who is this decorous woman you have with you?" Not to give away that they had already met before. Roselita and Gordon pretended it was their first time meeting each other. They both sensed that they should keep Brandon in suspense until the time is right to expose they've met before. Brandon filled with empathy said, "Well Mr. Gem this is my friend Roselita Macalaonez, as he smiled brightly." Roselita smiled as she stretched out her hand to greet Gordon. His head bent down to kiss the back of her right hand, as his eyes slowly rose up, both of their eyes locked. Roselita blushing as Gordon spoke softly as his voice deepened, "Miss. Roselita, Brandon has spoken highly of you, and it's my pleasure to finally meet you." Brandon, felt the heated tension amongst Roselita and Gordon as he felt resentment. He realized that maybe it wasn't a good idea for Roselita and Gordon to meet. He said, "Excuse me, I don't mean to interrupt this electrifying moment, I will go get three beverages." While Brandon turned to go walk towards the beverage table Gordon leaned forward whispered to her, "Miss. Roselita have you filled him in on our little secret yet?" Roselita blushed as she smiled saying, "No, not yet but he's bound to find out the truth if not sooner he'll know later," as she giggled. Gordon continued to hold a conversation with her. Once again he asked if she had put some thought into deciding if he is acceptable to getting to know him better. Roselita continued being Daphnean, answering, "Well I don't see why this handsome man named Mr. Gem shouldn't be acceptable." They laughed as they continued talking, just as they carried on Brandon re-approached them, he looked bewildered wondering what Roselita and Gordon were laughing about. He handed Roselita a glass, while passing Gordon the other one. Brandon sipped the beverage as he tried to resume back to the conversation. "Okay, what have I missed that is hilarious?" He added saying, "Roselita are you showing Gordon your allegro side again?" She laughed gleeful saying, "Yes, Gordon and I were sharing a moment of laughter. We're wondering if we had met before." Brandon, still bewildered, couldn't understand why they would be asking if they met each other before when this is the first time they're meeting each other. He shook his head in amazement, he felt stomped but finished talking along with them. Just as Brandon listened in Gordon quickly changed the dialogue to something more conservative. "Roselita...Brandon has spoken so well of you that I couldn't wait to meet you." Roselita smiled showing the whiteness from her teeth as she said, "Oh really...so what was so Intriguing that had you mesmerized over me." Gordon's smile lit up as if it was Labor Day and he is about to get his breakthrough. He couldn't wait to share his effervesce moment. "Well, Miss. Macalaonez it was how Brandon described your beauty and wit. See when another man can give precise detailing about a woman this makes the man inquiring go into suspense about her." As all three continued mingling amongst each other Brandon kept his attention focused on Roselita. Brandon noticed how her body language shifted as she became comfortable with the conversation. Brandon watched her eyes deepen with passion, her mouth curved while her mind seemed to be drifting away by lustful thoughts. The more she relaxed the more tense Brandon became as he stood next to her looking vexed. Brandon appeared frivolous on the outside while inside he quenched to make Roselita his woman. Brandon tried to laugh and be alert as they talked but his mind controlled his guiltiness. Leaving him wondering why he is so hesitated to say what's on his mind and in his heart. All of a sudden he noticed he was an outcast and his presence was no longer wanted. Brandon excused himself from Roselita and Gordon as he roamed the room. Brandon saw Sandy Rockwell across the ballroom. Sandy Rockwell was eyeing the crowd. It seemed as if she was waiting for someone to occupy her time. So Brandon decided to walk over in her direction he said, "Hi how are things going?" He added, "Are you enjoying yourself?" Speaking out loud, he didn't realize she could hear him. Sandy Rockwell yelled back, "Brandon its okay you can stop shouting because I can hear you clearly." The rhythm of his sound wave became mellow as he apologized, "I'm sorry but with the music blaring I didn't think you could hear me." Sandy Rockwell laughed, "Yes, I can hear you because you're standing close to me." Brandon Bright and Sandy Rockwell held a lengthy conversation when his attention of Sandy Rockwell talking became vague. Brandon tried to shake the corrupted thoughts of pretending Roselita is his woman. But the thoughts lingered making him become Vern able wanting to remove Roselita from Gordon's presence. Brandon realized that would be conspicuous on his part so he left the matter alone. Brandon resumed back to listening to Sandy Rockwell speaking, when out of nowhere she said, "Brandon would you like to leave the conference and join me back at my hotel room for coffee?" Being caught off guard Brandon said," Sandy Rockwell, that's a pleasant thought but I can't leave my friend Roselita all alone in the ballroom. Brandon tried to make up an excuse not to go with back Sandy Rockwell to her hotel room. Brandon said, "Besides Roselita would be wondering where I've disappeared too." Sandy Rockwell felt anguished but understood, realizing his love interest wasn't in her; instead Brandon had deep feelings towards Roselita. Sandy Rockwell saw the glow in Brandon's brown eyes; Sandy Rockwell could sense Brandon's mind is fixed on keeping a watchful eye on Roselita. After seeing Brandon's curiosity of how Gordon is becoming attached to Roselita. Sandy Rockwell knew at that moment that convincing Brandon to become her man wouldn't help the situation. There was no doubt that Brandon's heart longed for his friend Roselita. As Brandon watched Roselita's every move, while leaving Sandy Rockwell to feel left out. Sandy Rockwell excused herself from Brandon as she walked away. Brandon wasn't paying Sandy Rockwell any attention, realizing that she walked away quietly. Brandon tried shaking his exclusive thoughts of Gordon and Roselita becoming a couple. But the thoughts only deepen as Brandon saw a clear picture before his eyes. Brandon had finally realized he made a mistake he didn't mean for things to go smoothly between Roselita and Gordon Gem. Brandon could sense love unfolding into what could possibly lead to a walk down the aisle for the two of them, Roselita Macalaonez and Gordon Gem.

CHAPTER SEVEN

After all this time Brandon dreamt of marrying Roselita, he wanted it to be real and not his imagination. Brandon didn't want Gordon Gem to take his true love from him. Everything flashed before Brandon's eyes from the first time he met Roselita. To the times they've shared laughter, hanging out, eating, and being playful with each other but able to still be serious. Brandon reminisced on the night Roselita had cooked dinner for him. Brandon remembered all of the times Roselita went with him to his mother's house, in return how Brandon visited Roselita's family. The more Brandon went back in time over their bonding together, the more Brandon's flash backs increased leaving him speechless and uncomfortable. Brandon found out the more he shake away his thoughts the more he longed for her love and making her his wife. Brandon tried to pull himself together wondering what his next move is going to be and how can he win her heart back. For the remainder of the venting Brandon contemplated on how long he would be willing to keep silent by not exposing his true feelings towards Roselita.

***

Saturday morning arrived, beep…beep…beep…beep the alarm clock sounded as Roselita rolled over turning it off. Roselita sat up and stretched, she slipped her bare feet into her slippers. Roselita walked into her bathroom picking up her electric toothbrush while placing toothpaste onto the brush. Roselita brushed her teeth in a circular motion and swishing her mouth with cinnamon mouthwash. Roselita turned the knob to the shower on Luke warm as she placed her night clothing neat on the garment stand. Roselita stepped into the shower allowing the water to drip on her hair as she being to lather it with shampoo. While she shampooed her hair, she closed her eyes. Began to think about how she enjoyed herself last night talking with Gordon Gem. Once Roselita finished showering she dried off then put her clothes on. Roselita walked down the stairs to the first level of her home. The laptop ranged Roselita answered, "Good morning this is the Macalaonez resident may I help you?" The voice on the other end spoke in a sedated calmness but heavy, it appeared to be a male voice as he said, "Good morning to you too." The male continued, "Hi, Miss. Macalaonez this is Gordon, I hope you didn't mind me calling you?" Roselita being startled didn't know what to say. The first thing that slipped out of her mouth was, "How did you get my telephone number?" Gordon laughed, "Oh I'm sorry but I saw Brandon earlier this morning at the gym." I felt it would be impolite for a woman to be calling a man so I asked Brandon if it would be okay if I called you first." Roselita was still in a blank state of mind said, "Oh I see, so instead of asking me directly you decided to go undercover and ask my friend Brandon Bright?" Gordon assumed that this would happen. Roselita would be upset because he went behind her back without consulting her first to get her telephone number. Roselita continued, "Listen Gordon I don't mind if you call but since you're speaking from a gentlemen's point of view. It would have been in the uttermost respect if the gentleman would have been direct by personally asking the woman instead of her friend." Gordon didn't say another word for he had learnt that women love to have the last word. So Gordon left Roselita's statement remain closed as he proceeded with an apology, "Miss. Macalaonez I'm sorry if I didn't get your permission to call you but since I'm on the telephone would it be okay if we talked for a while?" Roselita's inside melted like butter as she smiled then returning his response. "Yes, that'll be okay; whew I needed to calm down." Gordon laughed, "You can add another whew for me too, for a minute I felt you were going to scold me for calling then send me away for good." Roselita's voice tone became mellow, as she sigh a relief of anxiety. Gordon and Roselita talked for hours until she realized she was running late for appointment.

Roselita forgot she had scheduled to meet with Mrs. Kingsley-Perez this morning. Roselita explained to Gordon that she needed to call her scheduled appointment; she'll call Gordon back when she is finished. After disconnecting with him she frantically dialed the numbers on her cell phone. Mrs. Kingsley-Perez answered, "Hello, this is Mrs. Kingsley-Perez?"...Roselita said, "Hi Mrs. Kingsley-Perez sorry to interrupt but I'm running late. Roselita added, "If you would like to reschedule your appointment with me that'll be fine." Mrs. Kingsley-Perez said, "No, darling I'm still coming, what time will you be at the office building?" Roselita said, "I'm leaving my home now, I'll be there in twenty minutes. "Mrs. Kingsley-Perez responded, "Alright darling I'll see you there." Roselita thanked Mrs. Kingsley-Perez for her patience while she quickly hung up from her cell phone. Roselita dialed Gordon's number by pressing the redial button Gordon answered, "Hello Gordon speaking." Roselita gasped for air while slowing her heartbeat down. "Hello Gordon, it's me Roselita sorry for the hang up but I needed to handle some business." Gordon said, "There's no need to apologize, if its business that needs attention then business you shall take care of while connecting other matters later." They talked for a while until Roselita asked if they could finish the conversation on her cell phone. Gordon said, "That'll be good that way it could feel as if he were really with her." Gordon added, "But on one condition, please don't talk to me while you are driving, I dislike when people talk and drive at the same time." Roselita laughed and said," Well Mr. Gem, we'll have to conclude this conversation later or at another time." Gordon said," How about continuing later tonight around seven thirty pm?" Silence filled the cell phone Roselita is shocked to hear Gordon asking her for a date on tonight. After putting some thought to his question Roselita playfully said, "Let me think about it." Followed by becoming serious she gave her final answer "Yes that'll be good." Gordon said, "Well that settles it I'll be at your place around six thirty pm, I'll see you then." Roselita's heart danced with delight as she smiled, she unlocked her car door and placed the key into the ignition. As Roselita slowly backed out of her driveway she waved to her next-door neighbor Mr. Hammer as he was picking up his newspaper. Mr. Hammer waved back as a smiled filled his face. Roselita then reached over to the glove compartment as she pulled out her tan and black CD case. Roselita shuffled through the CD's until she found some uplifting music; placing the CD carefully into the CD player she pressed number four. Roselita leaned back allowing the music to take over while staying alert, by keeping her eyes on the road ahead of her. Roselita turned right onto Edgerton Ave, passing several homes and code sacs, driving around curves and rolling over speed bumps. Roselita reached the end of Edgerton Ave as she made a right turn taking the back roads going to her job Welcome News Express. Suddenly her cell phone ringed as she pressed the button allowing her to hold conversations through her earpiece. "Good Morning, Roselita speaking how may I help you?" It is her mother calling to see how her daughter was doing, "Good Morning Mother, it is your mother calling to how her Mother is doing this morning?" Roselita said, "I'm good, mother." Mrs. Macalaonez continued, "Hum, sounds like someone has finally found a new love?" Roselita laughed as she said, "Okay, mother what's going on." Mrs. Macalaonez said, "I'm not for sure but would a thirty-eight year old woman named Roselita Marie Macalaonez care to explain who this man has stolen her from me?" Roselita said, "Mother, if it's Gordon Gem that you're inquiring about, why didn't you just say his name?" Mrs. Macalaonez laughed, "Oh Mother, now you know that handsome man Brandon Bright couldn't go one day without tracking your where about." Both women shared a laugh, they knew if they wanted to know anything about each other's business all they had to do was ask Brandon and he'll make sure the news is reported leaving no details out. Mrs. Macalaonez added, "So now that you know Brandon has been giving me the four-one-one on your where about and with whom, would you like to elaborate some more?" Roselita said, "Yes, mother.... Mr. Mouthy Brandon feels he made a final connection with his so called Love match making skills." Mrs. Macalaonez said, "Ah, so I hear... Brandon said he feels you have met your final match and from what it appears you could be seeing the alter sooner than you think?" Roselita answered her mother, "Well I'm not for sure as to walking down the aisle right away but there is a possibility besides we haven't even started dating. We are meeting up tonight at six thirty P.M?" Mrs. Macalaonez said, "Ah, so I see at least you're taking the opportunity to get to know this Mr. Gordon Gem; well I pray that things will work out between you two." Roselita thanked her mother for the blessing but she wanted to start off taking things slowly after all even though she was trying to explore the dating scene once again she couldn't release her heart from liking Brandon. Mrs. Macalaonez concluded, "Mother, I just pray that you'll make the right decision whether it'll be with this Mr. Gem or with Brandon, allow your heart to feel what it is you desire to open up and let out." Roselita said, "Mother, thank you again but only time can tell if Gordon or Brandon are fit for me, I'm a little scared but I know that I will get through this tough situation." Roselita had arrived at Welcome News Express as she finished holding a conversation with her mother. "Well mother I've just arrived at work, I'm meeting with Mrs. Kingsley-Perez today but I'll call you when I'm done." Mrs. Macalaonez said, "Good bye Mother, have a good day." Roselita pressed the switch off button on her cell phone as she placed it into her briefcase she pulled into the parking lot. She turned off the CD player, picking up her briefcase and belongs after pulling the key out of the ignition. Roselita opened the car door, standing outside straighten up her clothing while looking at her reflection from the car window, fixing up her hair, swiping her white teeth with the tip of her tongue. Roselita smiled at her reflection as she locked the car doors and began to walk toward the building. Once inside she greeted the security guards at the checkpoint before continuing walking towards the elevators. Roselita stood in front of the elevators as she pressed the button. Roselita saw Pomedra walking towards her; Roselita could see how Pomedra gained enormous weight by carrying her baby. Pomedra approached Roselita with her belly sticking out "Hey Roselita, what brings you by especially on the weekend?" Roselita said, "I have a meeting with Mrs. Kingsley-Perez besides shouldn't you be relaxing before the baby is due?" Pomedra said, "No, I whether work until he drops besides sitting around doing nothing becomes boring at times." Roselita continued, "I understand, so it's a boy?" Pomedra answered, "Yes, and it is Mr. Perez's baby it'll be my first of course and his sixth." Roselita asked Pomedra does she really know what she's doing, does it occur that she's breaking up a happy home and a good marriage filled with five children. Roselita wondered if Pomedra even cared enough to take herself, her baby and leave Mr. Perez alone to deal with the situation on his own. Roselita then realized that Pomedra is so convincing that Pomedra had no self-respect or cared enough that this will affect the life of her unborn child, teaching him that if mother can do this than it'll be okay for him when he becomes grown. Roselita went unto ask Pomedra, how Pomedra would feel if she was Mr. Perez wife and heard that her husband had gotten his secretary pregnant and she is going to do everything to destroy his life, wife and family. Pomedra answered with "Listen, I know everyone is upset that this has happened but one thing led to another so here we all are today, Mr. Perez and I are expecting our first baby together." Roselita flared up saying, "No, Pomedra things just don't happen unless you make them happen, first off you already knew Mr. Perez is a married man with a beautiful wife and has five children with her. Roselita continued, "So that was your first mistake, second what made you think Mr. Perez is going to leave his wife and family to be with you?" Pomedra said, "Well, why else would he have made me his secretary?" Roselita said, "So you can do your job and not be going around sleeping with the CEO of the company as a matter of fact I don't recall seeing sleeping with your boss as a job description." Pomedra said, "Well know matter what anyone said, Mr. Perez and I will be together and we'll be a happy family with our son." Roselita said, "Excuse me Pomedra I don't mean to say this but you have "I'm Ignorant written all over your forehead, why would you even waste your time with someone who isn't wasting any time on you." Pomedra said, "You know Roselita, I believe you are jealous because I have Mr. Perez. You've always wanted to get close to him but you're upset that I'm closer to him than you are, so close I'm carrying his child. Roselita laughed, "Listen Pomedra, the only closeness that I have with Mr. Perez is that he is the CEO of the Company and I work here. Pomedra, you are such a gold-digger, you are always sneaky, and you are always desperate. You are the type of young lady that seeks attention saying watch out for me; I'll take your man because I'm that conniving." Roselita added, "You know we've had this talk before but since I'm wasting my time. Pomedra, you are better off stuck in denial. Now if you'll excuse me I have a meeting to attend to but I hope you'll put some thought into what you're doing and realize you'll never be happy, until you free yourself.

CHAPTER EIGHT

* * *

Pomedra shrugged her shoulders and shook her head as she turned around walking away from the elevators. Roselita walked into her office turning the lights on as she sat at her desk taking a moment to reflect on the advice she shared with Pomedra. Roselita couldn't believe that Pomedra didn't comprehend being mature too well. Roselita sat remembering when she was Pomedra's age twenty-six years old and almost being caught up in a troubled relationship with a married man. Roselita reminisced on how she allowed herself to be caught off guard by the married man's sweet talk. Wrapping herself into his luxurious gift giving and dining on the best restaurants until it was time to get down to having sexual relations. Roselita knew she didn't want to go in that direction so she had pulled herself away from even seeing herself nine months later carrying his child. Roselita shook her head snapping out of her thoughts for the moment as she redirected her attention preparing for her meeting. Roselita is now ready and waiting for the arrival of her appointment Mrs. Kingsley-Perez. Roselita heard a knock on her door. "Come in, it's opened, to her surprise it was Pomedra coming back to apologize for not understanding why Roselita gave her the advice. Pomedra took a seat while Roselita explained that she is concerned about her life style since it seemed like there wasn't anyone else making an effort to reach out to Pomedra. Roselita felt the need to reach out; she explained to Pomedra that she had once stood in Pomedra's shoes. Roselita felt she was grown enough to make wise decisions realizing that they only lead to falsehood. An astonished look appeared on Pomedra's tanned face; she did not know that Roselita went through the same experience, except Roselita didn't get pregnant but Roselita felt awful realizing that the silly person was herself for falling head over heels for a married man. Roselita knew that most married men will always remain with their wife no matter how many times these married men cheated on their wives. Roselita knew some of these men's heart is with their wives while their boyish life style has the desire of chasing ladies. Roselita had always wondered what drove some married men to get married and then cheat after marriage. Until Roselita finally realized the cause is because some married men had never grown up and some of these married men are in desperate need to marry but not patient enough to find himself first. Roselita also noticed that after these married men have fulfilled their boyish ways their marriage is in jeopardy. Roselita always wanted to know how would some of those married men feel if the role were reversed and their wives spent most of their time chasing her girlish life style of playing games. Than when the wives had gotten tired the wives would return to their husbands love. Roselita felt playing with love's emotions is too risky and selfish. Roselita felt why not stay single whether than putting someone else through the heartache and pain because that person is un-happy with themselves. Roselita felt that after a while playing mind games becomes boring. The question that stands out to Roselita, "Is it worth cheating?" Roselita also realized that being in an unhealthy relationship like her parents, it is better to move unto other things, such as meeting a new love interest. Pomedra felt better now that she had a clear understanding. Pomedra said, "Roselita, I felt trapped and lost as if no one cared, it felt as if everyone from my family to my friends yelled at me and shunned me away. It seemed that the love I wants had from my family and friends was gone. So I decided to rely on myself and follow what I felt was best for me, but as you can see I ended up confused and now I'm having a married man's baby." Pomedra continued, Listen Roselita, I knew Mr. Perez wouldn't be with me completely because Mr. Perez would only lay his head at my place when he and his wife argued but just as soon as he felt ready to go back to her, he would leave my place. I know it's wrong and hard to take in. Roselita, I felt Mr. Perez had wanted someone whom he felt more attractive too. But after a while I realized Mr. Perez preferred experience over activeness and Mr. Perez wanted stableness over immaturity. Pomedra thanked Roselita again as she stood to her feet and walked to the door she turned around and said, "Roselita you really are a true friend, thank you for your guidance I'm glad we've became friends. By the way Bali and I have found closeness since my pregnancy and our father has reconciled with us so we are working on pulling our family together." Just as Pomedra finished thanking Roselita, Mrs. Kingsley-Perez came through the door, "Hello Miss. Macalaonez sorry I'm late...but I've made it." Roselita smiled as she stood up and walked from behind her desk closing her office door as Pomedra walked out. "Okay Mrs. Kingsley-Perez shall we get started I have another appointment at six thirty pm tonight." Mrs. Kingsley-Perez laughed, "Yes which tells me you didn't come to work on Saturday to waste all of your free time here, so I'll make it quick and ready for print." Roselita thanked Mrs. Kingsley-Perez as they got started on recording her information for the newspaper article.

***

Six thirty pm had arrived, Roselita fully dressed she wore a black business skirt suit, with her finest sterling leaving a radiant glow shine over her brown skin. The smell from her perfume of Rose, Jasper and Lilac filled the house where ever she walked. Roselita's hair flowed freely gracing her shoulders. Roselita's smile dazzled as she showed the whiteness of her teeth. Roselita's make up flushed with beauty of earth tones while her lips perked with a neutral color. Roselita checked the mirror one more time as the doorbell ringed. Roselita took her time answering the door, to her surprise as she opened it she saw a tall, handsome man standing with a dozen yellow roses and a small blue gift box. Roselita couldn't believe how handsome Gordon looked as she stood staring with a grin plastered on her face. Finally Roselita said, "Hi Gordon, please come in have a seat, may I get you something to drink." Gordon walked in behind her as he closed her front door, "No thank you just a seat would be good." Gordon took a seat on the maroon and cream leather sofa as he unbuttoned his suit jacket. Roselita entered the living room asking if Gordon wanted to hear some music or watch television. She laughed realizing that he was ready to take her out, and then later come back to her place to relax if she gives him the invite to come inside her house. Gordon said, "Listening to music would be nice." Roselita said, "You know what how about if we go ahead and leave that way we won't be late for our reservations." Gordon smiled in agreement saying, "Yes, that sounds a lot better did you need to do any final touches before we go." Roselita said, "No as she walked in front of him unlocking her front door and setting the alarm system. While standing outside of the restaurant, Gordon opened the car door of his beige Mercedes Benz waiting for Roselita to be seated. Gordon walked around to his side as he got into the car, he placed the key into the ignition then backed out of her drive way. He drove down the street and turned left then made a right onto another street. Gordon and Roselita by passed homes, schools and churches before entering highway eighty-five going north bound. Gordon turned on some easy listening music to set the mood for the evening. Roselita gazed outside the window admiring the scenic view. Silence filled the car as the music played she imagined sharing a dance with Gordon that would keep her in a daze. Gordon said, "Miss. Macalaonez can you tell me how we really ended up sharing our first evening together?" Roselita smiled and said, "If I'm correct we were somewhat forced to be together by this vicious man who was persistent by making this date work, would you happen to know his name? "Gordon said, "Yes, I believe it's your friend Brandon Bright and I must say he has done an excellent job by picking a good choice for me." He winked his right eye while gazing into Roselita's bubbling oval brown eyes. They both smiled as they continued to talk about how it seems that Brandon thinks he's doing a clever job. Roselita said, "You know for a minute I feel Brandon has made a wise decision with his predictions of love match making." Gordon said, "I agree, he has great taste and who would have known that the woman whom he introduced me to would be as stunning as he said she would be." She quickly turned her head to the left and said in a forceful tone. "What are you trying to say Gordon that you'd hope I wasn't unattractive?"

Gordon replied, "Oh no, I just felt that… um, well okay I didn't expect you to be this breathtaking. Roselita said, "Let me see if I can understand this, you wouldn't have wasted your time if I was unattractive?"

"Oh no that isn't the case, what I meant to say is...um."

"Yes, Mr. Gem what were you going to say if I hadn't measured up to what you felt would fit your standard of attractiveness?"

"You know what; let's just forget the whole thing of attractiveness." Roselita said, "Listen, I don't know but I usually like to finish a conversation through and not leave the other person that I'm talking with clueless." Gordon replied, "Roselita, I understand that you would like to continue this but baby, I feel that there really isn't a need to carry this conversation any further." Roselita said, "Okay, but you might want to be careful of the words you use when expressing yourself." Roselita continued, "Besides do you always go around searching only for the prettiest people and if you feel that they aren't attractive, you dismiss them." Gordon chuckled, "Woe, just a minute let's clear this up once and for all, first I'm not going to resin with you or will I give into this petty argument which there is no need to contend any further with." Gordon added, "Secondly, why must my mistake become our topic of this romantic evening, Miss. Macalaonez I have found you to be beautiful and attractive so that's all that should matter." She became furious, "Well Mr. Gem if you wouldn't have been so bold to make your statement clear then just maybe I would have saw the situation differently."

"You know Miss. Macalaonez it's my fault for starting this conversation which apparently has you upset over it, so I'm going to apologize and allow the remainder of the drive to be filled with music or silence."

"Oh so, now it's my fault for wanting an explanation, and because of this we won't have another conversation, we'll listen to music or deal with silence?" Gordon said, "Hold on a minute, I'm going to pull over to the curve, there is something I've got to do?" Gordon merged over to the right side pulling up along the curb, putting the car into park then turning everything off. He sat there watching Roselita's facial expression as she looked startled wondering why they had pulled over to the curb. Gordon leaned over as his voice lured her into a relaxing mood; the coolness of his fresh minty breathe took Roselita's mind far away. Gordon placed his right arm around Roselita's shoulders pulling her closer to him. Roselita's body became numb waiting to explode but instead she managed to suppress her urge from going deep. Gordon placed a gentle kiss on her forehead while he slowly moved down her nose, neck, then back up to her lips. With each kiss, he made sure she was enjoying herself. Gordon continued to slowly place love taps until she felt she couldn't take it anymore. Just as Roselita is getting comfortable Roselita placed her right hand over Gordon's lips, pausing the moment and said, "This is really nice but before we can become more then friends let's start off being friends first." Roselita continued, "That is if your sincere about being with me, I don't want to start something that neither you or I can't finish." Gordon, pulled himself back to his seat as he sat wanting to go further but realized she was making the right choice as to slowing things down. Gordon agreed rushing into a relationship could lead to frustration, ending with someone's feelings being hurt by the other person. Gordon straighten out his suit jacket as he apologized for stepping out of line, "Roselita, I'm sorry, I didn't mean to get carried away it's that you are so beautiful." Roselita give Gordon a playful response, "It's okay, I did enjoy the moment, I just want to make sure that you are the one for me as I'm for you." Gordon said, "Whew, I'm glad we have clarity on what we are doing and how we would like to go about it." Roselita smiled shaking his left hand saying, "Yes, I'm glad we're able to clear this up before things would have gotten out of hand and one of us would have ended up leading the other into something neither one is ready for." Gordon said, "You know I like the way you take your time and think things over before rushing into them. You have the uttermost respect from me because you are able to hold your own while having fun." She enjoyed being in his presence but wasn't for sure if what she was going through felt right. Roselita tried to put her thoughts of Brandon behind but they kept seeping through causing her to feel like she is making a mistake. Every time she looked at Gordon she would picture Brandon gazing into her dreamy brown eyes while caressing her every essence of life. She tried to shake the memories but each time the notion of Brandon would appear leaving her to feel afraid, she is misleading Gordon. The more she spent time with Gordon the more intense Roselita became she dreaded having Brandon to set her up with Gordon. Roselita felt by giving Gordon a try just maybe she could change the course from thinking of Brandon. But the more Gordon pursued her the more she felt he was turning into Brandon, realizing that she was thinking too much and she isn't allowing herself to explore being away from her close friend Brandon Bright. Roselita felt what is she supposed to do as Gordon draws himself closer to her, how is she going to put a Halt to the way he truly feels towards her. Roselita wasted too much time wondering what and how Brandon would have handled the situation if he were in her place. Just then Gordon interrupted, "Roselita dear are you okay, it seems you're zoning, from time to time you've been drifting in and out of a daze. "Would you like to talk about it?" Roselita quickly responded with, "Oh its nothing, I was taking in the scenery. Gordon made a right turn into the parking lot of Marlito's Restaurant, pulling up to the entrance. Gordon opened his side of the door, quickly getting out and rushing around to Roselita's side. As he opened the car door watching her get out of the car, Gordon noticed how attractive her legs were through her pantyhose. Next he watched how alluring her curve body fitted in her dress, Gordon enjoyed the roundness of Roselita's bottom while her breast made the dress appeared breathtaking. Roselita walked over to the entrance as she waited for him. Gordon ran around to his side of the car, placing the key into the ignition driving off to find a parking spot. Later that evening Gordon drove Roselita home, he pulled up into her driveway turning the car off. They sat talking for a while until Gordon said her beauty is radiant, and that someday he would love to be married. Which caused Roselita to go into a silence realizing that she could end up being married to Gordon instead of her close friend Brandon? Gordon continued, "I know this may sound awful but I can't get over how beautiful you are. I would love the opportunity to get to know more of you, who knows after a while you and I could be meant for each other." Roselita didn't know how to respond to Gordon, before Roselita could catch her reactions she blurted, "Yes, I would love to be that woman who becomes Mrs. Gem." Roselita mumbled to herself, "Oh what have I just said I can't believe that came out like that." Gordon smiled as he took her right hand and gently placed a moisten kiss on the backside. Gordon said, "Well, in that case I guess we'll have to start dating from this point on and later we'll make wedding plans?" Roselita paused as she sat in silence wondering what mess she had just caused knowing that her love life is about to take a thirty-degree turn. Roselita felt isolated but she knew she was the cause of making something out of nothing especially when she has control over the situation. Roselita also realized she had spoken too soon; Roselita wanted to make sure she was choosing the right man. Flashes of her past with Brandon clogged her mind, seeing all of the things they've been through together. To how Roselita would try and let Brandon know she is interested in him, feeling Brandon wouldn't take what she had to say to him seriously. Roselita reminisced about the beginning of their friendship including now, she wanted to weigh her options between both men. Roselita didn't want to make any final decisions that could lead to one man standing next to her, before family and friends. Or if she should remain being single. Roselita also wants to make sure that when the time is right some things will fall into place perfectly without any headaches. Roselita wants to make sure that what she is feeling is right for her and not some ordinary dream being deferred. Roselita wants to be happy most of the time and find peace within her marriage; Roselita wants to be told the truth without her spouse feeling guilty for telling lies. Roselita wants to know that they will work on their marriage and not have it sabotage by family, friends and outsiders, speculating what is true or false. Roselita wants to explore her marriage to every level imagined without the thought of divorcing. Roselita wants to feel drama free and not pulled in by rumors of family, friends or unknown people hating. Roselita wants children and she wants to give love unconditional and not sit around waiting to see when the sparks in her marriage will fly. Roselita wants patience and not jealousness; Roselita wants togetherness and not competition. All these things is what she wants and more, she knew after a while time will dwindle down and she is going to have to make that final choice. Until that time comes she turned her thoughts into a clear path, seeing what is in the moment and thinking about the decision later when or if she gets asked that martial question. Their evening came to an end as Gordon quickly got out and ran to her side of the car. Roselita took one last stare at how handsome Gordon looked then positioned her body to depart the car. They both walked up to her front door as she thanked him for having a lovely evening. Gordon placed a soft but slow kiss on the side of her cheek then gave her a hug while thanking Roselita in return for allowing him to have an opportunity to take her out on a date. After Gordon and Roselita exchanged courtesy, silence followed as the both of them parted ways. Roselita walked into her front door as she locked it behind her. Roselita set the alarm and walked into the kitchen turning on the light. Roselita walked over to her oak wood cabinets getting a mug cup out. Roselita placed it unto the counter top while reaching on the other side of the cabinet for her instant coffee cup packs. Roselita took the coffee cup packs and placed one into her coffee maker machine. Roselita leaned against the counter top thinking about the lovely evening that she shared with Gordon. Roselita thought about the joys of becoming Mrs. Gordon Gem but didn't want to rush head over heels. Roselita thought about how it would be nice to work as a team while they both ran the two companies he owns. Roselita tried to imagine carrying his children while practice saying her new last name Mrs. Gem. As Roselita dreamed the sound from the coffee maker beeped, Roselita came from her dreamy daze as she poured the coffee into her mug. Right when she was going to take a sip her computer laptop ringed. Roselita said "Good evening the Macalaonez Residence," The person on the other end was Gordon calling to make sure she had made it safely inside of her home. Gordon said, "I'm sorry to have disturbed you but I can't get you out of my mind. Roselita you may call it late night lust but I 'm calling it I believe I've fallen in love." As Roselita listened to him express his true feelings the first thing that came to her mind was, "It's ten O' clock PM, he had just dropped her off earlier and now he's calling her." Roselita felt any man that calls after nine thirty was horny and looking for a quickie just to crave his lusting urge. Roselita said, "Gordon, you mean to tell me after taking me out for dinner and returning me back home safely you feel you've struck gold. Now you are in love just like that?" Gordon said, "It may come to you as a surprise but I really do want to be with you in hopes of making you my wife. "Gordon concluded, "Roselita, you may not understand but I'm a grown forty-nine year old man, and some men at my age who are single are looking forward to settling down with the right woman." Gordon added, "This isn't a laughing matter but a serious one, you already know I'm the owner of two business's, I have my retirement money in investments, I've worked hard all of my life and now it's time for me to settle down with a potential woman." Being left speechless she did listen to him as he went on explain the difference between late night lusting and wanting to make her his wife. Roselita could hear how sincere he was explaining but a part of her felt nervous because she hadn't felt this way in several years. Roselita realized she was dealing with a genuine gentleman. Not someone like Brandon who had difficulty deciding what he really wanted out of life especially out of his relationships with the women he dated. Roselita knew Gordon had his credentials together, she knew he is finished living his lavish, boyish life style; she could sense he is ready for marriage. The games where just that, games that he'd played and lucked out every time realizing he can't fulfill his last goal. Roselita assumed by looking at his appearance, seeing how he conducts business, and enjoying hosting a weeklong conference that Gordon is definitely a man who is ready for marriage, which is to find a woman for himself and marry her. Because Roselita was deep into her thoughts, he assumed she had hung up the telephone after pausing from talking with him. He didn't hear her say anything so he asked, "Roselita, baby are you there?" Roselita answered softly, "Yes Gordon I'm still here and I'm still listening to you talk." Gordon said, "I don't want to scare you or force you to do anything that you don't want to do. But I really do have a liking for you and beauty isn't just what I saw, yes it was the first thing I've noticed but sometimes what we see as beauty can fade away and what do you have left?" Roselita answered, "Yes, if beauty isn't always important then what you have to go on?" Gordon said, "Love and what's inside of a person's heart, meaning love lasts forever and the heart can't help but to become compassionate." He went onto say, "Even an evil person has love because they wouldn't waste their time causing unnecessary commotion." Roselita laughed, "Hum, sounds like you have a little humor also?" Gordon replied, "Believe it or not once again I believe humor is in everyone, but some people don't express it enough." Roselita said, "Gordon, I'm sorry if I came at you, thinking that you were calling me just to have a reason to come back over to my home and have sexual relations with me then disappear into the deep night?" Gordon laughed, "Roselita, I could tell you weren't feeling comfortable that's why I let you know where I'm going and what I'm trying to do, say remember when I told you have been hurt before when we first met at the grocery store?" She answered, "Yes, that's when you told me you've seen the women in your family withdraw from men and at times they still feel bitter."

He said, "Will this is the last thing I would want to do is hurt any woman, first of all I'm a lover not a fighter, I only fight when it comes to protecting my woman." He said, "Throughout my forty-nine years I haven't lay a hand on any woman and today I still won't. But I do believe in spoiling her and allowing her to be in control of herself and of her feelings. He concluded, "So now you know Miss. Macalaonez that Mr. Gordon Gem makes sure that when he gives love to a woman she can feel the love. Roselita continued to sip her coffee as she walked up the stairs to her bedroom, while in her room she turned on the light stand placed beside her bed sitting the mug on a coaster. Roselita removed her clothing as she slipped into something more comfortable. Roselita stretched a crossed her bed and finished talking with Gordon into the wee hours of the morning. By time morning had arrived Roselita was snoring on the phone she had forgotten to hang up. Gordon had already released the receiver by hanging up the telephone on his end. All Roselita heard was beeping sounds which meant he had hung up and she needed to recharge her computer laptop.

***

It is seven o'clock pm on a brisk Thursday evening; Roselita and Gordon decided to go out for a second date. They were eating at Marlitio's Restaurant when they saw Brandon enter the restaurant. Roselita felt that was odd for Brandon to show up at a restaurant alone, she knew he very seldom went places by himself she watched as he sat at the table and ordered a beverage followed by dinner. Gordon saw how her attention was being captured by Brandon's presence, he said, "Roselita baby did you want to go say hi to him, after all you two are friends." She replied, "No, that's okay, I'm sure he is waiting for his date to come into the restaurant, he'll be okay." Roselita tried to resume her attention back to Gordon but she was curious as to who will be accompanying Brandon for dinner. Just as Gordon was about to speak she gasped quickly and saw her mother walk into the restaurant and sit in the empty chair across from Brandon. Roselita wanted to know what is her mother doing having dinner with Brandon and where Hayman was at. Roselita felt how Brandon could take her mother out and not her. Gordon noticed that her focus is completely on what's happening at Brandon's table. He said, "Roselita, baby I've had enough lets you and I walk over to Brandon's table and say Hi?" Roselita quickly diverted her attention back to Gordon as she responded, "Oh, that isn't necessary. I'm sorry Gordon if I wasn't paying any attention to you speaking." He said, "That's alright but if there is something on your mind which I can sense that there is why not get it out in the open and get clarity so you and I can enjoy a lovely evening." Roselita said, "You know Gordon I'm going to take your advice, yes let's walk over to Brandon's table and say hi to him and his guest." Gordon raised his right eyebrow in bewilderment he didn't know why all of a sudden she started to act immature but whatever she was feeling he wanted it to be over with. Gordon pushed his chair back as he placed his emerald napkin on the table and walked over to her seat as he pulled her chair out. Roselita stood then took a hold of Gordon's hand as she walked swiftly with him to Brandon seeing that his guest is her mother. While Brandon and Mrs. Macalaonez were sitting waiting on their dinner to come. The both of them noticed Gordon and Roselita approaching their table. They looked up to see Roselita and Gordon standing at their table, her mother said, "Hi Roselita...Mother what are you doing here?" Roselita filled with rage wanted to know what her mother was doing at Marlitio's Restaurant eating dinner with Brandon and not with Hayman. She tried to stay calm as she said, "Mother, you know that's the same thing I'm wondering, what are Brandon and you doing having dinner together at seven o'clock PM on a Thursday evening and where is Hayman, I suppose he is at work?" Mrs. Macalaonez, noticed her daughter's behavior, she sensed Roselita was getting jealous because she wanted to be with Brandon and she was having a hard time trying to get Brandon to be hers. She said to both men Brandon and Gordon, "If you two handsome gentlemen would excuse me I need to speak with my daughter?" Both Brandon and Gordon agreed, as Gordon looked at Brandon and said, "Listen, man I don't know what's going on but I think Roselita is in love with more than me." Brandon tried to deny that what Gordon said was true. He said, "Ah man she's definitely in love with you, besides you are all she talks about." Gordon said, "Well in that case what has her being upset especially towards her mother?" Brandon said, "Well let's just say Roselita is extremely sensitive which can cause her to become jealous quickly then she goes into this misfit and explodes for no unapparent reason. After a while Roselita will calm down and she'll be back to normal, it's confusing but I think she's never learnt how to deal with being herself." Gordon, had a surprised look upon his face as he said," Oh I see, well is there something that can keep her from exploding in her temperamental moments?" Brandon said, "Yes, she needs to feel secure and loved twenty-four-seven she needs to know that someone won't betray her and will be on her side because she stays to herself a lot. Why do you think she's always isolating herself, it's not because she's crazy or psycho but it's because she has a hard time trusting people." Gordon said, "Man Brandon this isn't good for her health at all then, she could cause herself to stay in hibernation for life. Even worst she could die from not expressing herself enough." Brandon said, "Yes, that's Roselita for you, she's a very attractive woman but she's allowed too many wrong men to cross her path then leave her high and dry." Gordon said, "Well I'm not the type of man who goes in for the bait and wait to destroy her later all because I didn't know what the hell I want for myself." Brandon said, "Gordon man trust me from another brother to another brother I can relate, this is why we're friends, I want her to rely on me for anything, well up until now, she can rely on you being there for her." Brandon wanted to cringe, he felt what was he saying, he is allowing the door to Gordon's world to open more so he could definitely sweep Roselita off her feet and keep her for himself. Brandon tried to figure out a way he could start leading Gordon to think Roselita can be his when actually he knew deep in his heart Roselita is for him. Brandon wanted her to be his wife and the mother of their beautiful children. He knew she is the only one whose able to cling to him, she depend on him, she felt loved by him, she felt comfortable, she felt like a woman, she knew if she needed anything he would give it to her. But his coward less self couldn't brave the strength he knew he had hidden in his heart. He knew if she wanted a good man or needed a good man, someone to protect her and make her feel safe he is the only one who knows how her soul longs to be stroked. The two men held a lengthy conversation while Roselita and her mother talked sitting back at Gordon and Roselita's table. Mrs. Macalaonez, said, "Roselita calm down I'm not dating your future husband Brandon. Besides he couldn't please me like your mama's man can that's none other than Hayman Borrow, she giggled." Roselita said, "Mother, I don't care to know how Hayman can whip it on you all I want to know is what are you doing with Brandon?" Mrs. Macalaonez continued to smile, "Mother, it's okay Brandon and I came here because Gordon called us to come here?" Roselita quickly looked at her mother as she said, "What, do you mean Gordon called for you and Brandon to be here, okay mother can someone tell me what's going on?" Mrs. Macalaonez, had a smile that beamed with a ray of light, Mother I'll let Gordon explain why we are all here." Roselita became startled, "Mother, what is Gordon going to do propose to me?" Mrs. Macalaonez, said still giggling, "You know I'm not for sure what Mr. Gem has going on with us and why he wanted us here, let's go and find out, shall we?" Roselita and her mother returned back to the table where Brandon and Gordon had stopped talking and looked at the two women. Both men stood up and pulled the chairs out for both ladies to be seated. Roselita and her mother took a seat as Gordon begin to talk, he introduced himself to everyone. "Hi everyone as you all know I've brought you all to this restaurant because I wanted to share something with you?" I've met Roselita awhile back driving on the highway then in the grocery store. I felt we could give it a try to make a relationship but after seeing the closeness of Brandon and her then coming to the conference together. Well let's just say I had put two together and realize that seeing Brandon's eyes attached to Roselita's where bout's up until now. Which made me go into suspense wondering are the two of you more than just friends? So my conclusion of this love triangle has made me realize that I could have been for you Roselita but your heart belongs to Brandon. So I'm standing here tonight to wish the both of you the best in your lives, Mrs. Macalaonez you have a beautiful daughter whom I can tell gets her radiant look from you. Brandon, from the first time you and I met and you tried to spice things up with informing me how wonderful of a woman Roselita is which you are correct. I sensed your emotions towards me wanted to say, "Gordon you can try to have her but I'm in love with her." Gordon continued, "You know I'm not the typical man who steps in to fill another man's shoes and takes the woman whom he's caught up into then desperately trying to make her their own." He laughed, "Brandon, I guess you never know how you feel about someone that's close to you until you stop being in denial." Mrs. Macalaonez sat smiling she looked into her daughter's eyes seeing that Gordon knew about Brandon and her affectionate love towards each other all this time. Brandon had a bedazzled look on his face he felt Gordon and Roselita were setting him up. He said, "So you mean to tell me that Gordon, you've already met Roselita before now?" Mr. Gem said, "Yes, this also explains why Roselita and I were talking and sharing laughter on Friday night, the last day of my conference." He added, "Brandon, since I could sense your love towards her I didn't want to go any further, I felt I would be jeopardizing the moment of you actually getting to keep her for yourself." Mrs. Macalaonez took a sip of her beverage as she continued to laugh saying, "Mr. Gem called me awhile back and inquired if you two had a thing going on, so I informed him that there could be some possibility between the two of you." The whiteness of Roselita's eyes widen as she looked at her mother. She said, "Mother how come you didn't say anything?" Mrs. Macalaonez said, "Oh Mother if I would have you wouldn't have gave Mr. Gem a chance, so I felt why not tell it to you until now." She concluded, "You see Mother, Brandon has dated several women while you and him we're just being friends, and I'm sure Mr. Gem has done the same but when it comes to my baby Roselita who isolates herself from testing the waters she'll stick to one man and settle with I'll wait for the next one to arrive...some time." She said, "Mother do you know how long that'll be before you decide to dip your foot in the water, it'll take you so many years, so why not start now while you're still young." Roselita respond back to her mother saying," Mother, why are you putting my business out here like that?" Mrs. Macalaonez said, "Oh Mother you know it's true, easy up a little." Brandon said, "I'm sorry I don't mean to interrupt this embarrassing moment but there is one question that I have to ask Roselita." Her eyes widen as Brandon took both of her hands and placed them into his squeezing them firmly. He said, "Roselita Macalaonez I'm not going to give a long drawn out speech so without further say my question that I want to know from you is well you marry me?" A tear began to roll down her flushed nutmeg cheek as she became stunned followed with a slow response of saying, "Yes, I would love to be Mrs. Bright." He opened the velvet small box with a white ribbon laced around it as he opened it her eyes beamed with splendor she couldn't believe what she was seeing. Her mother said, "Well don't just gaze at the ring, let's all have a look at how dazzling it shines. "Gordon smiled but felt it was supposed to be him proposing to her and not Brandon. Gordon felt a little jealous so he said, "Well isn't that lovely, Roselita would you want a small ring or a clustered ring as he pulled out of his suit jacket a medium Yellow box with a red bow sitting on top." Roselita looked at the ring Gordon had showed off; she couldn't believe she was being proposed to by both men she'd loved. Her mother leaned over to whisper in her daughter's ear and said, "Oh no we've got double the trouble, two engagement rings in one night, Mother I think you should thank both men then sleep on it." Roselita leaned over to return her mother's response, "I think you are right maybe I should take both rings home and sleep on it then give me answer in the morning. But which man is truly for me, I've weighed my options but I'm still having a difficult time choosing?" Roselita added, "Besides, both rings are gorgeous, mother tell me which one would you choose and which man do you see best that I should be with?" Mrs. Macalaonez said, "Oh no Mother is out of this it's up to you to decide just remember to follow you heart and let your mind feed you peace that will lead you being happily in love." Roselita continued to stare at both of her engagement rings as she looked at both men and said," If love was truly this easy don't you think I would have made my choice by now?" She closed her eyes then opened it as she looked at Brandon. Roselita said, "You and I have shared so much and been through so much only to have my heart broken into so many pieces. Because you weren't strong enough to tell me how you really felt towards me until tonight." Then she turned to face Gordon, "You and I haven't known each other long but long enough to know that if I marry you, you would be filling your selfish need knowing that you have to get married now because this is Gordon's ultimate goal." Finally she looked at her mother and said, "Mother you and I sit at this table caught in the middle of two grown men who could care less about me, they are only seeking to stay selfish. Not sharing their true feelings but wanting to show which one rules." She went unto say, "Yes two grown men who have been in competition with each other throughout this entire time. Wondering who could succeed at trying to make Roselita his." Roselita continued, "I'm sure the both of you talked about how you thought I was isolated. Here you two sit making complete fools out of yourself thinking that I should choose one of you because I'm supposed to be a isolated, obsessive, dramatized, and a semi-psycho woman whom you felt sorry for." Roselita carried on saying, "Please...how long did both of you think that I won't catch onto your irrational behavior. A behavior that is so ignorant that my mother is sitting watching two grown men fight feverishly over a woman who was never isolated she just knew when to say things while keeping silent on others. A woman who knows when she's being played and a woman who knows that true love is that which is shared by two people who find each other irresistible, that they wouldn't tear each other down but build each other up. I'm that woman who may seem odd but very intelligent, enough to know that the ring I chose is...Well...is...Hmm. She said, "The man of my dream is the man who can show value to a relationship and show that he's not competitive by pushing himself too hard by working on a plan to win me over. Roselita felt could this be a dream or was she about to enter into a world of reality. After all these years of keeping her feeling suppressed from the truth, is this the big moment that could change her life forever. She felt is she ready to take a step closer to fulfilling her love life by starting off by becoming happier. Roselita felt if she gives her answer now she could be making a mistake by choosing the wrong man, even though she loves them both. All sudden the words of what her mother said to her earlier, "Just remember to choose wisely, take your time, marriage isn't to be taken lightly." She wondered if she chose Brandon, how ebullient her family would be. But if she chose Gordon, she could lose her close friend Brandon forever. She realized the choice is yours and only can she pick the one who is right for her. She felt only God could give her heart what she so desired. Roselita had always wanted a husband but didn't need one to fulfill her needs. She thanked Brandon and Gordon for the rings. She thanked Gordon for the lovely evening. She turned to Brandon and said, "You will soon receive my answer." She said to her mother even though we've come with these men why don't we take a cab home together. Mrs. Macalaonez replied, "Roselita, that's it you're going to leave your answer mum?" She said, "Mother, I think it's best if I think about it some more before letting my mouth lead so quickly to speak." Mrs. Macalaonez didn't say another word she stood up from the table and thanked Brandon for a nice evening as she and her daughter Roselita paid their half of the meal and walked out. The Valet flagged a cab for them as he opened the car door for them to enter. Once inside of the cab, Roselita closed her eyes as she tried to sum what just happen up. Silence filled the cab as she wondered who she would choose, which man's dashing engagement ring belongs on her finger. While back at the restaurant both men paid for their dinners as they both discussed if giving Roselita their engagements was the right decision. Gordon said to Brandon, "Say man do you think that was fair for her to take both of the engagement rings, tell her mother let's get a cab then vanish, but come back later with her answer?" Brandon shook his head in astonishment as he returned Gordon's response saying, "Well you do have to admit she did shock us all and she was smart enough to say let her think about it then she'll get back to us." Gordon continued, "You're right Brandon but if that was another woman, we would have had our answer on the spot not putting us on hold until the next day." Brandon said, "That's true but I rather for her to think about it then say something she doesn't feel in her heart is right." Gordon said, "This is why I'm not married yet." Brandon said, "Then why did you just propose to her if you knew you aren't ready for this?" Gordon answered, "Because she seemed ready to be pleased by a man." Brandon said, "You know Gordon maybe Roselita is right, all you care about is yourself." Gordon said, "You know you're very comical Brandon because from what I understand Roselita mentioned you're selfish also." Gordon continued, "So selfish you didn't have the strength to let her know your deep feelings towards her." Brandon replied, "Well at least I didn't have to bribe her with material things or prove to her I was a Multi-Millionaire." Brandon added, "At least I've been there for her for over fourteen years, I managed to build up a relationship with her and not just pop-up on the scene at the last minute." Gordon laughed he said, "Ah, how funny and interesting, you would mention you and her long lasting friendship. He concluded, "I have a question my friend, if you and Roselita had been friends for this long. Then why did it take you this long to propose to her? Why not sooner and why did you wait until you had a feeling I was going to propose to her?" Brandon said, "Well Gordon, things take time and I wanted to make sure she felt comfortable about me marrying her." Gordon said, "Well as you can see, I haven't met her long but it also didn't take me long to propose to her either." Brandon said, "Well, I wasn't going to challenge you nor was I going to make this out to be a competition either, but since you wanted to go against the grain. I see you've been weighing the options on your own terms." Gordon said, "At least I'm man enough to be honest, instead of trying to play games wanting to chase after my boyish ways." Brandon said, "I rather would have gotten my boyish ways out of the way then bring them into a marriage with her and play the game then." Gordon said, "You are correct my man, but Brandon that should have been something you've gotten rid of years ago. When you knew it was time to become a man and settle you boyish ways down." Gordon continued, "Brandon, there comes a time in a man's life where he has to sort things out and figure out which direction he wants to go in. After a while he is going to need to think about his life on the long haul, retirement plans and having a family with or without children. In others there will come a time when a young man will have to grow up and make wise responsibility decisions about his life and his wife." Brandon became fierce, "Gordon just because you are a Billionaire. You may have all of what you wanted out of life, except for the wife and maybe children, this includes my woman Roselita. I' m an attorney, I have never asked of anything of Roselita, nor do I plan to ask of anything from her. However, I do know we are able to compromise on things, and balance our friendship out. I'm able to make Roselita smile and feel loved. I'm able to understand when she needs her space. I'm able to talk with her and not disappoint her. You see Gordon you are a stranger looking from the outside but never had a chance to see her inside. Who Roselita is, you've never experienced her mood swings, her happiness, her downs, and what makes Roselita the radiant woman she is today." Gordon said, "Yes Brandon you are correct again, but I also know that is doesn't take a scholar to sense her pains and know her gains. It doesn't take several years to see what type of woman she has mode herself to be. It doesn't take a lifetime to make a commitment to her love; all it takes is the right time. It doesn't take pumping and priming, it just takes the right man such as me to step into her life and the rest is history. Roselita could sense my love for her right away (Grocery Store). Brandon said, "I could hold this tedious conversation with you all night Gordon but I'm going to end with this, "I already know who she will choose." Gordon said, "Yes, we all know and it won't be you Brandon Bright." Both men walked out of the Marlitio's Restaurant fierce at each other for not understanding why Roselita didn't give her answer. Brandon and Gordon had gotten into their cars and drove off, leaving Roselita's last response to their question about who she should marry to penetrate on their minds. While Roselita went home to think about which engagement ring she is going to keep. The only thing both men; Brandon Bright and Gordon Gem could do, is wait to hear Roselita's decision…

TO BE CONTINUED….

CPSIA information can be obtained
at www.ICGtesting.com
Printed in the USA
FSOW01n2354151216
28654FS

9 781524 549572